Mysteries of Sparrow Island®

NIGHT SONG

Susan Plunkett & Krysteen Seelen

Guideposts Books

CARMEL, NEW YORK

www.guideposts.org
(800) 431-2344
Guideposts Books & Inspirational Media Division

Cover and interior design by Cindy LaBreacht
Cover art by Gail W. Guth
Map by Jim Haynes, represented by Creative Freelancers, Inc.
Typeset by Nancy Tardi
Printed in the United States of America

With deepest gratitude, we salute the families who keep the home fires burning for our men and women in uniform.

They also serve who only stand and wait .

("On His Blindness" by John Milton, 1608–1674)

ORCAS

To U.S.A.

LUMMI

N
W E
S

CYPRESS

GUEMES

To ANACORTES

FIDALGO ISLAND

*SPARROW ISLAND IS FICTITIOUS

CHAPTER ❦ ONE

WHY DO I KEEP HAVING THIS DREAM?
Abby Stanton slipped out of bed, donned her glasses and went to the open window. A soft sea breeze whispered over her five-foot-three-inch frame and ruffled her short brown hair. She took a deep breath and savored the faint salty tang laced with the scent of fir.

While the cobwebs of sleep cleared, she looked out of her second-story vantage. Summer's early dawn limned distant peaks of the Cascades. The golden light spread quickly, crossing the steely waters of Puget Sound and reaching south.

She lowered her gaze to the edge of the Sparrow Island property she shared with her sister Mary. Darkness still cloaked the shore. Unseen waves sloshed on the rocky beach, singing a farewell song to the night.

The susurration fed Abby's disquiet and she let the dream play in her thoughts. Set in the ornithology lab at Cornell, it was peopled with familiar faces. Some she'd known since her student days at the university. Others had joined the staff over the course of her thirty-five-year career.

In the dream, laughter and hugs abounded, along with high-fives and claps on the back as colleagues celebrated the final confirmation of an extraordinary event. The ivory-billed woodpecker, once thought extinct, was very much alive.

The astounding discovery had begun with whispers of a sighting in Arkansas. More sightings followed, changing the whispers into excited chatter. When the possibility of discovery was within reach, Abby led a team of investigators back to the source.

Tempering their high hopes with objectivity, the scientists conducted a careful search of the Big Woods in Arkansas. They returned with solid visual identification. The icing on the cake was a grainy video. Technicians at the University were able to enhance the images. The first showing prompted the spontaneous celebration at the lab.

Still replaying the dream, Abby recalled the uncharacteristic behavior of her friend and mentor, Jerome Winthrop. The Head of the Ornithology Department was a kind and thoughtful man with a deep physical reserve. He rarely touched anyone beyond the briefest of obligatory handshakes. Yet on this momentous occasion, he hugged everyone in sight, including two very startled professors. As the close-knit gathering burst into applause, the dream ended.

Abby leaned against the window jamb and sighed. The dream's abrupt termination left behind a sense of wrongness, as if someone was missing. Mentally, she matched the faces in her dream with the names of her former co-workers.

The second time through the list, she used her fingers to keep track, yet the result was the same. From Jerome to

Francine Keating, everyone who should have been there was there.

A longing tugged hard on Abby's heart as she thought of her colleagues at Cornell. *What new project is Francine working on? Does she miss me at the lab? Does Jerome?*

Abby pressed a hand to the sudden ache in her chest and chided, "Don't be silly." The bonds of friendship were as strong as ever. They'd weathered the winds of change that had brought the news of Mary's accident and swept Abby across the country. Moving from the East Coast back home to the San Juan Islands hadn't severed those precious ties. If anything, the maelstrom of events that followed only made her appreciate their relationships even more.

She still had her friends, and returning home had allowed her and Mary to resolve old differences and come to new understandings.

The lingering shadows of her dream faded as Abby got ready for work. It was Tuesday and she had a big day ahead conducting bird walks on the trails around the Sparrow Island Nature Museum. Sharing her birding expertise was one of her favorite duties. As the Associate Curator of the Sparrow Island Nature Conservatory, and the museum's resident ornithologist, the opportunity to lead bird-watching groups came often.

Downstairs, after her morning devotions, she checked on her sister. "Need any help or shall I start breakfast?"

From her wheelchair, Mary shot a glance at the hospital trapeze mounted over her bed, then flexed her bare arms. "What do you think?"

"About your fantastic muscle definition or making breakfast?"

With a pleased flick of her shoulder-length silver hair, Mary said airily, "Start breakfast."

"Your wish is my command." Leaving her sister laughing, Abby went to the kitchen with a light heart.

She admired Mary's determination to retain as much independence as possible since the car accident that had taken the use of her legs. The ability to lift herself in and out of her wheelchair required discipline and serious exercise. It paid off in freedom. Between her hard-won ability and her customized van, she could go nearly anywhere she wanted, at anytime. Today, her flower shop, Island Blooms, would be her first destination.

Abby finished her food preparations just as Mary entered the kitchen. "You're ready for the day awfully early."

"I have so much to do before Zack arrives. How am I going to fix his favorite meal and meet him at the ferry at the same time? I still have to go to The Green Grocer."

Knowing how particular Mary was when shopping for the right ingredients for her culinary specialties, Abby thought about how she could help as she put breakfast on the floral place mats on the table. "Hey, I'd be glad to pick up Zack."

"Would you? It would simplify things for me. I'd hate to burn dinner or undercook it."

"That would be bad for all three of us." *Especially Zack*, Abby thought. He so seldom had a chance to eat his mom's home cooking. Already looking forward to dinner, Abby checked the time. "He's coming in on the four o'clock ferry, right?"

"That's the plan," Mary said, visibly relaxing. "He'll call me if things change."

As they ate breakfast, Abby mentally juggled the day's schedule. She'd have to let Hugo know she'd be leaving early.

After they finished eating and cleaned up, Abby collected her purse and briefcase. "Unless you need me, I'll be heading out."

"Already?"

"Since I'm leaving work early, I'm going now so I can get a jump on the day. Will you be okay?"

Gratitude made Mary's blue eyes shine as bright as her smile. "I'll be fine. I promise. I have my cell phone and Finnegan, the wonder dog. What a great day. I can hardly wait till Zack arrives."

"Me too." Abby waved good-bye and left. Despite a sometimes overwhelming urge to protect, she'd learned to let her older sister define her needs. Mary was sensible about her limitations, as well as her capabilities, and didn't take risks that might jeopardize her mobility.

On the relatively short drive to work, Abby's spirits continued to lighten. The sense of something amiss in the dream was puzzling. *If You have something for me to learn, unlearn or do, Lord, lead me to it. I know You'll help me.*

Throughout the day, the warm and sunny June weather rewarded her little groups of bird-watchers with a lively show of flashing wings and melodious song. The thick stands of hemlock, Douglas fir and maple on the conservatory grounds hosted a variety of species engaged in fledging their chicks.

Generally, Abby let the experience and stamina of the birders on a particular tour determine the duration of the walk on the winding trails. For most of her fifty-five years, she'd spent every possible moment outside, studying God's feathered creations in their natural habitats.

In excellent shape from all the walking and hiking, she'd learned to adjust her pace for those who weren't as physically fit. This last group of eight seemed a little worn out so Abby decided to start heading back to The Nature Museum.

As the group neared the trailhead, Abby saw her boss Hugo

Baron coming toward her. Sunshine glinted on his white hair, eyebrows and mustache, accenting his patrician features and perpetual golden tan.

"Knock, knock," he called, the corners of his deep blue eyes crinkling mischievously.

Playing along, she responded. "Who's there?"

"Zack Reynolds at the ferry dock." Hugo's magnificent mustache twitched as he pointed at his wristwatch. "Mary called. His flight was early so he was able to catch the three o'clock ferry. I'll take over here."

Feeling a sense of urgency, Abby said, "Thanks, Hugo. Goodness, where did the afternoon go?"

After saying her farewells to the others, she hurried across the museum parking lot and didn't break stride until reaching her office.

The message light on her desk phone blinked. With the push of the button, she brought the voice of her nephew, Zack Reynolds, into the room.

"Hey, Aunt Abby. Mom says you're on taxi duty. I know I'm early, so I'm going to hang out at the park until you can get here. No rush. I'm self-entertaining."

It's great having a resourceful nephew. Abby dug her purse out of the desk's bottom drawer. *At least he has a fantastic afternoon to sit in the park.*

She envisioned her nephew trekking with his luggage up the hill to Shoreline Drive, then over to the park at the center of town. Shaking her head, Abby hurried out to her car. The influx of summer tourists would make finding a parking place a challenge.

Still, the beautiful day prompted her to keep things in perspective. Zack wasn't shivering in the rain with no protection.

He was no doubt enjoying himself in the sunshine and the fresh air of home. She drove carefully down Primrose Lane, past the Stanton Farm and into town.

In case he'd gotten bored and decided to walk around, she scanned the sidewalk on both sides of the street. In front of the businesses, flowers bloomed in window boxes and stone containers and hung in baskets from lampposts. The colorful petunias, geraniums, alyssum and lobelia gave quaint Green Harbor a festive air.

Parking near Holloway's Hardware, Abby was surprised to see the store's wide, covered porch empty. Usually three or four men gathered there, swapping stories, sharing a new fishing spot or giving out tips on how to do something like tuning up a lawnmower or an outboard motor.

She wondered where the men were today. They had been meeting there for as long as she could remember.

Walking briskly, she headed to the park. Halfway up the hill, she realized why the porch dwellers had abandoned their customary perches. Guitar music floated on the soft breeze. Surprised, she slowed to listen. Her nephew's perfect pitch wrapped around the chords, and she wondered who was accompanying him. As his voice soared, his heavenly gift amazed her anew. Only in her dreams could she sing an entire song on key.

The melody segued into another memory-evoking tune. Zack's rendition of "The Green Green Grass of Home" was the same version she and Mary often sang with their parents. Touched that he remembered, Abby paused and allowed her gaze to roam the hills and the harbor.

She wondered if Zack missed Sparrow Island as much as she had during her first few years away—before her life and career became so full. Perhaps a yen to touch the green grass of home, not to mention missing his family, was part of why he was here.

Abby considered it a minor miracle she and Zack were so close. Distance, and the joyful fulfillment of her calling, had made it difficult to spend much time with her niece and nephew. Although she'd made as many trips home as she could, she'd missed most of his and Nancy's childhoods.

Later, when Zack started touring with his band, Abby saw him more often. His music gigs on the East Coast gave them an afternoon here, an evening there, and occasionally a full day or two. The time together nurtured a special bond that continued to flourish.

Now who's being nostalgic? Smiling, she resumed her stroll up the park's pathway and met the hardware store's owner, Frank Holloway. A muscular, stocky man, his iron gray hair remained full below the edge of his teal Mariner's baseball cap. The case holding the glasses he needed while working the store's cash register peeked over the top of his blue denim shirt pocket.

"Zack's good on the guitar, Abby."

"Is he playing the guitar? I thought he had someone accompanying him."

"Nope. He's a one-man show."

"I knew he'd been practicing, but I hadn't realized how much he's improved." The members of his band often challenged each other to master different instruments. Zack's first love was the keyboard. Apparently, his hunger for music had been up to the dare and kept him experimenting and expanding his talents.

"Look at the people." Frank gestured toward the audience: two women with strollers, several moon-eyed teenage girls, a dozen kids of assorted ages, a handful of regulars from the hardware store porch and two women from Little Flock Church. "They love him."

"We do too—and not just because of his music. He's a good man."

"Couldn't agree more, but the music's reason enough for some. Not only does he sing as well as Glen Yarborough, he's almost as good on the guitar as Santo and Johnny." Frank raised an eyebrow for emphasis. "You just missed 'Sleep Walk.' Great song. Most of what passes for music these days is mumbo jumbo over electronic screeching. The songs of my youth were better."

With an ear cocked toward the music, Abby murmured, "He was born with a heart for rhythm and song."

"My hat's off to his father," Frank continued as though he hadn't heard her. "Jacob taught Zack an appreciation—a respect —for music the way we remembered it. And that's how Zack plays it."

Like-minded, Abby smiled an acknowledgement. "The band he tours with plays jazz, but Zack doesn't limit his musical interests. He loves everything from classical to bluegrass."

"Still, it's nice to hear the old songs played the right way."

She recalled her father's reaction to an upbeat remake of "Deep Purple." He'd considered the quick-tempo duet hideous and always changed stations when it came on. "It's highly possible each generation feels the same way."

"*Hmm.* Suppose so." Frank cleared his throat. "How about letting Zack play one more before you take him home to Mary?"

She noted the wistfulness in Frank's tone. "Do you have something special you'd like to hear?"

"He, ah, already played one for me."

And he didn't want to ask for another. Typical Frank. Always eager to lend a hand and reluctant to ask for special consideration. "We can ask." She nudged him with an elbow. "The worst Zack can do is say no." But she knew he wouldn't.

Looking relieved, Frank whispered the title he wanted to hear and she smiled. By his standards, this one was practically brand new. The two of them joined the half circle of spectators.

Singing "As Time Goes By," Zack sat unpretentiously on a picnic table. He was at home in jeans, scuffed running shoes, a faded red T-shirt and blue windbreaker with the sleeves pushed up his forearms. Built like a reed, at thirty-four, his even features made him seem ageless. A light breeze ruffled his thick, dark hair. The intensity of his blue eyes, so similar to his mother's, seemed to miss nothing. Neither did Abby's eyes. *Why had he traded his keyboard for a guitar?*

Pondering that question, she noticed Scott Kenai standing beside a tree. Delighted to see him, she waved and beckoned to him. The young man who sang at Little Flock shook his head, and she nodded her understanding. She knew the reason he avoided crowds, but apparently he couldn't resist the lure of good music.

After letting the last notes drift away on the breeze, Zack grinned broadly at the appreciative spectators. "Hey, Aunt Abby. Ready to go?"

The crowd groaned and protested, begging for one more song.

He shrugged and winked at her. "Okay, but my Aunt Abby gets to pick it."

"How about 'You Raise Me Up'?"

"Sure. It's one of my favorites." He adjusted the fret bar and strummed the intro.

"Thanks," Frank whispered.

"You're most welcome." Abby closed her eyes and let the melody carry her along with the praise to the Lord.

The song ended to a barrage of applause. Gracious as ever, Zack stood and took a bow, thanked his listeners, and then slipped the guitar strap over his head.

"Wait a moment, young man." Surprising everyone, Ed Willoughby rushed forward. He looked ready to jump out of his crisp, white soda jerk attire.

"What can I do for you?" Zack asked.

Radiating a palpable excitement, Ed stared at the guitar in Zack's hand. "Would you mind turning that instrument over?"

Zack's eyebrows rose. "You mean give it to you?"

Abby glanced around and saw several men from the audience move closer. "Exactly what are you looking for, Ed?"

"The back." The bold red bowtie at Ed's throat bobbed up and down. "Show me the back of it."

"Sure." Zack raised the guitar, flipped it over and let the pharmacist examine the back.

He gazed up at Zack in awe. "I was right."

"About what?" asked Abby.

"Look." Ed pointed a trembling finger at the neck of the guitar. "Look!"

"Somebody wrote their name on it." Abby leaned closer. "Now why would anyone ruin the lovely finish with silver paint?"

"This isn't just any guitar, Abby." Ed's voice rose half an octave. "Young Zack here is holding a rare piece of history."

Excited murmurs rippled through the audience.

"What's it say there?" called Frank from behind Ed.

"Neville," Zack answered.

"As in Neville Sanborne," Ed explained in an exaggerated stage whisper. "Surely you remember Neville and the Noteworthies?"

Startled, Abby blinked hard and stared at the silver letters spelling out Neville. "I remember them. They were popular when I was a girl. They sang 'Sparrow Island Night Song.'"

"That's right. They were good then and even better today," Ed crowed. "I still play their records on the pharmacy's jukebox. They're collector's items."

"Well, I'll be," said Frank. "Are you sure?"

"Of course I am. It took sixteen years to complete my collection."

"No, Ed. About the guitar being Neville's," Frank corrected.

"I'm positive it is. There's a nick on the edge of the scratch plate. I have a picture of him holding it when he and his band were here one summer." He turned to Frank. "You've seen the picture often enough. It's right over the jukebox. You come in and play Neville's music as much as I do." The finality in Ed's declaration left no room for doubt.

Zack put the instrument in its case and fastened the latches. "With all due respect, Ed, this has to be a knockoff. Think about it. If it was the real thing, it would be in a museum."

Shaking his head defiantly, Ed insisted, "I know I'm right."

"Well, where'd you get the guitar?" Frank asked.

"At a thrift shop over in Friday Harbor just a few hours ago."

"Afraid Zack's right, Ed," Frank said. "Neville Sanborne's

guitar sure as shooting wouldn't have ended up in a second-hand store."

Disgruntled, Ed marched toward the pharmacy.

Zack wheeled his suitcase around the end of the picnic table and picked up his purchase. Nodding a farewell to his listeners, he said, "Thanks everyone. I enjoyed it. Gotta go."

Abby waved too. Clearly, the matter was finished in Zack's mind.

They headed out of the park and down the sidewalk toward her car, his suitcase wheels clacking over the concrete joints. When they were well out of earshot of the others, Zack said, "It's funny. The Interisland ferry was delayed so I had half an hour to kill after the Anacortes ferry dropped me at Friday Harbor. I don't know why I went into that particular second-hand store, but I'm glad I did. This guitar's worth the two hundred bucks I paid for it."

Impressed, Abby eyed the leather-tooled case he carried as though it weighed a few ounces. "Goodness. I wouldn't think that amount would pay for the fancy case. It's beautiful."

"They were a package. Even under all the dust, it caught my eye."

Grinning, Abby shook her head. "I do believe you inherited your mother's shopping gene. She can spot a bargain at fifty paces."

"That's mom. You know, I didn't want to admit it in front of a crowd, but Ed may be right. This could be Neville Sanborne's long lost guitar. It disappeared around the time he died."

"For the life of me, I don't remember when that was."

"In 1967, before I was born."

The clock rolled back to Abby's teenage years. "Neville and the Noteworthies . . ." *Impossible. Or was it?* "You know, Zack, it doesn't seem logical. Someone had the guitar all that time. If they knew it was famous, why sell it at a thrift store?"

"You're right. Too bad it can't talk. Let's ask Mom what she thinks." Zack lifted his suitcase into the trunk of Abby's hybrid car. "We'll put the guitar in the backseat."

"Good plan. It'll never fit in here."

She pulled onto Shoreline Drive for the short ride home. "I had no idea you played the guitar so well."

"I've been practicing. Life as a traveling musician teaches you two things very quickly: versatility and adaptability. Without those, it's hard to improvise when a situation changes."

Abby parked the car in the Reynolds' garage, got out and opened the trunk. "Is that why you bought your own guitar?"

"Partly." He removed the case from the back seat, then stopped and stared at it. "Actually, Aunt Abby, I have no idea why I bought it."

CHAPTER ❧ TWO

With the sharp *R-R-RING*
hurrying her, Mary finished slicing a loaf of French bread
before cradling the phone between her ear and shoulder.

"Hi, honey," her mother said briskly. "I know you're busy
so I'll be quick. The oddest thing happened today."

Mary stuffed garlic cloves into the press. "What?"

"Sam was in the barn, cleaning out the back storage room
in the loft—you know, the one we almost never use?"

"*Mm-mm.*"

"Well, he found several boxes up there. Three of them . . . I
don't quite know how to say this, dear, but they're Jacob's."

Crushed garlic squirted across the counter. "Really? After all
these years? How did they get there?"

"Your father and I were hoping you'd know."

Mary dabbed a towel at the mess. "I . . . don't. What's in
them?"

"They're still sealed. The label says 'Jacob Reynolds for
Mary.'"

"How curious. Can you and Dad bring them over?"

"Not tonight. We're on our way over to the Alders' house."

"Oh, that's right. It's their anniversary party."

"I do so wish we could change plans, since I want to see my grandson. But they wanted to celebrate on their anniversary day."

The kitchen timer chimed. "You will." Mary eyed the oven. "We'll sort this out tomorrow. Okay?"

"Certainly, dear. Bye now."

The sound of the big garage door sent Mary into a flurry of activity. "They're home, Finnegan."

Sharing his mistress's sudden excitement, the golden/ Labrador retriever mix service dog stood at attention and wagged his tail. More than a helper, Finnegan was a trusted friend and companion who seldom left her side.

Mary quickly removed her apron, tossed it on the counter and rolled her wheelchair toward the laundry room. Across the small space, a closed door led to the garage.

As though sensing a special event, the blue-eyed, snow-white Persian Mary had adopted as a stray a couple of years ago jumped into her lap.

"You don't want to miss out on Zack's homecoming, do you, Blossom?" Watching the door, she stroked the cat's fluffy fur. "I'm sure he'll be glad to see you too."

The house door to the garage opened.

Mary's heart leapt at the sight of her handsome son. "It's so good to see you!"

In one motion, he abandoned his suitcase in the doorway, propped his guitar case against the wall and went down on one knee to give her a hearty hug. Mary savored the feel of his arms enfolding her, the faint scent of his morning's aftershave and the tang of the outdoors. This was her boy. Her child. He may have grown into a man years ago, but he was still her baby.

"It's good to be home and even better to see you, Mom."

She felt the kiss he placed on her cheek lodge in her heart. For a moment, she hugged him tighter. "I've missed you, son."

"Me too."

Before emotion swept her away, Mary patted him on the back. "You're here and so is dinner. I hope you're hungry."

Zack gave her another quick peck on the cheek and straightened. "I am. It smells like heaven. You made chicken piccata?"

"Of course." She always fixed his favorite meal his first night home and she always made enough so he could munch on the leftovers the next day. She pushed back to give him space.

"Not so fast." He reached down and greeted Blossom with a scratch behind the ears, then did the same for Finnegan. "Great welcoming committee, Mom." With a wink at her, he picked up the suitcase, leaving the guitar propped against the wall. "I'll take this right up to my room."

"Then wash up because I'm putting the bread into the oven. Everything else is ready." She saw Abby by the garage door watching the tender reunion with a big smile. Bless her heart. There was no one like her sister.

"Thank you," Mary said.

"My pleasure." Abby entered the house and dropped her purse onto the telephone table. "I got tied up on a nature walk and was too late to meet the ferry. By the time I caught up with him, Zack and his new guitar were serenading everyone in the park. Even Frank and the denizens from the hardware store porch were there."

Imagining the sight deepened the warmth around Mary's heart. "You know how Zack is. He loves sharing his music." She wondered where he'd left his companion, the keyboard. Thinking it unusual he'd come without it, she wheeled to the lowered kitchen workspace and reached for the baking sheet.

"I'll do this." Abby took the bread and put it into the hot oven. "You've done everything else. The table looks lovely. Roses, daisies, Japanese irises and baby's breath. It's a gorgeous arrangement."

"The lilacs you love have faded, so I cut roses instead." Mary made a mental note to fertilize the rosebushes hugging the deck rail. Perhaps she'd plant a lavender rose that would bloom all summer. It might remind her sister of lilacs.

Abby bent over the floral arrangement and inhaled. "Ahh. Thank you. You've thought of everything."

While washing up, she talked about Zack's impromptu concert in the park and Mary put the final touches on the meal. Before she could ask about the guitar, Zack came into the kitchen. He'd changed into a clean T-shirt. Damp locks of dark hair spiked around his forehead.

"What can I do to help, Mom?"

"Just take a seat. Everything's on the table." Words couldn't convey her joy. Mary led the little family in a thanksgiving prayer and expressed her gratitude for her son's safe arrival.

Listening to Zack relate the details of the places he'd been since his last visit kept her smiling throughout the meal. There was nothing like face-to-face conversation. Phone calls and e-mails were nice, but so much got lost when she couldn't see his expressions and body language.

When he'd called to say he was coming home, she'd heard a strain in his voice. He hadn't shared the reason for his spur-of-the-moment visit, but she could tell something weighed on his mind. Waiting for him to reveal what troubled him required patience, which wasn't her strongest virtue.

When they finished the meal, Abby cleared the table and put away the leftovers. "I'll get dessert."

Zack patted his tummy. "I'm stuffed."

"So you don't want the flan I made?" Mary teased.

"Whoa, I didn't say that. A man would have to be out of his mind to turn down anything you make, Mom. After seeing my family, your cooking is the next best part about coming home."

Carrying three desserts the way their friend Ida Tolliver did at the Springhouse Café, Abby brought the servings to the table. "Mary, the flan looks positively scrumptious. I'll have to conduct more birding tours just to walk it off, but I'm eating every bite."

"Hey, I'm going to go on one of those bird walks with you." Zack took two of the dessert bowls and put one in front of Mary. "It might do me a lot of good." He picked up a spoon, then put it down. "I need some thinking time."

Mary followed his glance to the back window. Beyond the deck stretching the length of the house, a grassy yard gently sloped to a hedge backed by rhododendrons. Clusters of pink and white impatiens bloomed at the feet of the big-leaved bushes.

Outside the informal hedge, a path wound down to the ocean. At this time of day when shadows began stretching, the water seemed bluer and the evergreens greener. Fresh leaves waved delicate and pale green in the breeze and the fair-weather clouds looked more promising.

Knowing her son's thoughts reached beyond the early

evening colors, she placed a hand on his forearm. "Don't think I'm not tickled pink about this visit, Zack. I am. However," she chose her words carefully, "I get the feeling missing us isn't the main reason you've come home."

His eyes narrowed with a concentration she'd often seen in his father. They shared many of the same traits. In her estimation, that was a good thing. Following his father's example had helped form the bedrock of Zack's excellent character. When Jacob needed another viewpoint, he always asked. She was confident her son would do the same.

"I think better here," Zack said softly. "There's just something about this place that helps me keep my head on straight." He covered her hand with his and squeezed. "It's safe harbor."

Mary knew the feeling well. There was nowhere on earth she'd want to live other than Sparrow Island. For now, she would not press Zack. He'd just arrived. "Take your time working through whatever's on your mind. There are no dragons chasing you here, son."

"I know." He picked up her hand and kissed her knuckles. "Thanks for being so tactful. The truth is—I'm sort of at a crossroad. I need to figure out what to do about . . . my relationship with Lily. My life.

"I can't see myself touring with the band twenty years from now. It looks like I have to make a choice between what I want and what I love."

The decision he defined left Mary wondering if his feelings for his girlfriend Lily had grown to the point he was considering settling down. She dared not ask. He had to open the door first.

"Oh well, as long as it isn't anything earthshaking," Abby quipped, waving her spoon.

"*En garde!*" Zack picked up his utensil and pointed it at Abby. "How dare you put things in perspective!"

While they engaged in a mock sword battle, Mary watched in wonder.

"I am not the enemy," Abby declared. "Guess again, *mon ami.*"

"If not you, then who?" The spoons clashed.

"It's an old foe everyone encounters."

"Zounds! Time is the culprit." Zack's spoon hit the table. He bowed his head in defeat.

Mary glanced from Abby to Zack and back. Without warning, the two of them burst out laughing. It was easy to forget the special relationship between them. Their bond had been cultivated miles away, after he had left home. They had their own peculiar way of communicating. Making light of a dilemma was their way of recognizing its importance.

"Is the duel over? May I pick up my ... sword? I'd like to eat my flan."

"The duel is done." Zack pulled his dessert in front of him. "My soul-searching battle has just begun."

Between bites, Mary asked, "Is there any way I can help you? Anything I can do?"

He heaved a sigh and shook his head. "Thanks, Mom, but no. This is a solo mission."

"As you wish," Mary acquiesced. He was a grown man and needed to make his own decisions. "I noticed you didn't bring your keyboard, but you did bring a guitar. When did you switch over?"

"I'm not switching, just expanding my expertise." He nodded at the case in the hallway. "It was an unplanned acquisition in Friday Harbor."

Mary glanced at the guitar case. Despite the scars and scuffs, it seemed regal, but was less intriguing than the reason he'd left the keyboard behind.

She listened as Zack and Abby filled her in on his performance in the park. What brought Mary up short was Ed Willoughby's assertion the instrument had once belonged to Neville Sanborne.

"You could say Neville and the Noteworthies put us on the map with one of their big hits," Mary mused aloud. "Would you believe 'Sparrow Island Night Song' was the theme of several high school proms?"

"Sure." Zack pushed away his empty bowl. "It's a classic. Oldies radio stations all over the country play it regularly."

"Classic? Oldies?" Abby asked slowly. "That sounds so . . ."

"Let's not even go there." Mary pushed her half-eaten dessert toward her son. "I have fond memories of dancing to Neville and the Noteworthies' hits. Is it possible you have his guitar?"

"Anything's possible, Mom. As I told Aunt Abby, the guitar went missing around the time of Neville Sanborne's death. More likey, it's the prop of a Neville Sanborne wannabe— maybe an impersonator. Elvis impersonators go all out. They even have conventions. But there was only one Elvis, only one Neville Sanborne." Zack polished off Mary's dessert, gathered the empty bowls and headed for the sink.

Mary wheeled away from the table and joined him and Abby. Finnegan went in the other direction, his nails clicking on the floor as he headed for the front door.

Mary caught Abby's eye as the bell chimed. "Were you expecting someone?"

"No. Maybe Henry—"

Mary shook her head. "Henry is at the Lopez Island sheriff's station tonight. He's covering for one of the men who took his son over to Bellingham for some medical tests."

"Oh dear, I hope it isn't anything serious." Sympathetic to anything involving children, Abby appeared distressed.

"No, no nothing like that. These tests are follow-ups for a corrective surgery done months ago." Mary turned her chair to make her way to the front door.

Surprise mixed with curiosity when she opened the door and saw Naomi Yardley on the front porch.

In her midforties, reading glasses dangling on a beaded chain around her neck, the head librarian and driving force behind the Sparrow Island Historical Society stood clutching her pocketbook.

"Hello, Naomi, won't you come in?" Mary searched her memory for a missed appointment or a meeting she should have attended and drew a blank. Perhaps the librarian wanted to talk with Abby.

Naomi stepped into the foyer and looked hopefully toward the living room. "Is Zack home?"

"Yes, he is." Her curiosity growing by the second, Mary pivoted her wheelchair and closed the door.

Abby poked her head out of the dining room. "I just made a pot of coffee. Or would you prefer tea?"

"No, nothing, thank you." The librarian held her patent leather purse like a shield, her knuckles white with tension.

Mary wondered if the purse would have fingerprints pressure-etched into the surface. "Is everything all right with you, Naomi?"

"Fine. Just fine. Although I'm at a bit of a loss...I mean..."

Abby took Naomi's arm and led her into the living room. "What is it? What brings you here this evening?"

"Zack! I could scarcely believe our good fortune when I heard the news. Oh, Abby, it's so exciting for Sparrow Island. I had to see for myself if it's true."

Feeling as puzzled as Abby looked, Mary asked, "If what's true?"

Naomi's excitement increased as Zack entered the living room. "Why, Neville Sanborne's guitar, of course."

Shaking his head, Zack said, "We don't know for sure it once belonged to him."

"Ed Willoughby told me Neville's name is on the handle."

The corners of Zack's mouth quirked and Mary knew her son was trying hard not to laugh. "A guitar doesn't have a handle, Naomi. It has a neck."

"I suppose it is important to get the terminology correct." She gave a thoughtful nod as though seeking the proper mental file drawer in which to store the information. "Okay, but his name is on it."

"Someone printed the word *Neville* in silver paint," Zack confirmed. "But that doesn't mean it was Sanborne's guitar."

Naomi dropped to the edge of the couch. "Ed Willoughby is an aficionado of the fifties and sixties. Why, just look at his store. It's authentic for the era. He knows more about those two decades than the rest of us put together. He assured me it was Neville's guitar. He even told me about the nick on the edge of the . . ." She paused as though searching for the right word. "The scratch plate," she concluded proudly.

Her curiosity growing, Mary said, "I didn't realize you were musically inclined."

"Oh! No, I don't want the guitar for myself, but for the

Sparrow Island Historical Society museum. Think of what a boon it would be to the Island's tourism to have such a piece of history on display." Tension pinched Naomi's features. "We don't have much of a budget, Zack, but we'll do whatever it takes to raise the funds to purchase it. That is . . . unless you'd be willing to donate it for the good of the community."

"Naomi, I don't think you can ask my son—"

"Just think of it, Mary. Neville Sanborne's famous guitar on display in Green Harbor. Why, people would come from all over to see it. And who better to donate it than Zack? Both he and Neville are musicians. Neville's home was in the East, but he had a fondness for the Northwest.

"I already have a display in mind at the library—a fifties and sixties motif. I'll bring in books, best sellers, from sister libraries. We could even have a sock hop at the high school gymnasium to raise money for the purchase price."

"Naomi, you're getting ahead of yourself," Abby cautioned gently.

"Think of it. It'll be fantastic, especially if you help us organize it, Mary. You have such a marvelous way of making events run smoothly."

Naomi's rapid-fire plans made Mary's head spin. "What if the guitar isn't Neville's?" She tipped her head at her son. "And what if Zack doesn't want to part with it?"

"I don't," he said softly. "It doesn't matter to me whether it was Neville Sanborne's or not. I like the sound and I'm going to keep it."

Naomi's shoulders drooped. "Please, please don't make your mind up tonight, Zack. Think about it. Think about the good it would do for the public to see the guitar, the memories it would conjure and the children it could inspire."

She opened her pocketbook and removed a business card. "Here. If you change your mind, please call me. Should you decide to sell, give us a chance. We'll get the guitar authenticated. That's all I ask."

Reluctantly, Zack accepted the card.

Naomi straightened her shoulders and headed for the front door. "Thank you, ladies, Zack. I'll see myself out."

Flabbergasted, Mary watched her leave. Naomi closed the door before Abby took a step toward it.

"What can of worms did I open this afternoon?" Zack muttered.

"I don't know," Mary answered slowly. "But I definitely want to see this guitar."

CHAPTER ✦ THREE

I'VE NEVER KNOWN NAOMI to be so tense and excited at the same time." Mary wheeled through the living room, following Zack and Abby back into the kitchen.

"Well, you have to admire her commitment to the Sparrow Island Historical Society." Abby finished washing the dishes.

"I'm not sure I can admire it." Zack put the case near the edge of the table and opened the latches. "She wants my guitar."

Mary quietly conceded he had a valid point. No one liked being hounded into doing something. She ran a fingertip over the buff stitching on the case. "This is very well-made. It looks sturdy."

"It needs to be," he agreed. "Anything traveling with musicians takes a beating now and then. The case must protect the instrument inside or both things wind up useless." Zack lifted the lid.

Surrounded by plush burgundy fabric, the blond guitar seemed to shimmer. A moment later, Mary recognized the fine grain of the wood as curly maple, one of her favorites. Only the scratch plate showed wear. "It appears this instrument has made a lot of music and someone took great care of it."

"You're right on both counts, Mom. The neck is rosewood and straight as an arrow." He lifted the guitar out of the case. "I used a flashlight at the thrift store to check the inside."

"What were you looking for?" Abby asked, wanting another look at the name on the neck.

"Structure. As far as I can tell, this one's in great shape. If there had been a cracked strut, I would've left it at the store."

"Can a strut be repaired?" Mary asked.

"Probably, but afterward, the sound is seldom the same." Zack flipped the guitar over. "Look, Mom. Check out the name."

Silver paint gleamed against the dark neck. "Neville," Mary mused aloud. "Not a common name today."

"It wasn't common forty or fifty years ago either." Abby bent over the lettering. "Come to think of it, I doubt it was popular when Neville Sanborne was born. I don't remember anyone named Neville."

"Will you play for us?" Mary sat back expectantly.

"Sure. What do you want to hear?" Zack ducked his head and slipped the guitar strap around his neck and shoulder.

Tongue-in-cheek, Abby suggested, "Gershwin."

Zack laughed and adjusted the guitar. "You really like to keep me off balance, don't you, Aunt Abby?"

She grinned back. "What's the matter? Don't know any Gershwin tunes?"

She laughed when he winked at his mother and began to strum, "Someone to Watch Over Me."

Abby remembered Mary and Jacob dancing to the tune at their wedding. They had looked at each other as if no one else existed.

Abby settled on the chair next to Mary and enjoyed the private serenade. Zack's fingers danced from chord to chord without hesitation. The emotion of his rendition would have melted the hardest heart. The purpose of this trip home registered keenly. He was seeking answers to questions that would change his life.

"Beautiful," Mary murmured, her voice breathless.

"Thanks."

"Let's take a closer look at the case." Abby wondered if it contained a clue to the previous owner.

"I don't know what they used as padding, but the interior feels like it's in good condition." Zack squeezed the nearest side. "Check out the resiliency."

Mary obliged. "Why, Abby, it's like the new foam they sell for beds these days. Of course, it couldn't be."

When her sister drew away from the case, Abby stood and ran her hand across the interior. A ridge under the plush bottom brought her up short.

"Something wrong?" Zack strummed chords for another song. "Tell me you didn't find a tear in it."

"No, I didn't," she answered slowly. "But there's something . . ." She slipped her fingers along the length of the ridge, then probed below. "Goodness, there's a pocket here." She glanced at Zack. "Did you know about it?"

He shook his head and played the intro of "Twilight Time."

"Anything inside?"

She reached under the flap. "Yes."

Mary wheeled closer and Finnegan came to attention. "What is it?"

Withdrawing the contents, Abby gave the loose pages to her sister and kept the wire-bound book. "Those look like sheet music."

Zack leaned forward. "Let me see."

"They're over fifty years old," Mary exclaimed, leafing through the pages and handing them off to her son. "Look at the price printed in the corners."

"Man, these are classics. Right out of your era, Mom. Grandma and Grandpa would love these too. What do you have, Aunt Abby?"

"It's a notebook." She opened it in the middle and her breath caught in her throat. "Oh my!"

"Notes on songwriting?" Zack asked expectantly. "I can always use some tips."

"I don't think so." Abby's pulse quickened as she carefully turned the thick pages. "It's a sketchbook. The title page says: 'San Juan Islands' and the main subjects are birds and their habitats."

"Oh."

"The detail is incredible, almost professional."

"That's nice." Mary held up two pieces of sheet music. "These are lovely. Framed, they'd make a great picture grouping."

Abby glanced up. Zack and his mother arranged the heavy old pages on the table. Their preoccupation with the exquisite art nouveau designs on the sheet music trumped interest in the sketchbook. "Do either of you know if Neville Sanborne was an artist or a bird enthusiast?"

Mary's brow furrowed. "Ed Willoughby might."

"Please don't ask him until I leave," Zack requested.

Understanding his reasons, Abby agreed. "You know, if this sketchbook was Neville's, it would go to the provenance of the guitar and enhance the value."

"Or the book might be something he picked up in his travels," suggested Zack.

"You're quite right." Abby turned another page. A Northern shrike perched on a branch and looked over his left shoulder, the curved tip of his beak in sharp profile. "Did the man at the store say how the guitar came into his possession?"

"He came to work one morning about five years ago and found it propped against the shop door." Zack resumed playing soft chords. "He took it to the sheriff's station thinking someone may have lost it or it may have been stolen and left there. They had no record of a theft complaint and nothing about someone losing a guitar. They held onto to it for months before they called him. If the store owner wanted it, it was his to do with as he wished."

"So he put it in his shop," Abby deduced. "And why not?"

"He watched the Lost and Found columns of the local newspapers for a couple of years," Zack continued. "Nothing and no one surfaced. He knew the guitar was a good instrument and would be of value to someone."

"Someone who played." Mary eyed her son.

"Yeah." Zack shrugged. "He had five guitars in a crowded space. This one was pushed to the back, probably because the others were electric and more saleable.

"Anyway, I called Chet from the band before I bought it to make sure it was as good a deal as I thought it was. He told me to jump on it and you know the rest."

He crossed his left ankle onto his right knee. "The music and sketchbook are gravy as far as I'm concerned."

"But if the guitar really was Neville Sanborne's and you later decide to sell it—" Abby started.

"Doesn't matter, Aunt Abby. The sketchbook is all yours, with my compliments. You'll enjoy it. For me, it's more baggage to haul on the road."

Abby flashed an uncertain look at her sister.

Nodding encouragement, Mary teased, "You can always give it to Naomi."

Feeling suddenly possessive of her gift, Abby sat at the table and started examining the contents anew. Meanwhile, Zack played and sang the tunes on the sheet music. His mother's clear soprano chimed in and filled Abby with warm contentment.

As Zack segued into another of Mary's favorite songs, his thoughtfulness further endeared him to Abby. She turned the pages of her gift quietly so as not to disturb or intrude. Toward the end of the sketchbook, she discovered two unusual drawings. The top of the page showed a cave set in a cliff. Below it, a small bat colony clung to the rocky ceiling of the cave's interior.

On the opposite page were intricate pictures of a bat in profile and a forward version. Measurements jotted between lines revealed that the little mammal was about the size of a man's thumb. An expert on birds, Abby's knowledge of bat species was limited.

"What are you poring over?" Zack asked, amusement coloring his tone.

"I'm not sure," Abby murmured, suddenly aware the music had stopped.

"What?" Mary wheeled closer, drawing Finnegan's watchful gaze. "A bird you don't know? Impossible."

"Thanks for the vote of confidence, but this is a bat. An extremely well-drawn one, I might add."

"Bats." Mary shuddered and Finnegan raised his head. She stroked his back, their signal everything was fine. "I know we need bats, but . . . ugh."

"This one is small. Very small. I wonder why the artist included it in a sketchbook of birds. He obviously thought it was important. It's drawn in great detail and precise measurements are given. It would be very interesting to find the cave in this picture."

Zack's laughter filled the kitchen. "Do you know how many cliffs and bluffs are on these islands? You'd have a better chance finding alligators in the Yukon."

"Maybe." Narrowing her eyes and staring at the ceiling, Abby considered that the sketchbook could be as old as the sheet music. The colony might not exist any more. But if it did, surely an expert at the Washington Department of Fish and Wildlife would know the best way to conduct a search.

"Okay, Auntie, you're wearing that I-know-more-than-you-do look. So, I give. What's so special about this bat?"

"I don't know." She tapped the page. "The artist annotated the drawing with the word *rare*. It just may be. First, I need to find out how many documented bat colonies there are in the San Juan Islands."

"Uh-oh," Mary said.

"What?" asked Zack.

"Sounds like your Aunt Abby has found another mystery to solve."

CHAPTER ❧ FOUR

Hoping to have breakfast with Zack before she left for work, Abby started down the stairs. When she was halfway to the foyer the front door opened, startling her into a full stop.

"Yoo-hoo, Zack. It's Grandma and Grandpa."

"Mom. Dad." Abby hurried down to greet them. "Good morning." She took a covered dish from her mother and gave her a one-armed embrace. Underlying the new perfume her mother wore, Abby caught the familiar scent of vanilla and cinnamon.

Thank heaven some things never changed, not even the way Ellen Stanton's short, curly gray hair always had a fresh-from-the-beauty-shop perfection. Her pale blue windbreaker highlighted her sparkling blue eyes and set off the nautical theme of her navy blue jersey top and flowing white trousers.

Abby hoped she'd age as well as her petite mother. Ellen possessed a youthful vitality belying her eighty years.

Mary joined them and reached up for an affectionate hug. "What did you bring?"

"Broccoli, cheddar and mushroom quiche." Ellen kissed Mary's cheek. "I hope you haven't cooked a big breakfast."

George caught Abby in a warm, welcoming hug. A wiry man with thick, whitish-gray hair and brown eyes twinkling brightest when around his family, her father gave her an extra squeeze before releasing her.

"Your mother and I couldn't wait to see Zack," he said, enveloping Mary and kissing the top of her head.

Abby closed the door and shepherded them toward the kitchen. "I'm glad you came early so I could see you too."

Zack's enthusiastic greetings delighted his grandparents. "Grandma, you always smell like you've been baking. Every time I pass a bakery with fresh cinnamon rolls, I think of you."

Abby chuckled to herself and quickly added two place mats and settings to the table. When she turned to get the orange juice, Blossom raced past, fleeing the boisterous family. In a fluffy white blur, the cat skidded around a turn and bumped into the coffee table on her way to the serenity of Mary's bedroom.

Finnegan, tail wagging, mouth open and looking as though he was smiling, remained beside Mary's wheelchair. He clearly relished the affectionate attention the elder Stantons bestowed.

Things settled when the family of five gathered around the table and George offered a prayer of thanksgiving.

"We have a meeting at the Senior Center this morning." Ellen started cutting and serving the quiche. "We decided to leave home early and enjoy breakfast with our wonderful daughters and our favorite grandson."

"Even though I'm your only grandson, I'm sure glad you

did." Zack lifted his plate for a generous slice of quiche. "And not just because of the good eats."

Gratitude for her family and her presence among them flowed through Abby, and she thanked the Lord again for the changes He'd made in her life. While she loved the years she'd spent in Ithaca, she was glad to be home. Her family's love and companionship enriched her. And she was available when they needed her.

SITTING NEXT TO ABBY, Mary listened to the conversation flowing around the table Jacob had made almost forty years ago. It was the first piece of furniture he'd built for their home. She'd been a new bride then and hadn't realized how much of their lives it would witness.

How many times, she wondered, had the Reynolds and Stantons gathered round and made it a silent partner to their conversations and celebrations, solemnities and sorrows. Their children had crawled around its legs. In time, it had held homework and the projects that always seemed to collect on its sturdy surface.

At the sound of her father's laughter and her son's answering slap on the love-worn tabletop, Mary temporarily closed the mental treasure box of the past. She didn't want to miss these moments. They polished another layer of joy into the table's surface.

"What are your plans for today?" George asked Zack after breakfast.

"Hang out with Mom. Spoil her a little." Zack gathered the last of the dishes. "Fix anything she needs fixing."

"Since you're willing to do a little work, you can bring in

your mother's boxes from the truck." George grinned at his grandson.

Mary shrugged. "It mystifies me how they got into your storeroom."

"We figured it out last night over dinner." Ellen glanced at her husband. "Lowell Alder put them there."

"Why?" Mary asked.

George touched her arm. "Do you recall the big rummage sale we had at the farm to raise money for Jacob's medical bills?"

"I'll never forget it," she answered, still grateful for the way the community had rallied behind the family after her husband was diagnosed with pancreatic cancer. Those had been the longest and shortest three months of her life. "People brought all kinds of things to your barn. It turned out to be more of a bazaar than a rummage sale."

"Right. Jacob had packed up the items you wouldn't need. It was a big load. The men from Little Flock Church came over, got it and brought the whole kit and caboodle to the barn. We sold all of his woodworking tools."

Ellen nodded. "We collected donations for weeks. After the sale, we had leftover items everywhere. For years, we considered having another sale. Eventually most everything was returned or donated or passed on to someone who could use it."

"The boxes?" Mary reminded her parents.

"We're getting to them," said George. "There were lots of people in and out of the barn. Everyone had their own idea of how it should be organized. On the big day, you brought Jacob."

"I remember it well," Mary said softly. "He insisted on being there."

"He found the boxes and asked Lowell to put them where they wouldn't get mixed up with the sale items. Lowell stashed them in the storage room."

"I wonder why Jacob didn't tell me," Mary murmured.

Ellen leaned forward. "I'm sure he meant to, dear. Things happened so quickly after that day."

"Lowell forgot about the boxes," George said baldly. "He didn't remember until your mother mentioned finding them last night."

"He feels very badly, Mary. I assured him you would understand," Ellen said. "Those weren't the only ones overlooked. We found half a dozen boxes from the rummage sale still up in the loft. I guess things just got piled in front of yours."

"When we're done delivering yours and the others, the rummage sale will be officially over." George sat back in open relief.

Ellen laughed softly. "After ten years. We certainly didn't rush into it, did we, dear?"

"Call it Christmas in June," George said.

"I'll get them out of the truck," Zack volunteered. "Where do you want them, Mom?"

"The craft room will be fine." A half-rueful smile lifted the corner of Mary's lips. She wished she could fetch the boxes herself. So many simple things had moved out of her control since the car accident landed her in the wheelchair.

Ellen hugged her grandson. "You're a good son."

"Thanks, Grandma. I've got a great family."

"And we'll see you later in the week." George planted a kiss on Mary's cheek.

In a final flurry of activity, Abby left for work and everyone else went outside. Once the boxes were stacked on the porch, Zack helped his grandmother into the truck.

Mary wished Jacob could see their son. He'd be so pleased. The knowing was strong, and yet, there was no sadness or sorrow attached. There was just a deep satisfaction of a life well-lived and the precious times they'd shared. Perhaps now, ten years after his death, she was ready to move forward.

Her thoughts turned to Sgt. Henry Cobb, the deputy sheriff courting her. *Courting* seemed such an old-fashioned, outdated term, but the only one that fit. And for that very reason, she knew Jacob would approve.

While Zack carried the boxes into the house, she went to answer the ringing phone.

"Hi, it's Henry. Did Zack arrive safely?"

"Yes. I was just thinking about you. Can you come for dinner?"

"Much as I'd like to, it isn't looking good. I have to keep this short, Mary. I'm in the middle of an investigation and we've gotten a new lead. I'll be in Eastsound for a couple of days before I head over to Whidbey Island."

"Oh, that's right." Mary shoved her disappointment aside. "Next week is the joint training session with the Island County Sheriff's Office."

"If there's any way I can get over to Sparrow Island, you know I will. I'd like to see Zack and I hate going so long without seeing you." Henry sighed. "I miss you already."

"I miss you too."

"I'm glad your son's there. He'll keep you out of trouble," Henry teased. "Until I come back and take over the job."

Laughing, Mary said, "I'll show you trouble, Henry Cobb."

"I'm sure you will. Oh, gotta go. Take care of yourself for me."

"You do the same."

Mary hung up hoping Henry managed a visit before Zack left. She went into the dining room where he sat.

"The boxes are in your craft room." Zack ran his palm over the tabletop. "I remember when Dad and I sat right here. He was sorting through some of his things, deciding who needed what, and where it would do the most good. He gave away quite a bit."

Mary pulled her thoughts from Henry and focused on her son's reflections. It was easy to imagine Jacob at his old spot at the head of the table. "Your father was a considerate and thoughtful man."

"I know." Zack tapped the wooden surface. "He walked the walk he talked."

Mary sat a bit straighter. "Well, that's what he'd want us to do, so let's take care of this piece of unfinished business."

"Sure." Zack stood and they both headed for the craft room.

He wiped the dust from the boxes labeled "Jacob Reynolds for Mary" with a damp paper towel, then put the first one on the low staging table she used for project preparation. A sharp crafter's blade made quick work of the sealing tape and she opened the top.

Startled, she gasped. "Oh my. I'd forgotten about Jacob's hat." She looked over at her son. "How could I? He wore it everywhere."

Zack removed the paper packed around the brown fedora, then picked it up. "It still smells like him." He offered it to his mother.

Tangy lime and mellow wood smoke conjured old memories.

"Don't go teary-eyed on me, Mom. I can't handle crying women," Zack teased.

"No reason to. My memories are good ones." Mary pointed to the pheasant feather peeking out of the grosgrain hatband. "Remember this?"

It was Zack's turn on the nostalgia merry-go-round. "Aunt Abby was visiting. She took me on a nature walk." His voice thickened. "What was I? Seven or eight?"

"Eight," Mary said softly.

"I found the feather and kept it as a souvenir. But a month later came Dad's birthday and I hadn't saved up enough allowance to buy him a good present." Zack lifted the fedora and examined the feather. "So I gave him my most prized possession. He put it in his hatband."

"He removed the feather only when he had the hat cleaned or when he bought a new one."

Zack nodded thoughtfully. "I don't recall him wearing any other kind of hat. This style of fedora was part of his personality." He met his mother's gaze. "Part of who he was."

"It's time for the feather to come full circle."

"What do you mean?"

"The hat is yours, Zack. If you want it."

Clearly torn between accepting the gift and questioning whether he should, he remained silent.

"Wearing your father's hat might help you consider how he would have handled your quest. Jacob can't be here in person to offer guidance or advice, but remembering him—how he lived, how he reasoned and the way he sorted through things —might help you."

She took the hat from Zack's hands and plopped it on his head. "Go look in the mirror," she whispered.

"Thanks, Mom. I— Thanks." Zack grazed his palm across the brim, then stood and headed for the door. "Be right back."

"You're welcome."

Mary pulled more packing paper from the box. At the bottom, she found a manuscript box. Curious, she lifted it out. Why did Jacob pack this one away? Was there something special about it?

"What do you think?"

The sight of her son took her breath and for a moment, all she could do was stare. "You're as handsome as your father and look so much like him in that hat."

"It does look good, doesn't it?" Zack's broad grin made her smile. "What do you have there?"

"A manuscript."

"Which one?"

"I don't know." She began worrying off the sturdy cardboard top. "I thought I had all of his works filed away." She paused before opening the box. "I couldn't bear to part with them."

"You helped him research most of them," Zack said reflectively. "You used to sit at the dining table and proofread his pages for him before we all went to the post office. I used to look forward to his finishing a book and all of us celebrating at Willoughby Pharmacy with malted milks, banana splits and hot fudge sundaes."

Nodding at the fond memories, she lifted the box top.

"Does that say *Untitled*?" Zack asked in a surprised voice.

Puzzled, Mary picked up the title sheet. "Yes. In big, bold letters. By Jacob Reynolds. How very strange. He never started a book until he had a title."

"Dad usually bounced around several before settling on one. I don't remember him ever changing a title, either. Not once he started writing," Zack mused, his tone thoughtful. "Maybe *Untitled* is the title."

Mary looked up at her son. "Why don't we read it? See what we can find out?"

"Sure. Want to use the dining room table?"

"It's such a beautiful day, let's go out on the back deck."

A short while later they sat outside. Blossom lay contentedly on Mary's lap and kept a sleepy watch for interlopers. Finnegan napped beside Mary's wheelchair.

"This is a different kind of story for Dad." Zack lowered the page he'd been reading. "In a way, it's more . . . him."

"I expected a mystery. I'm not sure what to call this. Maybe after I read another chapter it will come to me." Mary was in no hurry. The warm June day and the special joy of sharing this discovery with Zack filled her with absolute contentment. The only thing that could possibly make it better would be if her daughter Nancy sat passing pages with them.

CHAPTER ❦ FIVE

P LEASED AND A LITTLE surprised, Abby gazed at her gleaming desktop. Finishing the leftover paperwork had taken less time than she'd expected. A laugh tickled the back of her throat as she considered her unofficial bat project. In the past, the Washington Department of Fish and Wildlife had been extremely helpful in providing information. Before she contacted them on this project, however, she needed to expand her meager knowledge.

Propping the sketchbook on a stand at the center of her desk, she opened it to the intriguing pages of the cliffs and the bat cave. As she studied the pictures, the laugh in her throat bubbled out. Until yesterday, she hadn't put bat colonies and the San Juan Islands in the same thought.

An Internet search yielded considerable information. One interesting article tempted her to label the bat in the drawing a Keen's myotis. Instead, she resisted all labels and snap decisions. Further research warned that bat identification was far more complex than that of birds. She needed to keep her mind open to other possibilities.

For several hours, she studied bat taxonomy, along with the descriptions and comments made by noted experts. Most were quick to point out all bats are mammals and belong to the order *Chiroptera*, because *chiro* meant hand and *ptera* meant wing. Bats used their wings in much the same way as humans used their hands.

Abby took copious notes and methodically eliminated the species that didn't fit the details on the drawing. When she'd exhausted what she could find, she sat back and stretched. Bats were indeed elusive creatures. Some species had avoided detection so well that information on them was notably sparse. It was time to get help. She picked up the telephone and called the Washington Department of Fish and Wildlife. The operator transferred her to the resident expert on bats and their local colonies.

"Beth Bingham here. How may I help you?"

Abby had barely uttered her name and title when the bat expert exclaimed, "It's great to hear your voice."

Abby searched her memory. *Should I know this woman? Her exuberance doesn't make sense.* "Ah, well, uh—It's good to hear yours too."

"You probably don't recognize my last name," Beth said with a laugh. "You knew me as Beth Werling. Bingham is my married name."

"Beth!" The image of an eager college student with a love for birds popped into Abby's mind.

Beth Werling. Bright. Hungry for knowledge. Hard worker. A student when Abby was a professor at Cornell. What Beth had lacked in quick intellect, she more than made up for with diligent study and a willingness to go the extra mile.

"You're the bat expert?" The question came out before Abby gave it a thought.

"Yes. I've been with the WDFW for going on twenty years, which is almost as long as I've been Bingham instead of Werling. Personal stuff aside, you're the last one I thought would call for information on bats."

Abby provided a nutshell version of the reason for her interest. She concluded by asking, "If I e-mail a copy of this drawing, could you identify the species and tell me if you have a location for the colony?"

Beth's laughter made Abby smile. "You're presuming the drawing is sufficiently accurate. Generally, without a clear photograph—preferably a series of photos—pinpointing a species with absolute certainty is nearly impossible."

"I understand the necessity for caution," Abby agreed, her gaze fixed on the intricate drawings. "But, let me send you a copy. We might both be pleasantly surprised. Please call me when you receive it."

After hanging up the phone, she scanned and e-mailed the sketches to Beth. While waiting for her to call back, Abby straightened her research materials and organized her notes, her mind playing leapfrog with events from the past.

Beth Werling.

Something niggled in Abby's memory. Something she'd forgotten. The dream she'd awakened with resurfaced. She'd been looking for someone at the celebration. Was it Beth? Should she have been in the dream?

Abby propped her elbow on her desk and rested her chin in her palm.

Why wasn't Beth in the dream? Abby had always assumed the young woman continued in the field of ornithology and pursued her master's degree at a university closer to her hometown. Now, the discovery of Beth as a bat expert left Abby wondering why on earth she had changed fields.

Suddenly, the niggling bloomed into a clear memory.

Like a falcon returning to a perch, a mistake from the past settled on Abby's shoulders. Beth had asked for a letter of recommendation.

Whether due to the excitement of leaving on her first trip up the Amazon River or the traditional chaos surrounding semester finals and graduation, Abby had forgotten to deliver the requested letter.

Remembering it now made her uncomfortable.

The oversight was because of something as basic, as elemental as the need for letterhead stationary. There had been plenty in her desk at work, but none at home where she wrote the letter. Intending to print and mail it when her traveling companions gathered at the office for the trip to the airport, she'd dropped the diskette on top of her In basket.

It was still there when she returned from the Amazon four months later.

Immediately, she'd searched for Beth to apologize, to explain, but the student was gone and not a part of the master's program.

Now, Abby hoped there would be an opportunity for redress. Phone calls or e-mails seemed insufficient. She'd feel better with a face-to-face discussion.

Hugo arrived carrying two cups of coffee. "You've been in here all morning." He set a cup on her desk. "What are you doing?"

"Researching bats." She picked up the cup and took a sip. "Thank you. This is wonderful."

Hugo examined the sketchbook. "Very nice work." His white eyebrows rose. "Did you do this?"

"I wish my artistic skills were that good. I have no idea who drew it, but yes, it's excellent."

"Have you identified the species?"

"I'm working on it. I e-mailed a copy of the drawings over to Beth Bingham at the WDFW." Abby raised her coffee cup in a toast. "Here's hoping she can confirm my assumption that this might be a rare species."

Hugo set down the sketchbook, unbuttoned his suit coat, then settled on the visitor's chair. "Unfortunately, the general public is rather repulsed by bats and lump them in with spiders and snakes as undesirable creatures. Fortunately, not all cultures take that view."

"Really? Give me a for instance."

"For thousands of years the Chinese have used bats as symbols of good luck. In ancient Macedonia, people considered bats the luckiest of all animals. The bearers of bat bones were assured happiness."

"I had no idea," Abby marveled.

The phone rang and she picked it up.

"Abby, this is Beth at the WDFW. You were right. The drawings are first rate. Professional. The notes on dimensions and coloring are incredibly helpful. My colleagues and I give the subject a high probability of being a Keen's myotis, Latin genus *myotis keenii*. We'd like to talk with the artist." Excitement laced Beth's voice.

"So would I, but I don't know who it is. None of the sketches are signed or dated; they could be five months or fifty years old. The book is titled *San Juan Islands*. It came into my possession through a series of circumstances with my nephew. Initially, he didn't even know he had it."

"That's too bad. We want to learn more about this species. They're rare and elusive. Presently, we're trying to identify the location of all the bat colonies in the state. I'd love to come up there and search for this one, but I—" Beth paused and the silence lengthened.

"Why don't you? It would be wonderful to see you and talk about old times," Abby prompted. *And it would be a great opportunity to address my oversight.*

"I'm not mobile. I broke my leg five weeks ago and the cast doesn't come off for another few days. The doctor says I won't be climbing cliffs for several months. I suppose it's a good thing I'm buried in office work."

Her hopes of a quick meeting dashed, Abby heard what sounded like a pen tapping on the desk and sensed Beth's frustration. From deep inside, Abby felt a nudge to do for Beth what she couldn't do for herself—find the bats.

"Hold on a second." She covered the mouthpiece and looked at Hugo. "The bats are very important. Beth has a cast on her leg. Why don't we search for the cave?"

"But of course. Our mission is to conserve and protect wildlife, including bats," he whispered back.

"Beth, we'd be glad to start searching for the cliffs and the cave in the drawings." As soon as the words left her lips, Abby felt she was on the right path.

"Fantastic! The last colony of Keen's myotis was located up in British Columbia. These little guys aren't easy to find, Abby, but if anyone can, you will."

They spoke for several minutes before Beth hung up, and

Hugo asked, "Did she have any suggestions on how to conduct the search?"

"Not beyond looking for a spot that matches the drawing. She did say the Keen's myotis are a state candidate for conservation. Beth thinks there are bats on most of the islands. She mentioned the locations of two prominent sites. One is on Orcas Island in Moran State Park. The second is at English Camp, over on San Juan Island.

"Beth spoke to a representative of Bats Northwest. They're a nonprofit organization of scientists and lay people interested in protecting the bats in Washington, Oregon and British Columbia. A group just returned from English Camp where there's a bat house with around five hundred residents and an old abandoned house with a colony of seventeen hundred or so.

"I think we can logically assume the Keen's myotis are here—somewhere," Abby said slowly.

Hugo picked up the sketchbook and studied the pictures more closely. "We can eliminate Sparrow Island. The landscape doesn't match."

"True. This won't be an easy search. However, if I find the colony, Beth and her colleagues will jump at the chance to explore and validate it. Then, they'll do all they can to protect the site and the bats."

"Excellent. I sure wish I knew of a way to win the public's appreciation for our furry flying friends here." Hugo laid the sketchbook back on the desk. "Regrettably, I've never had anyone regale me with tales about a pet bat."

Neither had Abby. "What you said a moment ago about people having an unreasonable fear of them is true. The public doesn't realize how beneficial they are. Without them, we'd be overrun with moths, mosquitoes and other bugs. You might say they're our nocturnal cleanup crew. Perhaps doing a display for the museum about the benefits of bats would help."

"Excellent idea. Our role is to educate." He smoothed his white moustache. "Do you really think it's possible to find a colony of these elusive little mammals?"

"It won't be easy," she admitted.

"Well, let's see." Hugo cocked an eyebrow. "If we consider all the possibilities, there are four hundred and twenty-eight islands in the San Juan Archipelago. One hundred and seventy-two have names."

Abby laughed softly. "Thank you for not counting the ones submerged at high tide."

Eyes twinkling playfully, Hugo retorted, "Of course not. Bats don't swim. But seriously, Abby, it would be a tremendous coup for the conservatory if we found the colony in the drawing."

"Yes, and even better for the bats who may need protection." She went to the laminated map of the San Juan Islands covering a good portion of open wall. He joined her and together they studied the coastlines. "I'd hate to think of them being destroyed by a developer who didn't realize they were there."

"Or didn't realize their importance to the ecosystem," Hugo said thoughtfully. "Are you up for the search?"

Staring at the map showing the cliffs and bluffs along the islands, she said, "I'll admit to being a little daunted. But with the drawing as a reference, at least we have a starting point."

MARY DIDN'T KNOW what to think of Jacob's story about two young boys. She placed the final page of the manuscript back into the box. "Well, I'm blown away."

"The thing Jake and Gerry did with the coins on the railroad tracks was pretty neat," Zack said with a chuckle.

"If you or Nancy had sneaked off and put a coin on a track so you could watch a speeding train flatten it, you would have been grounded for life." Just the thought of two boys, ten and twelve, crouching down to see it happen sent chills through her.

She might not have taken it so personally if not for Jacob's compelling description. She could almost feel the rush of air as the train passed, smell the diesel fumes and hear the staccato clack of metal wheels on iron rails. Once again, Jacob had drawn her into one of his tales and held her captive.

Zack laughed. "You're assuming you'd find out. Neither of the boys told anyone. And if they did, the last ones they'd tell were their parents."

Recalling some of Zack's childhood escapades, she eyed him closely. "Fortunately, we have no trains on Sparrow Island."

The way his blue eyes twinkled, he appeared on the verge of laughing. "No, we don't."

"Is there something you want to tell me?"

Then he did laugh, startling Blossom who stretched and jumped onto the deck. "No, Mom, I'm sure there isn't anything about my childhood adventures I want to tell you."

Curious, afraid she may have missed something, she changed tactics. "Why not? You're too grown-up for me to ground you or send you to your room."

"No way." Still chuckling, Zack shook his head and gestured to the manuscript. "You know, we could make copies and send one to Nancy. She would enjoy reading it."

"I'm sure she would." Mary replaced the cover on the manuscript case and folded her hands over it.

"What's bugging you, Mom?"

She took a moment to form her thoughts. "Other than this being a coming of age story, was there anything about it that struck you as . . . odd?"

"You mean besides the fact it doesn't have an ending?" Zack rubbed his palms together. "The writing seemed to get better with every page, then falter. Sort of like Dad stopped and started. Maybe he wrote it in pieces."

"That's my impression too. I wonder why."

Zack shrugged. "Maybe he did—between the novels he wrote and sold. It feels, I don't know, different." He rushed to add, "And not because it isn't the kind of story he usually wrote."

Gazing down at the box, Mary agreed. "Your father obviously meant for us to take it out someday and read it."

"Otherwise he would have tossed it," Zack said. "Not packed it up for you to discover later. The more I think about it, the more certain I am that when the men from Little Flock took the stuff out of our garage for the rummage sale, they loaded the boxes without realizing Dad meant for these three to stay here. That's why he asked Lowell to set them aside and bring them back later."

"You're probably right," Mary said slowly. "The question now is what to do with Jacob's story." She looked over at her son. "What do you think about having someone work on it? You know, smooth it out. Polish it."

"Give it an ending?" Zack suggested.

Mary nodded.

"I'm no writer. Neither is Nancy. Are you thinking of taking a stab at writing?"

"Posh, no." She waved a hand at him. "But . . ." Mary's mind buzzed with possibilities.

Zack leaned forward. "It would be great if we could find someone to do it, then send the manuscript to his agent to sell. Just think of it—'A new book by Jacob Reynolds. The mystery writer's lost manuscript. At your bookstore now.'"

Mary liked the idea. A lot. "Step one is to get this copied. How about a trip into town? We'll go see Joe Blackstock at his print shop."

"If we have to wait very long, I'll buy you a malt at Willoughby's."

"You're on!"

As they prepared to leave, the phone rang. Passing through the kitchen, Zack said, "I'll get it. It might be Lily."

"Okay." Mary wheeled toward her bedroom to freshen up. When she came out, she asked, "Was it my favorite dog trainer?"

Scowling, Zack repositioned the fedora. "I wish. It was the music museum over in Seattle."

"Gracious, whatever for? Are they soliciting donations?"

"You might say that." Zack scooped up the manuscript box from the telephone table and motioned toward the garage. "I haven't had the guitar two days and people are crawling out of the woodwork wanting to buy it from me."

"They made you an offer?" Mary asked, incredulous. No wonder his mood had changed so dramatically.

"A lucrative one—if I can prove it belonged to Neville Sanborne." Zack stood in the laundry room and held open the door leading to the garage. "I tend to forget Sparrow Island has a hotline to the rest of the world."

"What did you tell them?" Mary slowed in front of him.

"It doesn't matter to me who owned the guitar before I

bought it. I'm not interested in selling and I don't plan to have it authenticated."

"Why not? I'm not suggesting you sell it, but aren't you curious?"

"Kinda. But the guitar isn't the reason I came home. If I let myself get caught up in all the speculation, I won't have time to spend on my quest. I need answers much more than I need to know if I got a bargain on a famous guitar."

"I understand." Looking at it from his perspective revealed the magnitude of his struggle. If he could ignore the possibility of owning a rare piece of musical history, then the issues he wrestled with must be monumental.

Still, it amazed her that news of the guitar had reached the museum in Seattle so quickly. Mary preceded him into the garage. "Well, you've made your position clear. That should end it."

"I doubt it," Zack said, opening the van door for Finnegan.

Always eager for a ride, the dog leapt onto the seat and Zack fastened the special seat belt around him. "Tell you what, Mom. If anyone else calls looking for a guitar, let's refer them to a music store—in Seattle or Hong Kong."

"Deal. No more talk about it. It's yours. You don't want to sell it. That's the end of it." She hoped. However, Mary suspected they hadn't heard the last from curiosity seekers.

CHAPTER ✤ SIX

Holding the sketchbook, Hugo murmured, "This really takes me back."

Abby leaned against her desk. "To where?"

"Australia. Different time and different bats. Different terminology. What we call colonies, they call camps. For a first-timer's introduction to the Chiroptera family, it was exceptionally memorable."

Intrigued, she paid close attention. Any time Hugo dubbed something as memorable, it was. She couldn't wait to hear this story. "Tell me."

"We don't have fruit bats here in the States. They fall into the realm of Mega-bats. Although the largest and most fierce looking of all bats, they feed strictly on fruits and flower nectar. As a result, they spread seeds, which grow into new trees and pollinate the flowers of native plants over long distances. They're essential to biodiversity."

"Mega-bats?" Abby tilted her head, absorbing the new information. "Just how large do they get?"

"As I recall, they can weigh more than two pounds with a wing span of around six feet." Hugo grinned. "If we were looking for *them*, they'd be easier to find. Fruit bats, or flying foxes as they're sometimes called, roost in trees and they're noisy."

"There's a lot to learn. While I was researching small bats, I wound up grateful the one we're looking for isn't as tiny as the bumblebee bat." At his raised eyebrows, she continued, "It's about as big as a real bumblebee, but with a six-inch wingspan."

"Speaking of wingspans, this is one of those times when I wish we had a small plane or a helicopter. If we did, we could visit the most promising places and start eliminating whole sections. A micro-bat, like this one, doesn't have a large range. Mega-bats can do twenty-five miles, but the smaller species are limited to five, maybe seven miles."

"That helps." Abby straightened and rubbed the small of her back. They'd been poring over the aerial maps for nearly an hour identifying areas with bluffs and crags. Already, they'd narrowed the search area by excluding Sparrow Island and those lacking the rugged terrain shown in the drawing. "We can eliminate one more spot." She drew an invisible *X* with her finger on the map.

"Are you sure?" Hugo pointed to a line of cliffs. "What about these?"

"Henry and I recently searched that island. It doesn't have any formations similar to the one in the drawing."

"Okay," Hugo said in a long exhale. "Every bit of information helps. This is still an enormous endeavor."

"I'VE BEEN GIVING SOME THOUGHT to what you said about the manuscript, Zack." Mary backed her van out of the garage. "I know the perfect person to help us polish what's there and put an ending on it."

"Who?"

"Ida Tolliver." Mary waited for the garage door to close before starting down the quiet street that connected to Oceania Boulevard.

"Isn't she a little young to have the kind of experience we need?"

"In most cases, I'd probably agree. However, Ida has considerable life experience for a twenty-four-year-old. She's supported herself since she was seventeen, after her parents died."

"I didn't realize she'd been on her own for so long." Zack shifted in his seat. "Still, last time I was here, she worked two jobs."

"I understand your concern. Her jobs are part-time and she's active with Little Flock. I agree her plate is already quite full. A task of this size might be too much to ask." Mary checked the rearview mirror before passing a group of bicycling tourists. "If it's too much for her, she'll tell us."

"Okay. What made you think of Ida, Mom?"

She glanced at her son and saw admiration mixed with curiosity in his expression. "You know how music is your dream?" Seeing him nod, she turned her attention back to the road. "Writing is Ida's big dream. Busy as she is, she's taking online college courses. Right now, she's enrolled in a creative writing program."

"Is she any good?"

Mary shot her son a puzzled look.

"I mean, just because she's taking classes doesn't mean she's capable of polishing and completing Dad's manuscript."

Mary turned onto Harbor Seal Road, then left on Kingfisher Avenue. "I've read some of her work. It's good. Very good, in fact. I think she has tremendous talent."

"Fair enough. Let's ask her then. From my own experience, I know when you want a dream badly enough, you make time to work on it."

Zack's introspective tone reflected his struggle to find a balance between his life goals and dreams. With a mother's prayer for him, Mary said, "Asking Ida will show we have confidence in her ability and believe in her potential."

Zack grinned. "All artists need encouragement and we'll take it anywhere we can get it."

Reaching over, she squeezed his knee. Like his father, her son had a good heart. She parked in front of Priority Printing, a small shop set between *The Birdcall* newspaper office and Edmonia Lewis's beauty shop, Silver Scissors.

"I'll get Finnegan." Zack released his seat-belt and freed the dog.

Mary made her way out of the van, then used the remote to retract the ramp extending from the side. "I've got the manuscript." She patted the embroidered blue denim bag fastened to the arm of her wheelchair.

A lingering glance down the street tickled a smile she felt growing on her lips. How she loved this little town, and how she wished Zack loved it enough to stay. Yet, even as the thought passed through her mind, she put it aside. Having both of her children live nearby was her dream. Theirs were different. Nancy's had taken her to Florida. Zack's took him all over the country.

The thought led Mary to hope she wasn't making a mistake. Ida had often expressed a desire to leave Green Harbor and explore the big cities. Perhaps meaningful work toward her dream would keep her on the island longer.

Large posters and smaller equally artistic pieces decorated

the buff-colored walls of Priority Printing. All were reproductions of advertising Joe had fashioned for clients. Hugo Baron's Sparrow Island Nature Conservatory occupied a corner with before and after posters showing the expansion of the facility. A gorgeous twilight poster of Sparrow Island in the bloom of spring colors commanded attention on the back wall.

The sounds of a printing press flowed through the open double doors to the work area. Unable to see over the high counter hosting the register, Mary skirted her wheelchair around it. "Yoo-hoo, Joe. Are you there?"

"Be right with you." His baritone carried a Brooklyn accent softened by twelve years on Sparrow Island. He sounded much younger than his seventy-four years.

"He does nice work," Zack commented as he moved around the room, examining each piece on the wall. "First rate."

Joe rounded the counter, wiping his hands on a red rag. "Hello, Mary. Sorry to keep you waiting. I had to finish up a job." A squarely built man of medium height, his thick, black hair showed only a hint of gray. His dark brown eyes smiled when the corners of his mouth turned up, as they often did. "How's the world treating you?"

"Couldn't be better." She gestured toward Zack. "You remember my son."

Zack had removed the fedora and now offered his hand in friendship. "Hi, Mr. Blackstock. It's been a while."

A guarded expression replaced Joe's usual joviality when he shook Zack's hand. "The young man with the guitar."

Mary thought she heard a soft groan before he quickly said, "It's at home."

Joe nodded. "What can I do for you, Mary?"

Finding Joe's sudden change of demeanor odd, she wrestled the box from her denim bag. "I'd like to make two copies of this please."

Joe checked for ink on his hands, then stuffed the rag into the front pocket of his black printer's apron before taking the heavy package. "This looks like a manuscript."

"It is." Mary explained about finding Jacob's unfinished story and wanting to preserve the original by making copies.

"A genuine Jacob Reynolds manuscript." Eyebrows raised, Joe opened the box. "All this time I thought the claims of people finding long lost works were bogus. I figured they were written by someone else. Guess I was wrong. The past does come alive." He glanced at Zack and frowned.

Her friend's mercurial changes troubled Mary. "Is something wrong?"

"What could be wrong?" Joe countered.

"I don't know." She looked from the scowling printer to her bewildered son. "You tell me."

Joe paused as though carefully choosing his words before addressing Zack. "The guitar you bought isn't Neville Sanborne's."

Mary blinked. Of all the things . . .

"I've never claimed it was." Zack moved closer to the counter.

Joe nodded once as though the matter was settled. "Good." He picked up the manuscript. "This will only take a few minutes. Do you want to wait?"

"Yes," Mary said.

"Sure," Zack answered at the same time.

Moments later came the rhythmic sounds of a high-speed copier making quick work of the pages. Mary met her son's confused gaze and he shrugged. Obviously, he was at as much of a loss as she over Joe's behavior.

The machine stopped and Joe returned with the manuscript and two white boxes containing the copies. Without a word, he rang up the sale on the cash register.

Mary paid him, saying, "I'm curious, Joe. How can you be so sure the guitar didn't belong to Neville Sanborne? Abby told me Ed Willoughby is positive it did."

Joe stiffened. "The day before he died, Neville gave a concert in Seattle. It was the last stop on a ten-city tour. He called from the airport when he reached New York. The airline admitted the guitar and his suitcase hadn't made the plane in Seattle. It would be on a later flight. They promised to deliver it in the evening. It never arrived."

Startled by the precise information, Mary blurted, "How do you know?" Then flustered she had challenged him, she rushed to add, "I mean, where did you learn that? You seem so certain."

"I am. Neville got on the plane. The guitar didn't. When he died in a car accident the next day, few people knew the guitar was already missing."

Mary hadn't pictured the printer as a nostalgia collector. Quite the opposite. Such things had never appealed to level-headed, down-to-earth Joe Blackstock or his wife Margaret. Still, Mary was confused over how he had acquired this information.

"Occasionally, there's speculation in the music trade about the missing guitar," Zack said. "You know, fillers."

"Yeah." Joe gave the receipt to Mary and pushed the boxes toward Zack.

"None of them mentioned your version of events." Zack scooped the boxes under his arm. "Not that I don't believe you, Mr. Blackstock. As a musician, I know firsthand that shipping instruments is the worst thing about traveling. The band and I carry ours with us whenever we can."

"You know a great deal about this guitar, Joe," Mary pressed. "Were you a big fan of Neville and the Noteworthies?"

The printer exhaled and looked away. Her curiosity on tenterhooks, Mary was afraid they wouldn't get an answer. She backed her chair to get a better look at Joe and realized he didn't appear so much angry as he did sad.

Finally, he said, "Yeah. A really big fan. You could say I was his biggest fan. You see, Neville Sanborne was a stage name. His given name was Mark Blackstock. He was my older brother."

"Your brother?" Had she been able, Mary would have come out of her wheelchair. "You never mentioned you had a brother, let alone that he was Neville Sanborne." Her good friend Margaret hadn't mentioned it either and Mary was determined to know why not.

Joe looked her in the eye, then turned to Zack. "There's no point in it. Mark's dead and I'm not the kind who rides the coattails of someone else's fame. Never did. Never will. I'd consider it a real favor if you'd keep the family connection private."

"Sure thing, man," Zack said.

"Of course we'll respect your wishes, Joe."

"Thanks." He turned toward the double doors leading to the printing press.

"Give my best to Margaret, will you?"

"Sure." Joe lifted his hand in a backward wave.

Feeling as though they'd stirred up a hornets' nest, Mary turned toward the street. *Lord, please help Joe work through whatever troubles him.*

CHAPTER ❦ SEVEN

"LOOK AT THE MAP." HUGO stepped back, dismay clouding his features.

Abby came to stand beside him. "It's a good thing we used color-coded markers." The abundance of red, blue, green and yellow dots reminded her of a child's artwork. "We can eliminate all the red and blue areas; they're the least likely. Our most promising sites are the green and yellow."

The phone calls she'd made and received throughout the morning helped to shape their search territory. One by one, she and Hugo marked the places where the WDFW, local wildlife enthusiasts and professional birding organizations had documented bat sightings.

"Hugo, there's a gentleman from the Parks Department asking for you in the museum," Rebecca Cody said from the doorway. Abby turned toward the sixteen-year-old. The part-time employee at the museum always wore a cheerful smile.

"Excuse me. I'll be back..." he glanced at the map as though reluctant to leave it, "as soon as possible."

After he left, Rebecca stepped inside. "What are you doing with all those colored dots?"

"Narrowing possible search areas." Happy to share her knowledge, Abby explained her hope of finding a Keen's myotis bat colony.

"Eliminating the populated areas is a good idea," Rebecca observed. "Most people would be grossed out by a bunch of bats flying around their houses. They'd want to get rid of them, like, yesterday."

"Unfortunately, that's true." Abby picked up a notebook and jotted a reminder to call pest exterminators. Homeowners would most likely contact them first. From her research, she knew few pest control companies had any idea how to remove a bat colony.

"Bats . . ." Rebecca said. "I'm glad I've never seen a live one up close."

Abby reached across the desk to a shallow dish in which she collected spare change. She selected two nickels and a dime. "Give me your hand."

When Rebecca did so, Abby dropped the three coins into the teenager's palm. "This is how much a Keen's myotis weighs."

"You're kidding!" Rebecca lifted her open palm and stared at the coins. "That's hardly anything. They must not be very big."

"About the size of Hugo's thumb. So they aren't anything to be afraid of. Besides, they eat moths and lots of insects."

"Mosquitoes?" Rebecca asked, brightening. She put the coins in the dish.

"About six hundred an hour," Abby confirmed, loving the way the girl's hungry mind absorbed knowledge.

"Wow. That's a lot for something so little. I may have to like bats after all." She turned toward the door. "Before I go, one more question?"

"Sure."

"Do they really, like, suck people's blood? Is that why they eat mosquitoes, because they have blood in them?"

Abby laughed. "You have an excellent mind. Actually, only three species of bats in the world live on blood. All three are in Central and South America. Hate to break it to you, Rebecca, but contrary to what you see in the movies, any respectable vampire bat prefers an animal over a human."

"Oh yuck. Vampire bats aren't my kind of birds."

"They aren't birds, they're mammals. Without them, we'd be knee-deep in bugs."

"Oh!" Rebecca lingered at the door. "I can tell I have a lot to learn about bats."

Pleased the girl was willing to keep an open mind, Abby suggested a trip to the library. "If they don't have the books you need, Naomi Yardley will order them through the library network."

"I'll do that. Thanks." Rebecca hurried out the door, heading toward the museum.

Abby turned back to her desk, picked up the telephone directory and leafed to the section on pest control. Too bad people thought of bats as pests. They were actually one of mankind's best friends.

She'd just finished her last call when Hugo returned. "I tried the exterminators in the yellow pages," she said. "It's a bad news/good news situation. None of them has tried to remove a colony, but no one has requested the service. They did agree to contact me immediately if they get any bat complaints."

"We'll stay alert for their calls," Hugo agreed.

"I suspect the best way to find the colony is to take what we know, make some educated guesses, then go looking," she said.

Joining him in front of the map, Abby began making plans. "We'll have to camp at the places we pick." The bats only left their shelters at dusk and returned before sunrise. The sense that the sketchbook fell into her hands for a purpose grew stronger. The Lord often used obscure things to either make a point or teach a lesson. In her case, she thought it might be both.

Hugo shoved his hands in his pockets. "It may be a couple of weeks before I can get away to accompany you. The Parks Department just asked me to be a consultant on a major project they're undertaking."

Abby's heart sank. "What about Beth?" *I can't let her down.*

Hugo looked at Abby sternly. "I can see searching for the bats is important to you, but you must not go alone."

Reluctantly, she conceded, "It wouldn't be smart."

"I don't want anything happening to you, Abby. Please wait until my schedule is less crowded."

Knowing he was right, Abby sorted through her alternatives. Maybe this was an opportunity, not a setback. Zack needed quiet time in God's company to sort out his dilemma. One of the best places to meet with Him was camping out in the majesty of His creation. "I've got an idea."

"Let's hear it."

"My nephew is here—"

"Ah, the man with the controversial guitar."

Another reason Zack might want in on a camping trip or two. "I'll ask him to come along with me—if Mary doesn't mind."

"Excellent."

THINKING FINNEGAN looked very regal in his bright blue service cape, Mary let him lead her and Zack into the Springhouse Café. The dog paused at the hostess station, waiting for a signal and Mary pointed to a table in Ida Tolliver's section. When they were seated, Finnegan took his position next to the wheelchair, his hindquarters tucked neatly under the table. Proud of him, she crooned, "Good boy."

"Ahem." A growing grin ruined Zack's fake scowl.

"You're a good boy too. The day you and Lily brought Finnegan to me was life-changing. It's hard to believe I put up such a fuss. I can't thank you enough."

"You don't have to thank me again."

"I do. I was so silly and you were so thoughtful. And Lily was so generous."

An image of the slender, honey-blonde dog trainer formed in Mary's mind. She liked the delightful young woman. Lily possessed a genuine warmth and friendliness that gave her a special light and drew people to her.

"You weren't being silly, Mom. Those were tough times. You had a lot of adjustments to make."

Life in a wheelchair did take getting used to. There are still occasions . . . She smiled and picked up the menu. "What are you going to have?"

"The clam chowder. It's been good here every time and it won't spoil my dinner."

Ida bustled up to the table. "Hi, Mary. Oh, Zack, how good to see you!" The waitress slid her flower-topped pen over her ear. "You're one lucky man. You have such a fabulous life."

"What do you mean?" Zack put down his menu.

"Traveling to all those cities with your band, meeting new

people all the time and seeing new scenery every day . . . it must be exciting." Her violet eyes gazed wistfully out the window. "Museums and art galleries, conferences and parades, something's always happening. Your life has to be way over the top."

"Trust me, it's not that exciting."

"Big cities are so cosmopolitan, so alive." She heaved a dreamy sigh. "You're probably just used to it."

"Possibly," Zack said with a shrug. "But people aren't close there, not like they are here on the islands. It can be lonely."

"Well," Ida plucked the pen from behind her ear and tapped the flowered end against her chin. "Between your music and Neville Sanborne's guitar, you don't have to worry about being lonely. You're a celebrity."

Dismay and puzzlement creased the area between Zack's eyebrows.

"A celebrity?" Mary echoed. She seldom thought about her son's growing fame.

"Yeah." Ida gestured at the empty restaurant. "If people knew he was coming in today, this place would be packed. Some folks want to touch the guitar. Others think if they touch Zack, they'll get some of his luck." She grimaced. "Anyway, a bunch of them went over to Friday Harbor to scour the thrift stores. They're looking for treasures like Zack's."

"I hope they find some," he said fervently. "In fact, I hope each of them finds something extraordinary."

Mary completely agreed. A new "treasure" of any kind would make the guitar old news and shift the spotlight of public interest away from her son. He'd come home for quiet introspection, not notoriety.

"That's so nice of you, Zack." Ida pulled an order pad out of her apron pocket. "And you just made my case. City life can't be all bad, not with people like you around."

After they gave their orders and Ida went to the kitchen, Zack said, "Are you sure she's the right choice for our project, Mom? She sounds like she's ready to take off any minute."

Mary toyed with her silverware and prayed for guidance. Young people often had trouble settling on what they wanted and seemed to change their minds with every sunrise. An inner conviction took hold and grew.

She looked up and met Zack's concerned gaze. "I believe we should stay with our original plan. Ida needs more time on Sparrow Island. The Lord is working in her. She's attending Bible study with Abby and me, and becoming active in the community. This is not a good time for her to leave."

"I see." Zack rubbed his hands together. "Don't get your hopes too high. She doesn't sound like she'd be interested in acquiring another anchor to keep her moored here."

"We'll go ahead and ask. What can it hurt?"

Zack sat back and put the fedora on a nearby chair. "You know, Mom, one of the things I miss when I'm away is your optimism. You always see the bright side and trust God to bring you there."

Mary's heart swelled with gratitude. After the accident, maintaining a sunny disposition had been a result of the Lord's working in her. "If we dig holes and hide every time life takes a bad turn, our days will be bleak. We are what we think. I choose to look for the good."

"Maybe things will come together."

"The timing is in our favor," she said.

"What do you mean?"

"When we broach our project, we'll want Ida's full attention. Look around. We're the only customers. Usually she's so busy she doesn't have time to talk." Mary smiled at the incredulity in her son's features.

He gulped. "And everyone who's gaga over the guitar is over on San Juan. Wow, Mom," Zack shook his head slowly, "this is almost unbelievable."

Ida served their beverages and steaming clam chowders along with a basket of fragrant herb and cheese scones. "Fresh from the oven," she boasted. "I'll be right back with the extra strawberry butter you like."

As she walked away, Zack said, "I'm amazed she remembered." His features brightened as he offered a prayer for their meal and Mary silently thanked the Lord for her son's faith. It had been a bumpy journey during his high school years, but he'd returned to the right road.

Ida brought a dish of pink-tinted butter and put it in front of Zack. "Can I get you anything else?"

Seeing her chance, Mary said, "If you have a moment, Ida, there's something Zack and I would like to discuss with you."

The conscientious server glanced around before giving them her full attention. "I'm all yours. What's up?"

Mary explained the boxes left in the barn loft. "Some of life's best gifts are right under our noses. Zack and I found an unpublished manuscript."

"A long lost Jacob Reynolds mystery?" Excitement turned Ida's cheeks a bright pink. "Would you let me read it? Please?"

Mary tilted her head. "What if it isn't a mystery? Would you still be interested?"

"He wrote in another genre?" Ida leaned forward. "Oh. My. Gosh. I've read and reread all his books nearly a dozen times.

He was so gifted. You didn't come here just to tease me with a solid gold carrot. Tell me you'll let me make a copy."

"I have one for you right here." Mary patted the denim bag on the arm of her wheelchair.

"It's uneven from all the stops and restarts," Zack warned, slathering strawberry butter on a scone. "We think Dad wrote it over a period of years."

"If you have the time," Mary said, "we'd like you to work with me on polishing the rough spots and giving the story an ending. Is this possib—"

Ida turned as white as her apron and Mary feared the girl might faint.

Zack jumped to his feet and took Ida's elbow to steady her. She leaned into him. Her knees buckled and he caught her. Easing her onto his chair, he looked at Mary. "What do you think, Mom? Is this a yes?"

CHAPTER ❧ EIGHT

THAT EVENING, ABBY JOINED Mary and Zack on the back deck. Overhead she heard a familiar night song. The *eeent-peeent* flight call was followed by another. "Hush," Abby whispered. "Don't move."

Above the shadows, she searched the twilight sky and spotted the boomerang shape of long, slender wings on an erratic flight. A territorial male sharply dove toward the grass, then pulled up at the last second. The air rushing through his wing feathers created a startling wallop of a sound.

"What kind of bird is that?" Zack asked.

"A common nighthawk," she answered. "They come from Brazil and other South American countries. It's winter there now. Like bats, they're voracious insect eaters, and sing when they fly and hunt at night."

"Oh my," Mary said. "That's a suitable postscript for a remarkable day."

Refocused, Abby considered the astonishing news they'd shared over dinner. As eager as she was to read Jacob's manuscript, she wasn't ready to part company with her sister and nephew. Not when there were so many unexplained details.

"I presume," Abby said, "after Ida recovered from her surprise, she was delighted with your proposal."

"Not quite." With a half chuckle, Mary pulled several feet of yarn out of her knitting bag and coiled it on her lap. Blossom's tail twitched over the canvas bag like a metronome moving from a slow waltz to a quickstep. Out in the yard, Finnegan dropped his ball, stood still and stared at the cat in silent warning.

Mary tickled Blossom under the chin and continued, "Once Ida heard what we have in mind, well, it was a bit overwhelming for her. She wants to read the manuscript before giving us an answer. I'm pleased she didn't say yes blindly. It feels right doing it this way."

It felt right to Abby too. She couldn't think of a better way to encourage the young woman than to demonstrate belief in her dream.

"Come to think of it, she was too awed for her own good," Zack reflected.

Mary's eyes widened.

Abby's attention moved from her sister to her nephew. "What do you mean?"

"Ida didn't ask what we intend to do with the book," Zack explained. "And we didn't make it clear we aren't asking her to work for nothing. We're hiring her. If it turns out we can actually sell the manuscript—" he looked at Mary, "Ida deserves a fair percentage."

Mary nodded agreement. "Good idea, Zack."

"It has an added benefit," Abby said. "Putting the work on

a professional level makes the experience more valuable for her. What made you think of it, Zack?"

"Too many gigs where I didn't get paid. Sometimes friends forget music is not only my passion, it's my livelihood. I learned that if I don't treat it as a profession, no one else does. The guys and I agreed long ago not to accept gigs without making the terms clear up front. We need to do the same with Ida."

"I can see why people would expect you to play for free," Abby mused. "They don't mean to take advantage, but it turns out that way."

"I intend to pay her, no matter what," Mary said. "But we don't know for sure if we'll be able to sell the book. "Or . . . if we'll want to sell it."

"Having second thoughts, Mom?"

"Not exactly. I just feel I'm overlooking something. When I decide what the something is, I'll let you know."

Feeling at a distinct disadvantage because she hadn't read the manuscript yet, Abby checked her watch. She could squeeze in a few hours of reading tonight.

"I trust your intuition, Mom. You certainly were right on with Joe Blackstock today."

Abby's curiosity spiked. "What happened with Joe? I thought you just got the copies made."

As Mary and Zack revealed Joe's relationship to Neville Sanborne, Abby's interest grew along with a sense of puzzlement. "I didn't know he had a brother. Let alone a famous one. Margaret never said a word. Neither did Janet."

"Not to me either," Mary concurred. "Of course, if Janet knew, she would have definitely mentioned it."

Abby met her sister's gaze and they shared a knowing grin over the church secretary who had trouble keeping a secret.

Janet's generous heart and enthusiasm for life demanded she share any good news she heard.

"Joe doesn't talk much about the old days in Brooklyn," Mary said of her good friend Margaret's husband. "I wish I knew if the brothers were close and what happened to make Joe keep his family history so private."

"I thought he sounded angry when he talked about his brother dying," Zack offered. "But what do I know? He seemed angry with me too. I sure wasn't about to ask him."

Abby rose and walked the length of the deck, then back. "I wonder if he knows anything about the sketchbook we found in the case."

Mary pulled out more yarn and wagged a warning finger at Blossom as Finnegan bounded onto the deck. "Joe is adamant that the guitar Zack has was not Neville Sanborne's. Maybe he's just in denial. It's been a long time since the guitar went missing. There's no telling how many hands it passed through before Zack bought it. Anyone could have put the sketchbook into the sheet music pocket."

"You're right." Abby sighed, trying to resign herself to the facts. "There's probably no connection." Still, the remote possibility niggled at her thoughts. "It's just that Hugo and I spent a good part of the day trying to figure out the location of the cave in the drawing."

"A clue's always nice," Zack said. "The sketch is so detailed it feels like you should be able to go right to the spot. As if you've seen it a hundred times. But that pretty much describes most of the bluffs in the San Juan Islands."

"Exactly." Abby removed her glasses and pinched the bridge of her nose. She could almost see the color-coded map and realized she must have memorized it. "Hugo and I did some checking and calling around and managed to eliminate several sections of shoreline."

Replacing her glasses, she continued, "We've narrowed the most likely possibilities down to three or four sites."

"You're going to check them out, of course." Zack rested his forearms on his thighs and leaned toward her. "When?"

His enthusiasm gave her a surge of energy. "Tomorrow morning I'll dig out the camping gear." Fortunately, it would only take a few moments. She kept it in a state of readiness for emergency bird rescues.

"Is Hugo going?" The lightness of Mary's tone betrayed her concern. She'd been alone on a remote stretch of road when her accident happened. Since then, she'd become a bit more cautious, preferring the safety of numbers.

"He's tied up for the next couple weeks." Abby glanced at Zack. The discovery of the manuscript had changed the dynamics of her earlier decision and now she wondered if asking him to accompany her was fair.

"Why don't I go with you?" Zack offered.

The soft clack of Mary's knitting needles ceased. "That's a very good idea, son," she said decisively.

Dumbfounded, Abby met her sister's gaze. "Are you sure? I don't want to intrude on your time together. And now that you have the manuscript . . ."

"I'm sure."

"Me too," Zack said. "Dad's book is Mom and Ida's project. Besides, according to Ida, half the island considers me a celebrity. If I stay here, I'll never get any peace and quiet. Neither will Mom and Ida."

Abby looked over to Zack, then back at Mary. "Of course, I'd love for him to go with me."

"Great, Aunt Abby." Zack stood. "Some of the camping you and I did in New York really helped me clear my head. I even wrote a few songs afterwards."

"You always did love tromping through the woods." Mary resumed knitting. "Go. Enjoy yourselves and the great outdoors. I'm sure I'll have plenty to do once Ida finishes reading."

The phone rang.

"I'll get it." Zack headed for the screen door. "It may be Lily. I left a message for her earlier."

When he was out of earshot, Abby asked her sister, "Are you sure you don't mind?"

"I'm positive." Mary put down her knitting, the yarn woven between her fingers. "If Zack stays here he won't get a chance to think about his future, which is why he came. He needs the serenity of the wind through the trees and the ocean lapping the shore.

"In fact, for a moment, I thought if I weren't in this wheelchair, nothing could keep me from going with you."

"Mary, if you want to come with us, we'll make it happen. Just say the word."

Laughing, Mary answered, "I know you would. But I remember now why I didn't do more camping. I don't like sleeping on the ground."

"Well come on. There's all kinds of great gear. You'll feel like you're in your own bed."

Light streaming from inside revealed Mary's self-deprecating grin. "No it won't. In my bed, I never worry about slugs creeping up on me."

"What are you talking about?"

"When Jacob and I took the kids camping, they slept under

the stars. Not me. I stayed in the tent. It had a floor. But, in the middle of the night, I'd sneak out with a flashlight and check them just to make sure there weren't any slugs sliming their little faces."

Abby laughed at her sister's foible. The sudden image of an army of slugs carrying little slime pails and marching to assault her sleeping bag popped into her mind. "Oh my. I never considered the dangers of a slug attack."

"Well, you should." Mary started knitting again. "I don't suppose bats eat slugs, do they?"

"Not that I know of. But from now on, thanks to you, I'll notice every silvery slug trail around my campsite." Pound for pound, she preferred slugs to bears or cougars.

"I don't believe it." Zack came out on the deck and closed the screen door.

"Lily?" Mary asked.

"I wish. She's introducing a new client to a service dog tonight. The girl's only ten. I'd rather hear how the meeting went than talk to some nut in San Francisco."

Mary raised her eyebrows.

"Yeah. He heard I have Neville's guitar and offered to buy it—sight unseen. That's nutty. He didn't want to take no for an answer. You know, Aunt Abby, camping out with you and hunting for bat caves is exactly what I need."

The phone call had irritated him, Abby realized. She couldn't blame him for wanting to escape the increasing number of inquiries. Like Zack, she had some thinking to do too. He was the perfect person to accompany her.

He turned on the yard lights and picked up the ball, signaling Finnegan he had a playmate. "No phones."

At the sound of the doorbell, Zack hurled the ball and raced the dog out to the grass.

WHILE ABBY ANSWERED THE DOOR, Mary put away her knitting and hoped their visitor hadn't come about the guitar. No wonder Zack was perturbed. The frequent contacts were even beginning to get on her nerves. There had been half a dozen calls on the answering machine when she and Zack returned from their trip to Priority Printing and lunch.

She breathed a sigh of relief at the sound of Ida's voice.

Abby offered the young woman a cup of tea, which she declined, saying, "I'm too excited to drink anything without spilling it all over."

They came out on the deck. Clutching the white printer's box, Ida waved at Zack and took a seat. Before Mary could mention their remuneration plans, Ida said, "I loved this story."

"You read it already?"

"I've done nothing else since you and Zack left the Springhouse. Fortunately, the rest of the afternoon was slow and I didn't have the dinner shift today."

Abby touched Mary's shoulder. "I'll be upstairs, reading while I have the chance. That is, if—"

"I left the other copy for you on the coffee table."

"Oh good. Thanks." Abby went inside, leaving Ida and Mary to talk.

"At first, I didn't think a tale about two brothers growing up in the country could be so rich and full," Ida continued. "I definitely want to be part of this project."

"So you think we can do something with it?"

"Absolutely. Positively. It needs some editing in the rough spots, polishing in others and some transitions between a few of the scenes."

Ida leaned closer. "I always considered Jacob Reynolds a superb writer. But this—" She splayed her fingers over the top of the box. "I laughed. I cried. I ached for those two boys. And now, I can't help wondering what happened to them. I can't believe Jacob just stopped writing."

Neither can I, Mary thought.

"Why?" Ida asked. "Why didn't he finish it?"

Mary shrugged. "I've been asking myself the same question and have no answer. Until this morning, I didn't even know the manuscript existed." And the fact Jacob kept it a secret bothered her more every hour. He'd discussed all his other works with her from start to finish. *Why not this one?*

"I keep wondering if he knew these boys," Ida said. "His insights went very deep, which is probably why they stirred up so much emotion."

"When it came to his youth, Jacob was a very private man," Mary said. "He often told me his life truly began the day he met me."

Ida clasped her hands over the box. "How romantic."

"I always thought so. But now I realize . . . he wasn't being romantic. He was being honest."

In retrospect, it was as though he'd drawn a line around those years. A line no one crossed.

CHAPTER ❀ NINE

Thursday morning Abby yawned without a twinge of regret over lost sleep. Next to her at the breakfast table, Zack yawned too.

"Goodness, what's with you two?" Mary asked.

"I stayed up late reading Jacob's manuscript. I couldn't put it down," Abby admitted. "Are you sure there aren't more pages somewhere with the ending?"

"We felt the same way," Mary said. "I'll check the other boxes later, but given Jacob's love for organization, I doubt he'd split up a manuscript."

"I think you're right, Mom. What we have is all he wrote." Zack turned to Abby. "Can I grab a ride into town with you?"

"Sure. I'm not going straight to work. I've decided to speak with Joe Blackstock about the sketchbook." Seeing Mary ready to protest, Abby added, "I know it may be a dead end so I don't have high hopes. But it'll weigh on my mind if I don't follow up."

"Good. I want to see Joe too." Zack cleared his dishes and headed for the kitchen sink. "Thinking about him, his brother and the guitar kept me awake most of the night."

"How come?" Mary gathered the remnants of her meal.

"I'm ... You know how it is, Mom, when we have our minds made up about something? It's easy to dismiss things that don't agree with our conclusions. I think Joe did just that. He was so sure Neville's guitar was gone forever, he rejected the one I bought without even seeing it."

Nodding, Abby carried the rest of the breakfast dishes to the sink. "What will you do? Show it to him?"

"Yes. If it was his brother's, then by all rights it belongs to Joe now."

"Will you give it to him?" Mary asked.

"Yes," Zack said with finality, then winked at Abby. "Maybe he'll reimburse me for the cost, and maybe he won't. Either way, it doesn't matter."

"You can cross that bridge if you come to it." Abby closed the dishwasher. "Your heart is in the right place. I'm proud of you."

"This is certainly the best way to settle the question of authenticity," Mary mused. "If the guitar wasn't Neville Sanborne's and word gets out ..."

Abby picked up her purse and briefcase. "Finish what you were going to say, Mary."

"We promised we'd keep Joe's relationship with Neville to ourselves."

"He knew that didn't include Aunt Abby. He's smart enough to know this family doesn't keep secrets from each other," Zack assured his mother. "And as for the guitar, I can handle any questions without involving Joe. If it wasn't Neville's, I can honestly say I heard it from an unimpeachable source."

"I see," Mary said. "And if it is?"

"Again, I'll tell the truth—that I returned the guitar to the rightful owner. I don't have to name names."

Mary reached up and squeezed her son's arm. "You're not only a good man, you're a smart one."

After giving her a kiss good-bye, Zack loaded the guitar into the backseat of Abby's car and they headed for town.

"This time of day we're most likely to find Joe tinkering with his boat," Abby told her nephew as she parked near the Green Harbor Marina.

Gulls squawked, their graceful bodies soaring on the sea breeze. The floating dock gently rose and fell with the mellow waves. Nearby, a pair of Canada geese basked in the morning sun. Overhead, blue sky pushed a melting line of fog toward the horizon.

"Is it true Canada geese mate for life?" Zack asked as they walked down the dock toward the *Island Hopper's Delight*.

"Yes. They're remarkably faithful and mourn when a mate dies." Abby spotted Joe in the cabin of the thirty-four-foot Bayliner. "They're rather predictable, like Joe. He's one of those people who enjoys polishing and maintaining his boat as much as he likes taking it out on the water."

"Just the kind of man who should own one."

"Ahoy, Joe," Abby called from the dock.

"Hello, Abby." Joe bustled out of the cabin onto the deck. His cheery smile melted when he saw Zack with the guitar case. "I thought we finished this business yesterday."

"Well, sir, we did and we didn't. I had trouble sleeping last night. You and this guitar were the reason. So I need your help."

Joe's surprised gaze darted suspiciously between Zack and the leather case. "To do what?"

"Look at the guitar. Thoroughly. If you tell me it wasn't your brother's, I'll be satisfied. I'll sleep tonight. But if it was Neville's —Mark's, then it should belong to you," Zack said evenly.

"You really know how to corner a guy." Joe cocked an eyebrow at Abby. "Sometimes it's best to let things be."

She returned a thin, quiet smile. Zack was his own man and Joe knew it. She could only surmise the controversy around the guitar had sparked long-forgotten memories. Unfortunately, she didn't know if they were good or bad.

Not budging an inch, Zack pressed, "How about it?"

"I suppose you'll hound me until I look at it."

"I can be persistent."

"All right. Let's see it and get this done. I have a deck to swab before I go to the shop."

Zack went down on one knee, laid the case on the dock and flipped open the fasteners. Abby watched Joe for a sign of recognition, but his expression remained unreadable when Zack lifted the guitar out of the plush interior.

Joe took the instrument and stared at the stringed surface for a long time. Slowly, he tilted the guitar to see both sides.

Just when Abby was about to ask if it was Neville's, Joe turned the instrument over. A flash of sunlight glinted off the shiny surface and let her catch a glimpse of the tears in Joe's brown eyes.

She glanced at Zack to see if he noticed. He seemed barely breathing, his full concentration devoted to Joe.

Finally, the older man spoke. "You opened Pandora's box, Zack. I'd know Mark's guitar anywhere."

A surge of excitement coursed through Abby. She had dozens of questions to ask him about his brother, but she kept a firm rein on her tongue. This moment belonged to the two men. Zack let the silence lengthen.

Joe shifted the guitar and held it with his left hand. His callused right forefinger traced the silver letters on the neck. "I remember the day Mark did this. He thought Neville sounded British and had a more memorable ring than Mark Blackstock. He wanted people to really listen to his music, to remember it and him."

"He succeeded," Zack said respectfully.

Joe shook himself. "And you're getting there too." He held out the guitar. "Here you go."

Zack shook his head and folded his arms. "Like I said, you tell me it was your brother's—"

"It was. It's the genuine article."

"Then it's yours."

"And I'm supposed to do what with it? Hang it on a wall? Turn it into a curiosity?" Caressing the instrument with his gaze, Joe shook his head slowly. "This was meant to be played. It made people happy. Made 'em sing and dance. I don't have that talent, but you do, Zack. You keep it. Use it like it was meant to be used."

The conviction in Joe's refusal took Abby by surprise. However, he could not have made his position any clearer.

A brazen gull lit beside the case and looked inside. "No, you don't," Abby chided, bending to shoo the gull away. He eyed her defiantly before waddling down the dock.

"Thank you," Zack said as he took the guitar. "I won't be selling this or hanging it in a museum."

With a tight nod of approval, Joe turned away.

"There's something else," Abby said hurriedly and stood up. Opening her briefcase, she removed the sketchbook. "I realize the guitar may have passed through many hands, but considering this revelation I think it's best to ask you. Do you know anything about this?" She offered the book to Joe.

His hands trembled when he took it and Abby felt a wave of empathy. Seeing the guitar after all the years of believing it lost forever must have been an emotional jolt. Without uttering a word, he opened the cover and turned the pages carefully, looking at each drawing. When he finished, he said, "This is Mark's work too. Where'd you get it?"

She explained how she found it in the sheet music pocket.

Amazement filled Joe's expression. "I can't believe it was still there."

"Could be no one discovered the pocket," Zack said. "It's a custom design. This is the first case I've seen with one."

"I'd like to ask you about some of the drawings."

Joe handed back the sketchbook and Abby carefully turned to the pages showing the bats. "Do you know where and when he did these drawings? It's important."

Joe scratched his head and shrugged. "Whenever life got hectic, Mark came to the San Juan Islands with his hiking gear and the guitar. He loved it here, called the islands his quiet refuge. He wrote his best songs here.

"I can't remember a time when he didn't have a pencil in his hand—composing lyrics or sketching something. Mark never owned a camera. To him, photos couldn't capture emotions like a drawing." Joe thrust his hands into his jeans pockets and studied the pictures again.

"What a talented man," Abby said.

"Yeah, Mark was one of those special guys who lit up a

room the minute he entered. He was eleven years older than me and I idolized him. For my high school graduation—" Joe gazed wistfully out at the blue sea—"Mark brought me with him on a trip to the San Juan Islands."

Pleased that at least some of Joe's memories were happy ones, Abby gave an encouraging smile.

He sniffed and squared his shoulders. "Back then, it didn't matter where we went as long as he took me along. We did a lot of climbing. He liked the bluffs where a man feels suspended between the sky and the sea. That's where he felt closest to God."

"Can you remember which islands he favored? Was there one in particular? Or a special area he liked?"

Joe scrunched his eyes and rubbed his forehead a moment, then looked at her. "We usually hung out in the Rosario Strait. He liked Decatur and Blakely Islands." Joe shook his head. "I haven't thought about this in years. Why is it important now?"

Abby looked down at the drawing. She and Beth had discussed the artist's notation beside the bat and the arrows pointing to the short dark brown hair on the back and shoulder patches. A second entry noted the underhair was a lighter brown. "Beth Bingham at the WDFW thinks this is a Keen's myotis. If it is, these little guys are rare and possibly endangered."

"Ahh. I should've figured something like that since you're involved. If I think of anything helpful, I'll let you know. How about selling the sketchbook to me?"

Suddenly seized with reluctance, Abby wanted to hold onto the book, at least for a while. "May I keep it until we find the bats?"

"OH, MARY, these boys were so close." Ida pushed back from the Reynolds' dining table, wistfulness pinking her pale cheeks. "I always wondered what it would be like to have a sister—or even a brother. Someone to play with and share secrets would've been terrific. I guess that's why I like Jacob's story so much."

Mindful of the seven long years Ida had been without any immediate family, Mary covered the young woman's hand with her own. "You're a little sister to me."

"Goodness." The pink in Ida's cheeks deepened into a rosy blush. "What would Abby think?"

"I know she feels the same way. Love always has room for one more."

"That's what I mean. It's neat the way you two often know each others thoughts."

Mary squared the corners of the pages in front of her. "It wasn't always that way. Like the boys in this story, when we were little, the bond between us was tightly woven. And like them, we had our differences. Then adolescence hit and we walked a rocky road for a while. Now, with the Lord's guidance, we've come full circle and resolved past misunderstandings."

Sensing that Finnegan needed activity, she bent toward him. "Go get the paper."

The dog trotted off to the handy pet door built for him and Blossom.

Mary returned her attention to Ida. "You know, I think you've touched on what's missing at the end of Jacob's manuscript— the aching intimacy contained in these first sections."

Ida tapped the pencil eraser on the table. "Do you think the accident with the swing happened to someone Jacob knew? Maybe he was there and saw the whole thing."

"Or maybe he was drawing on the emotions he and I experienced when Zack had his first bad accident. Talk about fear. Holding your injured child in your arms is truly an unforgettable experience."

The pencil tapping stopped. "What happened?"

"We were in the front yard watching Zack learn how to ride his bike. At the driveway, he looked over and saw us, grinned from ear to ear and tried to wave. He went head over handlebars. Fortunately, he had no broken bones, although he did have a concussion.

"After we took him home from the emergency room, Jacob stayed by his side day and night for the next three days while the concussion took care of itself."

"He must have been a very sensitive man," Ida mused. "No wonder he wrote with such feeling."

Mary looked down at the manuscript. In the story, Jake and Gerry took turns on a backyard swing to see who could go the highest. Jake had just topped his brother's record when the tree limb holding the swing broke. He'd landed hard, the branch crashing down on top of him. A large splinter pierced his upper arm.

"I wonder . . ." Mary's voice trailed as her thoughts sped through the past.

"What?"

She checked her watch. They had time. The Springhouse didn't expect Ida until eleven o'clock.

"Come with me." With Finnegan at her side, Mary wheeled through the living room, down the short hall and into her bedroom. She selected a photo album from the dozen lined up on the bottom shelf of the nightstand. Flipping through the pages, she found the faded photo of Jacob on the beach.

"Oh. My. Goodness," Ida exclaimed, looking closely at the photo. "Is it my imagination, or is Jacob's scar in the same place as Jake's in the story?"

Hearing her thoughts confirmed raised more questions in Mary's mind. "I once asked him how he got the injury. He told me he was swinging on a tire swing and it broke."

"Just like in the manuscript!"

"I didn't make the connection the first time I read it. The story captivated me . . . but as we were talking, it struck me as familiar, as something I'd known about for a long time. Then I remembered Jacob's scar."

Ida ran a fingertip across the photo. "If he was writing from experience then we have a real mystery on our hands."

"I think we can safely assume Jacob patterned this scene around himself."

"If that's true, it raises another question." Ida closed the album. "Who is the other boy? Did Jacob actually know a kid named Gerry?"

WITH THE KEYS to her father's boat in her pocket, provisions from The Green Grocer stashed in the trunk of her car along with their gear, Abby led Zack into The Nature Museum.

"Glad to see you again." Hugo clasped Zack's extended hand in both of his. "You're looking fine. Excellent hat."

"Thank you, sir." Grinning broadly, Zack stroked the brim of the fedora. "It was my father's."

Abby thought Jacob would have enjoyed his son's quiet pride of ownership. "Zack's going on the bat hunt with me. We've decided to leave this afternoon and want to go over our itinerary with you."

"Excellent. I'm sorry to miss the adventure but relieved you two will be looking out for one another. By the way, Zack, the sketchbook you gave your aunt provided the impetus for our next exhibit. We've decided to call it 'The Benefits of Bats.'"

Abby beamed at her boss. "When people discover all the good bats do for us, they'll want to protect them." Hugo's enthusiasm for the exhibit added to her optimism. They'd find the elusive little critters. She was sure of it. "We'll concentrate our search efforts along the coastlines in the Rosario Strait."

Hugo's white eyebrows knit with perplexity. "Why there?"

"Come with me." She took the men to her office. After closing the door for privacy, Abby told her trusted friend and employer about Joe's connection to the guitar—and the sketchbook.

Zack explained Joe's request for confidentiality and added, "I don't blame him a bit. People are all riled up over this guitar."

"I see," Hugo murmured. "I know Joe prefers a simple, quiet life with Margaret, their boat and his print shop. If it becomes common knowledge he was Neville's brother, their lives will turn upside down. William Jansen at *The Birdcall* would press him for an interview."

Zack grimaced. "If people know, they won't leave him alone. I even had to change the message on Mom's answering machine."

This was news to Abby, welcome news. "What is it now?"

"If you're calling about the guitar." Zack spoke in an imperiously official tone. "Look elsewhere, there's nothing for sale at this number."

"You're so good at that, Zack, you're scary." Abby gave him a mock punch on the arm.

"I was tempted to do it in Mom's voice, but I didn't think she'd approve."

"She wouldn't mind. Not much anyway. I hope your message works."

"Me too," Hugo added solemnly. "No one will hear about Joe's connection with Neville from me." Turning to the wall map, Hugo tapped the Rosario Strait. "In light of this new information, it makes good sense to start here. How long will you be gone?"

Zack looked at Abby. "Two nights?"

"Definitely. We want to make the most of it." Thinking of the changing tides, she glanced at her watch, then pointed to a bay on Decatur Island. "We'll begin here and work our way down the coast. There are several good vantage sites where we can scan long stretches of shoreline."

"Right," Zack agreed. "Then, if we find something reasonably close to the bluff in the drawings, we'll cut in toward the shore and check it out."

Hugo smoothed his mustache. "Sounds like a good plan."

"We'd better get moving," Zack urged. "We want to take full advantage of high tide and we still need to load Grandpa's boat."

"Right you are," Abby agreed. "I feel much better about this, Hugo. We've narrowed the search area drastically. There's only forty miles to explore."

Their gazes met and she could see an unspoken concern in his deep blue eyes. They both knew forty miles of squiggly coastline meant unpredictable eddies and sharp rocks lurking beneath the water. In the ever-changing conditions, a single moment of inattention could be disastrous.

CHAPTER ❦ TEN

MARY HAD JUST FINISHED freshening up when Ida returned to the house with her overnight bag. "Welcome back. We are all delighted you could stay with me while they're camping. It's such short notice."

"Not to worry. I'm glad to be here." Ida put her little duffel on the steps next to the basket of freshly laundered sheets. "When I first started working split shifts, I didn't think I'd like it. Now, I love having free time during the day. I can run errands, visit friends and take online classes."

"I see," Mary said, heading for the kitchen. "Those are advantages I hadn't considered. And your writing instructor?"

"Thinks I'm one of the luckiest girls in the world to work on a Jacob Reynolds manuscript." Ida carried the tea tray to the dining table where they'd left the pages earlier in the day. "And I definitely agree. If I don't stop pinching myself to make sure I'm not dreaming I'll be black and blue all over."

Mary chuckled, then turned her attention to the page of notes she'd started. The paper was only half filled. "I've been trying to come up with an end to the story, but I'm not making any real progress."

Ida turned sideways on her chair and faced Mary. "I'm stymied too. I think our trouble is that we don't understand the real meaning of the story."

"*Something* is missing," Mary agreed. "Until we discover what it is, we've hit a wall. Good heavens, we've barely started. Is this writer's block?"

Ida laughed. "Perish the thought. It means we need to do some research. Did Jacob leave anything else with the manuscript? It doesn't have to make sense—at least not right away. We simply need a clue as to why he wrote this story."

"Let's go to the craft room." Mary turned her chair. "I've been meaning to open the next box, but between the fedora and the manuscript, I didn't get any further." *I've been afraid of what I might find.*

"Ohh, good! Maybe Jacob left us a clue or more pages."

Grateful for Ida's upbeat attitude and trying to draw on it, Mary quipped, "Get out your magnifying glass, Sherlock Holmes. The game is afoot."

In the craft room, two sealed boxes sat on the table. Mary tossed the empty one on the staging stand aside. "If you'll get box number two, we'll see if we can solve this mystery."

Ida obliged and set it within easy reach. "This feels like a game show. You know—are the answers in box number one or box number two?"

Mimicking a television announcer, Mary said, "Stay tuned to find out." With her heart in her throat, she ran a sharp craft knife across the sealing tape.

Together, they folded back the flaps and removed wads of

packing paper. A third of the way down, they found a treasure wrapped in a thick towel.

"My goodness, it . . . it's extraordinary," Ida whispered as she lifted out an exquisite teak box and gave it to Mary.

Perplexed and feeling a growing hurt, Mary nodded. She recognized Jacob's workmanship. *Why haven't I seen this piece before?*

Like the manuscript, the box carved another question mark into her heart. Her pulse racing, she ran her fingertips over the sides and corners. "Smooth as glass," she murmured.

"It's so perfect," Ida breathed.

Mary remembered how Jacob frequently came in from the garage covered in sawdust with only one thought on his mind—sharing the beauty of a particular wood grain with her. "He believed certain pieces of wood reflected bits of God's glory. He wouldn't carve on them because it would be like defacing a masterpiece. Instead, he'd spend hours on the finish, bringing out the natural luster." Mary caressed the rounded edges and corners. Everything about the box felt fluid. *Why didn't he share this one with me?*

"Where are the hinges?" Ida bent down for a closer inspection.

"Hidden inside."

"Aren't you going to open it?"

Apprehension swirling, Mary slowly lifted the lid. Immediately, she realized it was a presentation box, the two halves of equal size. On the right, four swivel fasteners held an old horseshoe against a pale blue velvet lining. On the left, flat clips held a yellowed envelope.

"Oh. My. Goodness," exhaled Ida. "A horseshoe. Just like in the story."

"Ida, will you get that chapter off the table? Bring it in here and read it to me?"

"I'll be back in a flash."

While Ida read aloud, Mary held the box on her lap and traced the outer edge of the horseshoe.

Heat waves shimmered off the sand surrounding the steel pole in the horseshoe pit. Jake ignored the pain shooting up his arm and concentrated on the opposing team. He and Gerry couldn't afford to lose this final round of the competition. They'd made a bet with their father and their whole summer was at stake.

Just the thought of spending those golden months inside the family store made the knot in Jake's stomach tighten. He hated make-work jobs like sweeping up after the janitor, repainting walls they'd done last year, or recounting the stock their father checked every morning.

Last night was the worst. He and Gerry got stuck rearranging the storeroom for the third time in as many days. Father was afraid of losing the bet and having to close the doors for one measly day, so he'd come up with the ridiculous project. The ache in Jake's heart grew, surpassing the throb in his arms.

Please, God, let us win so we can prove to Father there's more to life than work. Just once, make him spend the whole day doing fun things with Gerry and me. I don't care what it is, Lord. Fishing, playing catch, a picnic in the park, even the silly miniature golf park would be all right. Just let us do something together where we can wear old clothes, get dirty and laugh a lot.

The opposing team scored a leaner and Jake's hopes sank. For them to win, his brother would have to score and Gerry looked done in. His face was pasty-white and sweat trickled down the side of his neck. "Oh man," he moaned, his eyes filled with worry, "we're in trouble now."

Jake put his arm around Gerry's sagging shoulders. "Nah. It's okay. We're the best. We can do it."

A snicker rolled through the crowd and Gerry grew paler. "I can't. We're gonna lose."

The quaver in his younger brother's voice struck deep, promising there was more at stake than the bet. Somehow, Gerry mistakenly feared their friendship was on the line.

"Maybe we will," Jake agreed softly. "And maybe we won't. Whatever happens, you're still my brother. Still my best buddy. And best buddies don't give up without trying."

"I suppose." Gerry looked up, his expression waffling between hope and anxiety. "You promise? Whatever happens we're still tight?"

"I promise." Jake crossed his heart. "Always."

Gerry's chin came up and he drew a deep breath. His first attempt fell short. The second slipped out of his grasp and landed halfway down the lane. The opposition began congratulating each other and elbowing their friends.

"You can do it, Buddy. I'm right here with you."

"Okay." Gerry took two steps back then led off with his left foot while drawing his right arm down. His form was perfect. One step, two and a stumble on the release.

The crowd gasped and Jake's insides turned over. He

didn't want to watch but couldn't look away. The horse-shoe arced up and out and hit the ground in front of the box. The iron bounced into the sand, then rolled on an edge to a stop. As it teetered in the sand, Jake saw himself mopping a corridor that stretched into forever.

He grabbed his brother, held him tight and whispered, "No matter what."

The horseshoe wobbled over, landing with a soft plop and circling the iron pole neat as a ring on a finger.

As Ida's voice trailed away, Mary opened the aged envelope and took out a royal blue ribbon lettered First Place in gold. Fighting tears, she slipped the satin trophy beneath the flat clips. "I'm so confused. Right now, I'm getting angry with Jacob. I don't like not knowing what this means."

Ida knelt and clasped Mary's forearm. "In my first writing class, the instructor put five items on his desk. Everyone had to choose three, then write a story around them. Although we were free to select any three, they had to connect in the story."

She touched the side of the box. "Maybe that's what Jacob did here. Maybe the manuscript is a collection of pages he wrote about seemingly unrelated items to get his creative juices going."

Mary sighed. It didn't sound like something Jacob would have done. Still . . . "All right, we have the horseshoe and the ribbon. How do they get us closer to writing the last chapter?"

Ida tilted her head, her gaze on the horseshoe. "Let's go on a scavenger hunt."

"Huh?" Mary set the presentation box on the craft table.

"Let's look around the house for any items Jacob mentioned in his story. If we find some, it'll help settle the question."

"You mean, if it was a writing exercise?" Mary didn't believe Jacob wrote the story for practice, but she liked the idea of a scavenger hunt. One way or the other, she needed an answer to a much bigger question. Was the book fiction or not? If Jacob was Jake, were the vignettes wishful thinking? Or were they something more?

ENJOYING A LONG AFTERNOON on the Stantons' boat, Abby and Zack took a second turn around Decatur Island. She'd noted three areas deserving a closer look.

Pointing to an islet about a half mile across, Zack said, "I always thought of Center Island as small, but look over there." A twin engine Cessna approached and landed on an airstrip beyond the trees.

"I suppose it's a matter of perspective." Changing the focus on her binoculars, Abby scanned the bluffs below the landing field. "To me, *small* means The Pointers or Black Rock—any of those chunks of rock rising out of the sea."

"Yep. They're picturesque, but in the fog, or during a storm . . ." He shuddered and steered the boat around tiny Trump Island. "I remember the day Dad, Grandpa and I had a run-in with one."

A sense of being left out fluttered over Abby's heart as she trained her binoculars on the cliffs above Brigantine Bay. She'd only heard about the mishap after the family males reached home safely. "I remember many prayers of thanks that none of you got hurt."

"You were at Cornell then, right?"

"No, I was at a spill site, rescuing oiled birds."

Keeping Decatur Island on their right, Zack guided the

boat into Thatcher Pass. "Oh yeah, I remember now. Grandpa said you were the reason our rescue came so fast. Since you were taking care of His birds, God sent the fisherman to take care of us."

Abby laughed and felt lighter. "Dad tends to give me way too much credit."

They rounded Fauntleroy Point, motored past a flat stretch of shore, then threaded the narrow pass between Decatur Head and little James Island. Abby studied the steep bluffs around the jut of land on the bigger island. A quick check of her notes confirmed she'd put it near the top of her list.

"I'm glad we made this second pass, Zack. This spot has potential, but the north end of Reads Bay is more promising. We'll go back there after we set up camp and have dinner."

"Did we decide to camp on Spencer Spit at Lopez?"

"It seems our best choice," Abby said. "It's near our search area and easily accessible."

"Sounds good. I'm getting hungry." He nudged the throttle forward.

After they'd dropped anchor and gone ashore, a short hike brought them to their campsite. Abby liked Zack's suggestion of sleeping under the stars. Even better, he proved he hadn't forgotten Northwest camping basics and put up a just-in-case tent.

Meanwhile, she got busy at the fire pit. Knowing they'd need a stout meal, she put foil-wrapped potatoes and corn on the cob on the coals and seasoned the meat.

While they waited for the vegetables to cook, Zack brought out his controversial purchase. Giving her a conspiratorial wink, he began strumming familiar ballads from the 1970s.

It was just like him to bring his music along. "Most people would be flabbergasted if they knew you brought Neville Sanborne's guitar on a camping trip."

"I won't tell if you won't." Zack executed a complex sequence of chords, paused and looked at her. "It bugs me not knowing why I went to the thrift store. Why I bought this particular guitar. I'm not an impulse buyer. The last thing I want to do is accumulate stuff I have to drag around when we tour."

With no insights to offer, she tilted her head, inviting him to continue.

"The more I think about it, the more it comes down to just feeling like I should."

"I have to admit, it's easier to tote around than your keyboard. And," she glanced at the trees, "there's no need for an electrical outlet."

"The crazy thing is, I left my keyboard behind so I wouldn't get distracted by my music. I need to concentrate on figuring out my future." Zack folded his arms over the guitar and shook his head. "I called Lily before we left home. She's on cloud nine. The pairing of the little girl and the dog went even better than she'd hoped. Of course, she's a little sad too. You can't train dogs like she does without loving them. Giving them away to a new owner means giving away a piece of her heart."

Abby felt a rush of affection for Lily and her generous nature. "Is she still working part-time for the veterinarian?"

"Yes. He wants her as a full-time assistant, but she's committed to Pet Partners. It's her sweet spot. Despite the time it takes, she refuses to call what she does work."

"When we love what we do it doesn't feel like work." Abby paused for a moment, then asked, "Are you serious about Lily?"

Zack set down the guitar. "At this stage of my life, it wouldn't be fair to get serious about any woman, let alone Lily. Don't get me wrong. I really care for her, but . . ." He looked away. "Isn't it time to start the meat?"

Realizing she'd struck close to the core of his problem, Abby let the subject drop. Perhaps later, after the peace of their surroundings settled in, he'd be ready to talk. She hoped so. Lily had a hold on his heart whether he wanted to acknowledge it or not.

Abby went to the fire pit and tested a potato. "The veggies are ready. Do you want to do the honors and grill the meat?"

"Doesn't every guy?" He stood. "You know it's my favorite part."

While she put the rest of their repast on the picnic table, Zack put on a virtuoso performance at the grill.

After a leisurely dinner, they took the boat back to Reads Bay and dropped anchor where they had the best view of the bluffs. Abby's anticipation built as the sun dipped toward the horizon.

"Did you ever do anything you regret, Aunt Abby?"

"I think everyone wishes they could say no to that question." She chuckled sadly. "Me included. In fact, I was just thinking about one such incident. Only this one wasn't something I did. It was something I didn't do."

"Are you willing to share?"

The weight behind her ribs felt heavy and she glanced up at the sky. Ironically, the sun seemed to hang in place, promising all the time she'd need for a little soul baring. She took a deep breath. "Funny, I remember it so clearly now. I was at Cornell. A student had asked me to write a recommendation letter.

"Late in the afternoon, just about this time of day, I sat at home, composing the letter. It took a while. I wanted the recommendation to be positive without excessive superlatives. Most of all, I wanted it to be an honest assessment.

"I was quite pleased when I finished. Then I couldn't find any university letterhead. I kept meaning to get some, but other things got in the way—preparing for finals, graduation and my first trip to the Amazon."

Her shoulders slumped. "In a nutshell, I got so busy I forgot about the letter. Didn't remember it until I came back from the Amazon and found the draft in my in-box. The person who asked for it hadn't entered the master's program there at Cornell. She'd left the school.

"Now, I'm wondering if my oversight was the reason." She wished she could go back and finish the job she'd left undone.

"Wow," Zack breathed. "It reminds me of the poem: for want of a nail the horseshoe was lost, then the rider, and all the way up to the battle. So what happened to the person?"

"She finished her education elsewhere. I'd always assumed she'd continue in ornithology, but she took up a completely different field."

Suddenly, the setting sun shot vivid streamers of orange, gold and purple through the high clouds.

"It's time. If the bats are here, they'll fly out any minute," Abby said.

Together, equipped with her best binoculars, she and Zack studied the cliffs, searching for any dark wisp of motion against the pale rock.

As the sky's color faded into night, Abby struggled to hide her disappointment. Finding the bats on the very first attempt wasn't a realistic expectation. Like raising the old issue with Beth, neither endeavor would be easy.

Later, Abby and Zack snuggled in their sleeping bags. A fire burned in the pit, the flames dancing in the soft breeze.

"This is great, Aunt Abby. It's been way too long since I slept out under the stars."

Zack started humming "Amazing Grace" and Abby joined in singing.

With Zack's sure tenor leading the way, they made it through three hymns before Abby hit a clinker of a sour note that set them laughing.

As the night deepened, the flames died back to a toasty bed of coals. She cocked an ear to the song filtering through the trees and echoing out on the water. "Listen, Zack. There's a Swainson's thrush. He must be restless tonight."

"I hear it. Hey, there's a flying tiger."

She smiled into the darkness, pleased he'd remembered what she told him about the fearlessness of the great horned owl and his nickname.

They listened to the night songs for a little while before Zack spoke again. "Dad's manuscript keeps running through my head."

"He does bring childhood to life on those pages," Abby murmured.

"He and Mom gave Nancy and me great childhoods. In my travels, I've seen a lot. I know it isn't easy being a parent today. I doubt it ever was. I wonder how Dad managed to make the right choices every time."

Abby grinned at the stars. "I doubt he thought he did. The important thing is you think he did."

Zack chuckled. "I remember a few times when he and Mom butted heads."

"Would one of those be when you tried to buy a motorcycle?"

Abby had been on the phone with her mother every night for a week. Ellen hadn't wanted to take sides, but like Mary, she was terrified of seventeen-year-old Zack getting hurt.

"It was a sweet machine. And Dad was on my side. He knew he couldn't protect me against life. Mom wanted to keep the padding around me for a while longer. Until I was fifty-five, I think."

Abby laughed. "She's done a good job of letting go and trusting you."

"She's the best." He paused. "So was Dad. I can't tell you how much I wish he were still here. Or how many times I've wanted to ask his advice. When I was younger, I didn't realize how well he ordered his priorities. He knew how to balance his love in life and his love for his art."

"Jacob was many things," Abby reflected, "a true Renaissance man. Best of all, he was eager to lend a hand whenever someone needed it. That's quite a legacy."

CHAPTER ❦ ELEVEN

Ida's eyes widened as she looked at the miniature carvings. Pigment enhanced the intricate designs engraved on ivory and whalebone. "Jacob made all of these?"

"And the cabinet." Mary opened the wood-framed glass door of the three-tiered display case. "Scrimshaw was his winter hobby. He wasn't much for television and considered scrimshanding an appropriate pastime for someone who loved whale watching like he did."

"What does one have to do with the other?"

Mary recalled his patient explanation when she'd asked the same question. "In the early 1800s, whalers didn't have a lot to do between hunts or at night. To fill the long hours, they made their own tools and engraved elaborate pictures on whatever was handy—usually the bones and teeth of whales or an occasional walrus tusk. It was a long tradition. Herman Melville referred to scrimshanders using whalebone in his novel, *Moby Dick*."

"Gosh, I wonder how I missed that. I guess I was too caught up in Ahab's story, because I always connected scrimshaw with elephant ivory. Come to think of it, elephant ivory and old whaling ships really don't go together."

"No, and there's an embargo on ivory. Some ivory with pre-embargo status is still legal to purchase. That's what Jacob bought."

"I see. So scrimshaw is a lost art?"

"It almost was. America banned commercial whaling in the Pacific around 1824. Shortly thereafter, the American Whaling Fleet ceased to exist and the art of scrimshaw sort of died out too. Today, many of those old pieces are found only in museums.

"It might have slipped into total obscurity if President John F. Kennedy hadn't been an avid collector. His interest brought scrimshaw back into the public eye."

"Good, because these are beautiful."

Mary took a small but powerful magnifying glass off the shelf. Next, she picked up a whale tooth engraved with a stand of iris. Giving both objects to Ida, she said, "If you look closely, you'll see how each petal and leaf is comprised of many tiny lines."

"The detail's amazing," Ida breathed. "All that work. It must have a very special meaning."

"Jacob made it for my birthday. It was his last piece."

Ida reverently handed it back. "Do all these commemorate similar events?"

"In a way. They're mementos of special times we had together." Mary selected a piece of whalebone with a three-masted schooner tossed on a stormy sea.

She offered it to Ida and said, "He carved this the winter

Nancy had measles. She was miserable and only quieted if I held her and Jacob sang to her. After a week he was so hoarse he couldn't talk."

Ida examined the carving before returning it to the glass shelf. "And the others? Would you mind telling me about them?"

While Mary took a trip down memory lane, Ida studied Jacob's scrimshaw with the appreciative yearning of a girl who'd lost her family much too soon.

After the last piece, Ida said, "How wonderful you have such beautiful reminders."

"There's one more item." Mary took it out of the back of the cabinet and held it up to the light.

Two laughing boys played on a tire swing. The one soaring into the air looked over his shoulder at the other whose arms were still extended from providing a mighty shove. She'd always thought the image charming and never questioned its presence in the midst of their family treasures. *Until earlier today.* "This is the one I wanted you to see. I don't know the story behind it. Or I didn't until we found the manuscript."

"I see what you mean," Ida said softly. She stroked her thumb over the piece. "The texture feels different. And the image doesn't go with the others. They're all landscapes or seascapes, not people."

"You're very observant, Ida. Jacob used elk horn for this scene."

"When did he carve it?"

"A few years after Zack was born. It was one of his first pieces."

Finnegan yawned noisily.

Mary glanced at the clock and was both surprised and relieved to find the hour was late. No wonder Blossom had disappeared. She'd undoubtedly curled up in the middle of the bed.

Suddenly very tired, Mary said, "Let's turn in and start fresh tomorrow."

"Okay. It's been a long day for me too. Sharing your memories was a very personal and generous thing, Mary. Thanks for trusting me with them."

"You're very welcome, dear."

A short time later, Mary lay in bed unable to sleep, the impromptu scavenger hunt heavy on her mind. Jacob intended her to follow his clues. Of that, she was certain. The trip to the scrimshaw cabinet was her idea and turned out to be a very insightful one.

Sharing the story of each piece had taken her back in time and allowed her to relive the joys that had given their love and youth such color.

She saw again how he'd tried to prepare her during his final months. Often he spoke of her moving on with her life—remembering him, but being open for new love, fresh opportunities and the full joy of living.

How well he had known her. Although she no longer grieved, she'd been afraid to let go and move on. Who would love her, and whom would she love, with the total commitment she and Jacob had shared?

The words he spoke a decade ago echoed clearly in her mind. *Every love, like every person, is different. God made us for love. To love Him. To love each other.*

An image of Sgt. Henry Cobb rose in her mind. What she felt for him was different from her feelings for Jacob.

Was it love? She wasn't ready to say, though she conceded it was a mature emotion and it ran very deep. Henry had a way of showing how he felt. He was steadfast. Loyal. Loving.

She had no doubt he'd walk through fire to help her. He'd been the first person on the scene of the car accident that put her in the wheelchair. Their relationship hadn't developed until after she could no longer dance and hike, run or even walk.

She punched the pillow again and Blossom kneaded the blanket in a show of annoyance at her restlessness. Mary stroked the cat's soft fur and realized that, for several reasons, she needed to solve Jacob's riddle.

Her night prayers included a plea for understanding why he hadn't told her about the manuscript. It seemed every time she turned around, she discovered things she didn't know about him and it hurt.

THE SECOND DAY of their search, Abby lowered her binoculars and glanced at Zack at the helm of the boat. He stood with his stubbled chin thrust forward and was as quiet as he'd been all morning. Other than a few necessary snippets of conversation, he'd barely spoken since they broke camp.

The rapid changes in his expression reflected an intense inner dialogue. For Abby, those faraway looks, negative head-shakes and confused sighs were familiar symptoms of a young person chewing on a problem.

She suspected Zack's thoughts centered on last night's discussion. Considering his admiration for his father's ability to prioritize, her nephew had a great deal to contemplate.

The situation reminded her of the years at Cornell when she felt like a lightning rod for students seeking guidance. She'd quickly learned that most often, the answers lay inside the seeker. Uncovering the truth was the challenge and silence was her most potent ally. For now, Zack needed to search. When he was ready to open up, he would.

In the meantime, she had her own issue to contemplate.

She raised her binoculars, scanned the cliffs and thought about her telephone conversation with the WDFW's bat expert. Beth had sounded genuinely happy to hear from Abby and eager to renew their acquaintance.

She swallowed hard, again wondering if her oversight had contributed to Beth being excluded from the master's program. Either way, she owed Beth an apology. It was the best way to clear the slate.

Gulls circled overhead, crying a challenge to the raucous crows chasing an unconcerned eagle. With a disdainful flex of his powerful wings, the raptor caught a wind current and sailed toward the crags. From the shore, songbirds trilled to the rhythm of the waves.

"Those cliffs look promising, Aunt Abby." Zack pointed to a jut where blue-water waves broke at the base.

She checked the map. If they were cruising along the southern tip of Blakely Island . . . "That must be Armitage Island. Let's check it out."

"Whoa, look there!" Zack turned the boat in the water and cut the engine. A pod of Orcas swam lazily between them and the island.

Enthralled by the sight, Abby and Zack momentarily abandoned their quest and watched the magnificent black and white whales. Their sleek bodies glided effortlessly through the water with a flick of their powerful tails.

The scene felt eerily familiar and Abby hastily flipped the pages in the sketchbook. When she found the one she wanted, she rushed to show Zack. "Mark Blackstock drew a pod of Orcas in this exact, same spot. Look. The coastlines are nearly identical."

Zack looked from the page to the cliffs and back. "We must be getting close."

"It's been decades since Mark made these drawings. I thought erosion and weather would have taken a bigger toll on the topography. Seeing that it hasn't helps us a lot. The cliffs we're searching for shouldn't have changed much from the sketch either."

Waves from the wake of the passing Orca pod sent the boat rocking. Off balance, she reached for a handhold and dropped the sketchbook. "Oh no!"

"I got it." Zack scooped up the drawings.

"Thank you. Thank you." Her heart had nearly stopped when the book tumbled close to the edge of the deck.

"What do you say we check out this chunk of rock?"

"Excellent, as Hugo would say."

Shortly after noon the dam of Zack's silence broke. "I've been thinking . . ." he started, then his voice trailed.

Abby gave him a "no kidding" look, which brought a faint smile to his serious expression. "Care to share your conclusion?"

He settled onto the captain's chair and steered the boat into the current.

"I knew I had to figure out what I was doing with my life when I woke up one morning and realized I was thirty-four. Time's rushing by. I'll be old enough to be president on my next birthday. What have I accomplished?"

Abby forced a smile into submission. He made it sound as though his age was on par with Methuselah's.

"I'm not married, don't own a house, and I haven't planted any roots. My life has been centered on my music."

"Do you want a wife, a family, a house and roots in a community?"

"The thing is, I didn't think so, until . . ."

"Lily?" Abby prodded gently.

Zack nodded. "She encouraged me to take this time off. She's a smart woman who knows what she wants. But she never pressures me."

"I suspect you do that yourself."

"Only recently," Zack admitted, then shifted his weight. "You know, Aunt Abby, when I was a kid, Dad was a champion of the idea anything is possible. I saw my life as a hallway of doors, each one representing a possibility. I ran past many of them—fireman, policeman, engineer. They didn't interest me. I wanted the golden door labeled music.

"Dad encouraged me to follow my passion. I did. Now I think I've followed it too single-mindedly. No, lately, I know I have. Especially when I look at Lily."

Again, Zack shook his head. "Marriage is a big commitment. As things are now, there's no way. She's too fine to take on the road. Besides, she has her own career. People come to her from all over the country for the dogs she trains."

"Finnegan. He's a prize," Abby agreed.

As if she hadn't spoken, Zack continued, "We have a married guy in the band, so I've seen the problems of leaving a family behind and going on the road. The burden falls on the wife. That's not fair, not right.

"Being home reminds me of the way Dad struck a balance in his life and tells me I have a long way to go. Getting there requires big decisions and hard choices I'm not sure I want to make."

Abby understood his difficulty. "Some choices are harder than others—particularly when the two things you want seem incompatible."

"The thing is, not making a choice *is* a choice." Zack tapped the steering wheel with a closed fist. "While I've been on the road I've missed important stuff in the lives of people I love. Birthdays, anniversaries, Christmas, Easter—the kind of things I'd like to be part of. But I'm just . . . absent."

"You're not forgotten," Abby offered, though she knew only too well it was a small consolation. Nothing on earth shone as brightly as the love in a family member's eyes. Or felt as full and right as their spontaneous hugs.

"Each year I'm missed less and I rationalize more." Morosely, he stared at the deck. "My absence has a price I didn't count on."

Thinking of the triumphs, tribulations and celebrations she'd missed while pursuing her career in New York, she murmured, "Hidden costs. I know exactly what you're talking about. Honestly, every decision has them. Sometimes compromise is necessary. Do you have any thoughts in that direction?"

Nodding slowly, Zack ran his palm around the boat's steering wheel. "About a year ago we got together with some other musicians for an after-hours jam session. One of the players was a cellist." A sudden grin lit up Zack's face. "Man, could he play."

"Jazz?" Abby asked.

"And classical, rock, bluegrass. You name it—he played it. I think part of the reason he was so good, so relaxed and comfortable, was because he'd found the perfect gig."

"Which was?"

"The symphony. It got me thinking about how a stable spot

like that would change my life." Zack tipped his head. "I wasn't sure, so I prayed about it. I'm more suited for the pops orchestra, so I wrote a letter, filled out an application and waited for them to schedule an audition."

Abby's stomach tightened. "What happened?"

"Nothing. I didn't hear from them." He shrugged. "I figured God closed the door. I was supposed to stay on the road. Or look elsewhere. Maybe teach music privately or in a high school or college."

"You'd be an excellent instructor," Abby said. "You interact well with people and your passion for music comes through."

"I suppose. But I'm not sure teaching is the right choice. I need to play. To make music with other musicians." With a despondent sigh, he stood and shook himself. "You're a great listener, Aunt Abby, but I think I've had enough heavy stuff for now. Let's go set up camp, then explore Armitage Island. We'll either find your bat cave or scratch that pile of rock off the list."

CHAPTER ❦ TWELVE

SATURDAY MORNING, MARY faced another uncomfortable truth.

Because Henry's case was taking him from Orcas Island to Seattle, he didn't have time to see her. The real problem was the relief she felt at the unexpected reprieve.

On one hand, she ached to tell him about the manuscript and the subsequent discoveries. She wanted to hear his opinion. On the other, given his nature as an investigator, he'd ask questions she couldn't answer.

She didn't like feeling so torn.

Out of sorts, she glared at the ringing phone and waited for the answering machine to inform yet another caller there was nothing for sale at this residence.

Instead, she heard, "Yoo-hoo, Mary. Are you home?"

Welcoming the interruption to her warring thoughts, she answered the phone. "Hi, Mom."

"I saw the flower arrangement you did for Margaret yesterday. It's gorgeous. What a sweet thing for Joe to do—send flowers for no reason other than he loves her."

Being the owner of a flower shop could be particularly satisfying. Yesterday had been such an occasion. Joe had come in search of something special for his wife. He said he owed her a special thank you. Mary had taken great care with the arrangement for Margaret. "Thanks, Mom. I'm glad you liked it. It *was* a sweet thing for him to do."

"The reason I called is to find out if Henry will be coming over after church services tomorrow."

"I'm afraid not." Mary caught her mother up on Henry's caseload and busy schedule. "He'll be back next weekend."

"You must miss him. I certainly do."

"I do." *More than I can say. But there's so much I don't feel I can say—especially over the phone.*

"Are you sure you're all right dear? You sound . . . distracted."

"I suppose I am. I'm waiting for Frank to come by and fix the washing machine. When I came home from work yesterday, I went to run a load. It made strange noises and died."

"How awful. I'm sure Zack and Abby will have plenty of laundry when they come back. They are coming home today, aren't they?"

"Yes, and—Oh, Mom, there's the doorbell. Gotta go."

"Okay. But if you need a machine, come by and use mine. Bye, dear."

Mary opened the front door and saw the owner of Holloway's Hardware. "I'm glad you could come on such short notice, Frank."

"It's lucky for both of us Aaron computerized the inventory system. We rounded up the most likely repair parts lickety-split. I'll have you in clean towels before you know it." Frank closed the front door and gave Finnegan a friendly pat on the head.

With the service dog at her side, Mary backed away to give Frank free access then followed him to the laundry room. Just inside the door sat an overflowing basket of soiled towels.

Frank and her mother had guessed right. With two additional overnight guests in and out of the house, they'd nearly emptied the linen closet.

"This mechanical friend of yours has seen a lot of suds." Frank put down his toolbox, turned off the water to the washing machine and unplugged it. "In a few more years, you might have to think about a new one."

Mary waved the thought away like a pesky mosquito. "As long as you can fix it, I don't need to think about it."

Frank tossed her a grin before embracing the machine and wrestling it away from the wall. "When I can't get parts, you can put it in a museum." He selected a screwdriver and stretched over the top to unfasten the back plate of the controls.

"Then I'm in good shape, because, Frank Holloway, you can repair or patch almost everything I own."

"One of these day's I'm going to retire and you'll have to call Rick DeBow." He looked over his shoulder. "Good man."

"Reliable." Mary agreed. "Like you."

"Harrumph." Frank changed his screwdriver for a pair of needle-nose pliers. "I hear Zack went off on a bat hunt with Abby."

"They're due back this afternoon. You'll have the machine fixed, and I'll have the towels washed and dried by then. Perfect timing."

"I wouldn't call Zack bringing Neville Sanborne's guitar to the park and letting everyone see it an example of good timing."

Mary groaned softly. "You cannot believe the phone calls we

get. I let most of them collect on the answering machine. Of course, if it's for me, I pick up."

Frank removed a piece with wires and springs, held it to the light, then tapped a scorched spot. Apparently satisfied it was the culprit, he tossed it into his open toolbox. "That guitar of his has folks arguing all over town. It's becoming quite a controversy—one Green Harbor doesn't need."

Mary silently thanked Zack for taking the instrument on the bat hunt. That way, she could honestly tell people it wasn't there. "I don't see why one little guitar causes so much talk."

"You're kidding, right?"

"No, I'm not. It can't do anything on its own. It—"

"Was Neville Sanborne's." Frank removed the new part from the box. "A lot of folks think Zack ought to give it to Naomi Yardley for the garage collection she calls a museum. Then again, they didn't pay for it. Seems to me some folks can be mighty generous with someone else's hard earned money."

"No argument here."

"Some of the guys think your boy ought to sell the guitar to a collector, like the music museum over in Seattle for a lot of money."

A thin smile tickled Mary's lips. "Interesting."

Frank seated the new part and picked up a screwdriver. "Aaron thinks Zack ought to put it on that bay thing and auction it off."

"eBay," Mary corrected automatically.

"That's it. All these new-fangled ways to buy and sell gives me the heebie-jeebies."

"Aaron and the information age are the future."

"Guess I'm the past." He grinned over his shoulder. "I plan to be part of the future too. But all the computer stuff is

Aaron's bailiwick. I give him a free hand and he teaches me what I need to get by. One day, Holloway's Hardware will be his. May as well start running it for the next generation."

"Nice side step, Frank."

"What do you mean?"

"I mean talking about Aaron and the business to divert me from asking what *you* think about Zack and the guitar."

"Didn't work, did it?"

"No. Now that you've expressed every other opinion in town, why don't you tell me yours?"

"Simple. Stick it in the closet until he can take it back to Chicago. Green Harbor has enough tourists. We don't need more attractions."

Normally Mary would have disagreed. She and many of the other business owners in town were always on the lookout for interesting ways to draw more seasonal visitors. "In this case, I'll agree with you."

Frank attached the back panel. "Let's test this puppy." He reconnected the power, turned on the water and adjusted the controls. The machine started immediately. After trying several settings and ensuring it moved through the cycle, he jockeyed it back into place.

Not wanting to waste time or water, Mary loaded the towels and added soap.

Frank closed up his toolbox. "Do you know what he's going to do with it, Mary?"

"Keep it and play it, although I suspect it's been more of a distraction for him than for anyone else."

"Fair enough. He's a smart young man."

She reached into her denim pouch and withdrew a checkbook.

Frank refused payment for anything beyond the cost of the new part. "Don't know why you keep trying to pay me for what I'm doing out of friendship for you and Jacob. Just because he's been gone a decade doesn't mean our friendship ended." Frank winked at her as though reminding her of a secret. "It's not like I don't plan on seeing him again."

Mary counted on it too. Too bad she would have to wait. She had more than a few questions she'd like to ask Jacob right now. With her mind refocused on his manuscript, she saw Frank out.

As the truck with the hardware store logo on the side purred away, her thoughts churned through the mystery Jacob had left for her. Finnegan stood at her side, waiting for a command or for her to choose a direction.

Suddenly certain the answers she wanted weren't in the old pages spread across the dining table, she rolled to the craft room. After pushing the empty cardboard box off the staging table, she managed to pull the last of the three boxes from the main table. The box landed catawampus on her lap.

As she adjusted it on the staging table, she congratulated herself on how far she'd come since leaving the rehabilitation center. The counselors and therapists had taught her more than she'd realized.

"I'm doing fine," she whispered with a prayer of thanks for those encouraging people.

With three swipes of the craft knife, she opened the box. Near the top, wrapped in crumpled packing paper she found the item she half expected. "Oh! There you are. You're more important than I ever knew."

Finnegan came to attention.

"It's okay," she assured him. "Look at this." She held up the clear paperweight that had always sat on Jacob's desk. Blue felt covered the bottom. Suspended in the center of the half globe hung a flattened penny.

She dropped the paperweight into her lap and pivoted her chair. "Come on, Finnegan. I want to read the story about the flattened coin again." Energized by determination and the growing certainty she was on the right trail, she wheeled to the dining room table and found the pertinent section of the manuscript.

"Ya think anyone saw us?" Gerry peered around the trunk of an apple tree laden with fruit ready for picking.

Jake cast an apprehensive look over his shoulder. If they got caught sneaking away from the orchard, they wouldn't have a free minute for two months. They'd be stuck working in the store. "I think we got away clean." A combination of nervousness and excitement put a squeak in his voice. "C'mon, they won't miss us if we hurry."

They darted from tree to tree, putting more space between them and the apple pickers scattered through the orchard.

In the distance a train whistle blew, sounding a call for the boys to run faster. At last, they broke through the trees and saw the railroad tracks playing peek-a-boo through the scrub.

Panting from exertion and perspiring from the late summer heat, the boys scrambled up the embankment to the graveled tracks. Triumphant, they stared at the steel rails as though they were a golden prize.

Heat veils shimmered, distorting distance. The sharp smell of tar and creosote hovered around the big ties. The scent of perspiration and damp hair filled Jake's lungs, and he wondered why fun sweat smelled different from work sweat.

Gerry put his ear against the track. "Ow. It's hot."

Jake dropped down next to him. "Can you hear it?"

"Yeah." He pointed into the shimmer. "Look! It's coming."

"Got the quarter?"

Gerry searched his pockets. Each thrust of his sweaty hand into his denims became more frantic. "I can't find it."

"You'd better. Quick! We haven't got much time." The rippling ball of black coming toward them grew larger.

"I must've lost it." Gerry's features crumpled as he sat on his heels.

Jake stood and rummaged through his pockets. Amid the gum wrappers, yo-yo, penknife and a red kerchief, he found three pennies.

The whistle blew, loud and urgent.

"Forget it," Gerry shouted. "We gotta get off the tracks."

Jake laid the pennies on the rail then grabbed his brother's hand. Together, they scrambled down the short embankment and threw themselves on the ground. Before they could push away the dry summer grasses tickling their cheeks or the scrub brush poking their arms, the train slammed out of the shimmering heat and thundered in front of them.

The whistle shrieked steadily, stealing the scream in Jake's throat, urging his heart to beat faster. The hard smell of metal on metal stung his nose. His ears rang with the driving noise of the high-speed engine and the great churning wheels roaring over the shining steel road.

A spit-stealing hot wind surged down the embankment, yanked at his hair and sanded his face with dirt. Refusing to close his eyes, he squinted into the train's hellish breath. He didn't want to miss a single second even if he forgot his own breath and his heart hammered all the way through his chest.

Then the train was gone and the caboose disappeared like a ghostly red specter into the afternoon heat. The hot wind chased after the shimmering image, leaving the bushes and grass still.

Shaking from head to toe, Jake rose up on his elbows. Every part of him seemed to vibrate as if his whole body was rushing into the next minute. He looked at his brother. Awe and wonder looked back. "Wow!" Gerry breathed, his eyes wide and dirty cheeks flushed.

"Wow is right." Jake pushed to his knees. "Let's go find the pennies and see if they're flat."

They crab-walked up to the tracks, then stared down. Two of the pennies were gone. The third was no more than a wafer-thin copper disk with a small split on one edge. Jake tried to pick it up, but it wouldn't budge. Hoping it wasn't fused to the rail, he dug out his penknife and pried the disk free.

"Jeepers," Gerry whispered. "You're amazing!"

Jake knew he'd never forget the love and hero worship on his brother's face.

And he never did.

"Okay, I get it now." Mary relaxed and closed her eyes. Her fingers stroked the paperweight. The message of the manuscript made sense if Gerry was Jacob's brother. A real flesh and blood brother he never told her about.

CHAPTER ✿ THIRTEEN

I KNOW BETTER THAN TO be disappointed, but I am." Abby set two glasses of iced tea on the deck table then plopped onto a wicker chair beside her sister. "We eliminated large sections of coastline, found several promising sites and made a few interesting discoveries. The drawing is so clear, it seems we should have found the bat cave."

"You'll find it next time," Mary encouraged.

"I hope so." The simmering urgency to locate the colony left Abby feeling restless. She knew the situation would bother her until she had a definitive answer for the WDFW and Beth.

"I'm confident you'll succeed." Mary squinted at the sliding screen door. "Where did Zack go?"

"To do laundry. Then he's going to call Lily."

"Good." Mary picked up her iced tea and raised it in a toast. "Thanks for this and for taking him with you."

"It was my pleasure." Abby sipped her tea. "Although he didn't find the clear answer he's looking for, he did discover an excellent direction." She shook her head. "I am glad for that. The way God works never ceases to amaze me."

Mary's eyebrows rose questioningly.

"Think about it. Zack's need to assess his life brought him home at the same time Sam found the boxes. From the moment you put the fedora on Zack's head, he's been thinking about his father, about his ability to prioritize. Jacob's a great role model for the questions Zack's asking himself now."

"I see." Mary traced a water droplet down the side of her glass. "Yes, timing is important."

Sensing her sister's strange mood, Abby leaned closer. "I don't recall reexamining my choices during my thirties. Earlier . . ." She smiled at the memory of her one-time beau Perry Nelson and the unexpected turns their lives had taken. "Did you have a time of reassessment?"

"Once I met Jacob, my life was set and I never questioned my direction. Do you remember me dithering about my future when I got out of high school?"

Abby grinned. "You wanted to see the world without leaving the nest of Green Harbor."

Mary laughed. "Well put and very true. After Jacob came into my life, I had everything a woman could want. Even after he got sick, in ways I didn't fully grasp, he took care of me until we both had to let go."

"How are you and Ida doing on his manuscript?"

Abby listened in rapt attention as Mary told her about the scrimshaw piece and the paperweight with the penny. She described in detail a presentation box holding a horseshoe and ribbon, every word clipped and tight with tension.

"What's wrong? What aren't you telling me?"

Mary's lips pursed as if she'd swallowed something sour. "I'm afraid. I don't want to believe Jacob lied to me by omission."

Abby stilled. "What do you mean?"

"The pieces I'm finding, together with the manuscript, tell me the boy Jake in the story is Jacob. The brother in the book is his flesh and blood brother."

Seeing the steel in Mary's expression, Abby tried to imagine Jacob with a brother and couldn't. "How can that be?"

"Nothing else makes sense. I'm so upset, I could throttle Jacob for not telling me he had a brother." Mary took the paperweight out of her denim bag. "This is like a slap in the face. It sat on his desk every day, so it's not like he forgot he had a brother the way he forgot to tell me about the boxes."

"Oh Mary, he meant to tell you about the boxes or he wouldn't have asked Lowell to bring them back to the house," Abby said, wanting to ease her sister's pain.

"Granted. But he didn't tell me about his brother. Now I'm questioning everything." Mary folded her hands in her lap and stared at them. "I hate feeling like this."

"You and Jacob had something very special, something rare and precious. Don't tarnish it with speculation. Cherish it for the treasure it was." Abby leaned forward and placed a hand over her sister's. "Do not, for a moment, doubt Jacob's love for you."

"That's part of what makes this so difficult."

Abby searched for the right words, some consolation or explanation to give Mary a bit of peace. "Let's think about this logically. If you're right and Jacob had a brother, something drastic must've happened." A new realization moved Abby back in the chair. "Goodness, did he die?"

"I have no idea. Jacob never spoke about his family. When I asked, he changed the subject." Tiny furrows appeared on Mary's brow. "After a while, I stopped asking. Eventually, it was like they never existed."

Uncertainty clouded her blue eyes. "Now I wish I'd been more persistent. Then I might know if the events in his manuscript actually happened the way he described . . ."

"Or if he described the childhood he wanted and didn't have," Abby finished.

"Exactly. I don't know if the work is a memoir or fiction. Even worse, I'm afraid I've violated a trust. I've shared the manuscript with what feels like everyone." Mary shuddered and rubbed her hands together. "Jacob wrote it in secret. Even in death, he kept it a secret. Maybe I should've left it that way."

Abby wrapped her hands around Mary's cold fingers. "If he hadn't intended for you to see the manuscript, to read it and share it, to delve into it and ask questions, he would've gotten rid of it. He knew *you*—knew he could trust you with the story, that you'd sift it with gentle hands."

"I hope it isn't too late for me to do what he wanted. It sat in darkness for much longer than he could have anticipated." Mary sniffed and disengaged her hands to reach for a tissue. "And I'm still in the dark about his family."

SUNDAY MORNING, Abby, Mary and Zack drove to Little Flock Church. The tall, narrow wooden structure with arches over the windows and white doorways always lifted her spirits. Above the weathered metal cross at the peak of the shingled steeple, high white clouds sailed the ocean blue sky.

Walking behind Mary and Finnegan, Zack and Abby went up the ramp to the right side door of the sheltered portico.

They waved at friends and exchanged greetings with the pastor, Rev. James Hale.

Inside, sunlight streamed through the windows, lighting their stained glass borders with brilliant color. Smiling at her parents and Sam, Abby slid into the last pew, shortened to accommodate Mary's chair. While they shared hellos and hugs, nostalgia swept over Abby.

How many of life's seasons and cycles had the old pews and wooden floor witnessed? The patina of time gleamed on the dark woods and the spare lines of the handmade altar at the front of the church. Constructed of madrone, the loving gift from a former pastor stood near a piano almost as old as the church.

In their solid presence, generations had prayed and sung, shared sorrows and joys with each other and with the Lord. Feeling connected to all the blessings there, she watched the maroon-robed choir take their positions.

The congregation hushed. The intricate chords of a guitar blended with the piano and soared to the rafters. Then a marvelous baritone wove through the notes, singing praises to the Lord. The hairs on her arms stood up as the four-part harmony of the choir joined in humming backup.

When the song ended, Zack nudged her. "Who's the soloist? And why can't I see him?"

Leaning close to her nephew, Abby whispered, "He's behind the choir. I'll introduce you later if you like."

"Please," Zack answered softly.

Rev. Jim's teaching about the lilies of the field and relying on God to provide seemed tailored just for her. She'd find the bat colony in His time and not one second sooner. Content and thankful for the reminder, she sang along with the choir and even managed to stay on key most of the time.

In what felt like the blink of an eye, the service ended and she followed Zack and Mary from the church.

A soft breeze rustled the rhododendron hedge between the church and the parking area. Zack drew his mother and Abby aside. "What's the deal on the guitar player with the great voice? He should be out front, leading the choir, not hidden in the back row."

Empathy tightened Abby's chest. "Scott Kenai's spirit is as beautiful as his voice, but he prefers the background. He doesn't sing anywhere else."

"Why not?"

"He's shy and self-conscious about his appearance, Zack," Mary said softly. "He has some congenital problems and the medical profession has done all they can. He believes people will focus on the message in his music if they aren't distracted by . . . the messenger."

Abby ached for the unfortunate twenty-four-year-old. His flat face and bulbous nose often made him the object of curious stares. She winced inwardly at the ridicule he must have endured as a child in school. "He just wants people to think of him like a regular guy."

"But he isn't a regular guy," Zack protested, scanning the parishioners filing out of the church. "His gift makes him exceptional."

WITH ZACK IN THE KITCHEN sampling everything Ellen made, Sunday dinner at Stanton Farm took on a festive air. "I saw you with Scott after the service," Ellen told her grandson.

Immediately, Mary refocused her attention. She'd missed that conversation. She'd been chatting with her good friends, Janet and Margaret, when Abby introduced Zack and Scott.

The encounter with the shy musician was short, with Scott keeping a low profile in the shadows on the side of the church. When his sister finished a brief visit with friends, the two of them had hurried away.

"Scott sure seems like a nice guy," Zack told his grandmother. "I get why he's self-conscious, but doesn't he know he's among friends at Little Flock?"

"I suspect meeting you, whom he sees as a stranger, brought back his shyness." Ellen handed a big bowl of salad to her grandson. "He's a bit awed by you."

"By me? Why?"

"Because you make a living with your music. Scott would love to do the same." She donned padded mitts and opened the oven to remove the bread. "His medical condition makes it impossible."

"Too bad." Zack carried the salad to the table and returned for the cruets of oil and vinegar. "What's on the outside shouldn't matter. It's the inside that counts."

Her son's righteous compassion lightened Mary's mood. Scott occupied a permanent place on her prayer list and a little corner of her heart. Perhaps he'd claimed part of Zack's too.

The screen door at the back of the kitchen squeaked as it opened, breaking her reverie.

"Hey, Sam," Zack called. "Hope you have a good appetite."

"You're just in time. Dinner's ready." Mary waved, then wheeled to the table with the bread.

Sam joined her at the Stanton's dining table. Upon his

release from prison eleven years earlier, George had hired him as a handyman. Sam had made the most of his second chance.

In a low voice he said, "I never expected to see those boxes in the loft. When I did, I wondered why you moved them there. Now I know you didn't. It's too bad they got lost like that. They were special."

Startled, Mary regarded him closely. Short, stocky and wearing his fifty-two years of hard living like a badge, he radiated the peace of a man confident in his destiny. "What do you mean, 'special'?"

Puzzlement kinked Sam's forehead. "Well . . . the first time I saw them, Jacob had me move them from his office to the garage."

"Did he say why?"

"He wanted them available for you, but not in your face. Hey, Mary, I figured he told you."

"I wish he had."

"Have you opened 'em yet?"

"Yes," she admitted.

"What'd you find?"

"Memorabilia. His newest fedora and an unfinished manuscript, among other things."

Sam groaned. "Shoot. I hate to think of one of Jacob's great stories sitting in the loft so long."

"So do I." *Why didn't he just leave me a note with instructions?*

CHAPTER ❦ FOURTEEN

MARY DECIDED TO LEAVE Jacob and his doggone mystery alone for a while and enjoy Sunday dinner. Later, she'd take Sam aside and see if he could recall anything that might help her understand Jacob's reason for leaving the boxes.

The family gathered around the table, and George offered a prayer of thanksgiving. Afterward, she took a piece of hot bread and passed the basket. "It feels strange not having Henry here today."

"It does," her father agreed. "What's he doing and how long will he be gone?"

"He's conducting joint training seminars with the Island County Sheriff's Office. He'll be back next weekend." Mary missed her absent beau. She was past being embarrassed by what she didn't know. Henry would have good suggestions to help her figure out this mystery.

Sam's gaze fixed on Mary. "Have you read the story Jacob left for you?"

"Zack, Abby and I have read it. In many ways, it's the most mysterious book Jacob ever wrote."

"Is that so?" George asked. "You've certainly got my attention. When may your mother and I read it?"

Abby caught Mary's eye and remained silent.

Knowing she couldn't deny her parents, Mary said, "You can borrow the copy Abby read. I'd like to keep it in the family, including Sam, of course."

"Its okay, Mary." Sam waved away the offer.

For a moment, she was affronted by his rejection, then saw his open sincerity. To hide her confusion, she took a big bite of salad.

"Tell us about it, Zack. What was your favorite part?" George inquired.

"There's a spot where the two boys decide to play hooky," Zack answered. "It was September and very hot in Yakima. They went to their favorite swimming hole."

"Those naughty scamps," Ellen murmured. "Did they get away with it?"

"Not exactly." Zack winked at his mother, and she couldn't help the small smile tugging at her lips.

"It never crossed my mind to play hooky," Abby said.

"That's because you liked school, otherwise you wouldn't have gotten all those degrees," George told her, then addressed Zack. "What happened to the boys?"

"They had one of those great days where they did everything they wanted. Skinny-dipped so they wouldn't get their clothes muddy. Climbed trees. Played games. Laid in the grass and spun stories about the cloud shapes in the sky. Shared dreams about what they wanted to do when they grew up.

Gerry was set on the stars as an astronaut. Jake preferred solid ground and intended to chronicle Gerry's adventures in space."

"Ah, boys being boys," George said fondly.

"They might have gotten away with it except for one thing." Zack leaned back stretching out the story. Like his father, he used suspense to make a point.

Ellen took the bait as she often did when anyone tossed a story line her way. "Let me guess. The school notified the parents."

"Sorry, Grandma." Zack folded his hands on the edge of the table. "Gerry, the younger of the two boys, was walking in the creek to wash mud off his feet before putting on his socks and shoes. Jake waited on the shore hollering at him to hurry up. Then Gerry started shouting and the creek turned red."

"Dear me," gasped Ellen. "What happened?"

"Gerry stepped on a broken piece of glass. It sliced open the bottom of his foot," Zack explained.

"Uh-oh," George said.

"They argued about what to do," Zack continued. "Gerry wanted Jake to go home. Just pretend he'd gone to school. No point in both of them getting into trouble."

"And he went," Sam said.

Mary eyed him closely. *How could he know a story in a book he hadn't read? Or was he guessing?*

"Yeah," Zack agreed. "But Jake didn't get far before he went back. He didn't think Gerry could get home even though they'd used his shirt to bandage his foot. Good thing Jake did, because he was right."

Sam nodded thoughtfully. "Had to carry him piggy back."

Her curiosity bubbling over, Mary inquired, "Now how would you know that?"

Seemingly mystified she would ask, Sam answered, "How else can one kid carry another?"

"Makes sense," George agreed.

"What happened to the boys?" Ellen asked, bringing them back to the original subject.

"They fessed up to playing hooky," Zack answered. "Tearfully. And asked for forgiveness. Guess that and the ten stitches Gerry got in his foot were enough, because they weren't punished and never played hooky again."

"Sometimes we punish ourselves more than anyone else can," George said. "Seems the more painful the lesson, the more likely we are to use what we learned from it. And that's a good thing, because then we aren't likely to make the same mistakes again."

Mary felt like she was back to the beginning, but with an added complication. Sam's sparse comments suggested he might know more than he let on. Did he or didn't he?

She sighed. The whole guessing business felt like swimming in mud.

MONDAY MORNING, eager to check in with Hugo and make plans for her next cave hunting trip, Abby rose before the alarm clock sounded. Further invigorated by her morning devotional, she found herself ready for work and the first one in the kitchen.

While pondering ways to approach Beth about the past, Abby made coffee and started breakfast. When no solution to her thorny problem emerged, her thoughts drifted.

On another Monday over a decade ago, after Jacob's diagnosis, she'd flown home for a visit. She'd used her mother's car to take Sam over to the Reynolds' home and her sister out to lunch for a much-needed break. They lingered over the meal, then visited friends before filling a cart at The Green Grocer.

In retrospect, Abby realized how much Mary had needed the time away from the house and Island Blooms. The interlude had provided an oasis of normalcy in the desert of circumstances beyond anyone's control. Jacob had surrendered to God's will and Mary was trying hard to do the same.

Hours later, when Abby drove Sam back to the farm, she'd been struck by the serenity in Jacob—and in her passenger. The streetwise ex-con had clearly drawn strength from the man whose life was fading quickly.

He'd commented that getting Jacob in and out of the shower was no big deal. When Jacob asked if he would trim his toenails, Sam had given it a try. Sam had said if Jesus could wash the apostles' feet, he could do the small task for a man in too much pain to bend over.

Abby never forgot Sam's kindness, knowing it's the small things we do or don't do that can have the greatest impact.

"Morning, Aunt Abby." Fresh from the shower, Zack's damp hair spiked on his forehead. He made a beeline for the coffeepot.

"Good morning," Mary echoed from the doorway, Finnegan at her side. "I smell breakfast."

Abby dropped bread into the toaster. "It's ready. And good morning to you too," she said to Blossom. The white Persian lifted her tail and leaned against Abby's calf. "You want to be fed, don't you?"

"I'll take care of the critters." Zack sipped his coffee before gathering the food and water bowls.

Breakfast became an organized dance of morning hustle with

the three of them discussing their plans for the day. Before they started cleaning up, Zack offered to accompany Abby on another camping venture. Mary gave her enthusiastic approval.

The sound of the doorbell startled them.

"I'll get it." Abby left Zack loading the dishwasher.

She opened the door and found Scott Kenai standing on the porch. His deer-in-the-headlights expression softened somewhat when she gave him a cheery, "Good morning!"

"Hi, Dr. Stanton," He pulled his baseball cap from his head and finger-combed his hair. "I'm here to see Zack. But if I'm too early, I'll come back after work."

"No, no." Hiding her amazement at the presence of the reserved young man, she beckoned, "Please, come in."

"Hey, Scott," Zack called as he hurried into the foyer. "Glad you came by, man."

Abby stepped aside and noted how Zack's friendly greeting put Scott at ease.

Their guest wiped his feet on the porch mat, then checked the soles. "I, uh, need to be over at the hardware store in a little bit. Mr. Holloway has some work for me in the stockroom. But, if it's okay, I'm taking you up on your offer to let me see the guitar."

"Sure thing." Zack gestured toward the living room. "Right this way."

"Hello, Mrs. Reynolds."

"I'm happy to see you, Scott," Mary beamed.

With a shy smile, he moved carefully into the living room.

"Have a seat." Zack put his famous purchase on the coffee table and opened the case.

"Gosh." Scott scooted to the edge of the couch and stared. "This is, like, a piece of history."

"Guess so." Zack lifted the guitar out of the case. "Here. Give it a try."

The color drained from Scott's flat cheeks, leaving his over-sized nose a bright pink. "Me?"

"Sure. This is a musician's instrument and you're a musician, right? Here. Go for it!"

Abby could have kissed Zack right then and there. Instead, she sat in a chair beside Mary.

Awed, Scott took the guitar. As soon as he did, it was apparent nothing else existed in his reality. He played several chords, grinned, then adjusted the strings. A moment later, the opening bars of "Sparrow Island Night Song" filled the room.

"Oh, I love this song," Mary murmured.

Scott sang softly at first, then his baritone swelled with the music. At the refrain, Zack sang along, taking the easy melody while Scott slipped into the trickier, moving harmony.

Abby felt her sister take her hand and they exchanged a look of wonder. Playing and singing transformed Scott. It seemed a million-watt light-bulb burned inside him.

The song ended, but Scott wasn't ready to return the guitar. Grinning at no one in particular, he segued into an intricate Flamenco Abby knew to be difficult even for a seasoned professional. The speed and precision of his fingers on the fret bar captivated her. It didn't seem possible to make so much music with one instrument.

Suddenly, the notes faded and the concert ended. Self-conscious, Scott lovingly placed the guitar into the case. "Gosh. Thanks, Zack."

"Where did you learn to play like that?" The awe in Zack's voice matched the emotion lingering inside Abby.

"My sister bought me some books and I taught myself. I don't guess—"

"Taught yourself?" Shaking his head, Zack confessed, "Your talent, your drive—you blow me away. Hey, man, I'd be honored if you'd jam with me sometime."

Hope filled Scott's eyes. "Really?"

"Really. Absolutely my privilege to play with you," Zack assured him.

"Thanks. I will." Scott checked the clock on the wall. "I gotta go. Don't want to be late."

"Oh," Abby said, suddenly realizing the time. "Me too. Would you like a ride over to Holloway's, Scott? I'm going right by."

"Gee, Dr. Stanton, I'd appreciate it."

"And we appreciate you taking an ordinary Monday and making it special." She squeezed Mary's hand, then let go. "Starting the day with such beautiful music is truly a treat."

Abby gathered her purse and briefcase. It's the little things, she thought again. Like Zack's extending the invitation to Scott after church yesterday morning. Who knew how greatly God would bless them all for a simple act of kindness?

CHAPTER ❦ FIFTEEN

MARY TOOK A LAST LOOK at her reflection in the bathroom mirror and dropped her hairbrush in the drawer.

Hoping her son wouldn't notice her nervousness, she scooped up her purse and headed out to the living room.

Zack gave her a wolf whistle. "You didn't have to get all dolled up. We're just going over to Grandma and Grandpa's." He opened and held the door leading to the garage.

"There's nothing wrong with wanting to look nice." She breezed past him and signaled Finnegan to jump in the van's open door. The lift was down, waiting for her.

Zack wanted to show his grandparents the sheet music they found in the guitar case.

She wanted to talk with Sam. If the handyman knew anything else about Jacob's boxes, it might help her quest.

She boarded the van and locked her chair in place. After Zack hooked Finnegan into his safety harness and clambered inside, she said, "Seeing Scott this morning was a delightful surprise. And hearing him play—oh my!"

Zack launched into an oratory of praise for the young musician. Since she was in complete agreement, Mary listened with half an ear. The rest of her attention she devoted to driving.

In town, she turned onto Municipal Street and barely slowed until she pulled into the driveway at Stanton Farm.

No sooner had she turned off the engine than Sam emerged from the barn. He leaned on his rake, watching her as the side lift lowered her wheelchair to the ground. "You go ahead," she told her son. "I'd like to speak with Sam for a few minutes."

"Sure thing, Mom. Don't take too long or Grandpa and I will eat all of Grandma's cinnamon rolls."

"Ok, I'll be right in," Mary said.

Zack bounded up the steps into his grandmother's enthusiastic hug.

Mary called a cheery hello to her mother, then headed toward the barn and Sam.

Immediately, he put down his rake. One of the things she liked about him was the absence of pretenses. When she saw him checking to see who drove into the yard, she suspected he'd been waiting for her. Now, seeing his purposeful stride, she was sure of it.

"Hello, Mary." He tipped his sweat-stained ball cap.

"Can you spare a few minutes, Sam?"

"As many as you want." He gestured to the big maple in the backyard. "Let's go over there." He moved behind the wheelchair, pushed her off the path and across the freshly mown lawn.

Thanks to Abby's patient tutoring, Mary recognized a pair of house wrens and a Bewick's warbler flitting through the sheltering branches of the old tree. The reminder of her sister's unconditional love strengthened Mary's resolve. She didn't know if Sam could tell her anything helpful, but she had to try. She'd had enough uncertainty and supposition.

He parked her chair close to the wooden picnic table, straddled the bench and faced her. His blue eyes were alive with expectancy, yet he sat quietly.

"I've been thinking, Sam. The first year you were here was also the last year of Jacob's life. You two spent a lot of time together."

"I was a ship trying hard to stay afloat in strange waters. He was like a lighthouse for me. He lived his faith. He couldn't be shaken. Not even when the doctors told him he had the Big C."

Mary closed her eyes, remembering the serenity and deep conviction Jacob exhibited at what had been their darkest times. "I'm not sure I ever told you how much we both appreciated your help."

"You did. There's no need to say more, Mary. He helped me much more than I ever helped him."

"You were there for him, Sam."

"I considered him a brother. Sometimes when I visited with him, he'd tell me stories, just like he was writing a book. Talking that way seemed to take his mind off his pain."

"Ah, yes, creative escapism. He used to recite song lyrics to me," she reminisced. Then, returning to her purpose, she continued, "Would you mind answering a few questions about that time?"

"Not at all. Fact is, I figured you might have some. You and your sister usually do." A knowing, patient smile softened his rugged features.

"Yesterday you said the boxes were special. Did you know what was in them?"

"I helped Jacob pack them up. I carried them down to the garage for you."

"Why didn't he just leave them in his office? I would have found them there."

"It would've been too soon. He loved you, Mary. He knew you'd grieve, and he knew there'd come a time when you'd be ready to clean things out and move on. No one figured the boxes would get lost for ten years."

"Reading the manuscript has taught me there were a few important things I didn't know about my husband. I've been following the clues he left. Did Jacob say why he left them for me? What he wanted me to do?"

"He said you'd know."

She shook her head. "Did he ever mention his . . . brother?"

"You know about Gerald?" Sam's eyebrows rose in surprise.

The confirmation felt like a claw closing around her heart. "Is that his name?" *Gerald. Gerald Reynolds. Jacob's younger brother, Gerry.*

"Yep."

Mary struggled for a deep breath. "Is he alive?"

"I don't know. But Jacob did say he was heartbroken about the rift between him and Gerald." Sam tilted his head. "Jacob invited him to your wedding."

Mary gasped. "He did? He never said a word."

"Course not. Everybody'd be asking what happened when he didn't show, wouldn't they? It would've put a damper on the day."

Understanding dawned on her. "I see."

"That's right. Jacob figured it was his duty and privilege to protect the woman he loved. Couldn't have you starting your marriage fretting over something nobody could fix. The choice to come or stay away was Gerald's."

"When you put it that way, I see how typically *Jacob* it was," she said, recalling the beauty of her wedding day. "We were so happy. God truly blessed us with each other and our children."

"See? No reason to mention Gerald and cast a dark cloud."

"Do you know why he didn't come? Did Jacob tell you?"

"All I know is the rift ran deep. Jacob stopped trying to mend it sometime after Zack was born. The way Jacob talked, something big happened around then and he knew his family didn't want him."

"*Aargh*," Mary cried, fighting the frustration creeping into her heart. "And he never said why?"

"Nope. Course, I didn't ask either."

Mary shaded her eyes with her hand. *Men never got the details.* Taking a deep breath, she lowered her hand. "Do you know if he sent word to his family when he was dying?"

"Far as I know, he didn't." Sam's brow furrowed with concentration. "Sometimes we care more when folks are gone than when they're here and we can see them. I figure it'll be the same for Gerald."

"Why do you say that?"

Sam heaved a long sigh and looked at his worn work boots. "I don't like thinking about my time in prison. But I can tell you this. Even the hardest men care about someone. It doesn't matter what kind of front they put on. When somebody they loved dies, has an accident or winds up in the same prison, all those feelings come out. They can't hold them back and they blubber like babies. Seems to me, as close as Jacob and Gerald were, a piece of that love would've lasted."

"Ten years have passed. I wonder if Gerald knows Jacob's gone," she murmured, feeling cold and shaky inside.

Sam shrugged. "The stories—the ones about them playing

horseshoes, working in their old man's store from dawn to dusk, picking apples, putting pennies on the train tracks and playing hooky—"

"He told them all to you," Mary marveled.

"I hate that this hurts you, Mary. I wouldn't be telling you now, except he told me to. When you asked."

"What?" Finnegan popped to his feet at the sharpness in her voice.

Sam raised his hands in a gesture of surrender. "Don't shoot. I'm just the messenger."

Mary reeled in her wild emotions and gave Finnegan a hand command to sit and stay. "Could, ah, you explain what you mean, he told you to tell me?"

"As best I can, I will. But first . . ." Sam dug in his shirt pocket and pulled out a plastic bag filled with chunks of red apple. He lifted an eyebrow and looked at her. "I knew you'd be upset. Okay if I give this to him?"

"Yes." She gave Finnegan the proper signal.

He wolfed down the apple chunks and Sam soothed, "It's all right boy. No one's gonna hurt your mistress while you and me are around."

When the bag was empty and Finnegan lay contentedly next to her chair, Sam continued, "To tell you the truth, Mary, when you never said a word about Gerald, I figured Jacob had changed his mind and tossed the manuscript." Sam shrugged. "If he had, it wasn't my place to say anything. I didn't know it was lost."

"Lost," she murmured, "or waiting for the right time. Funny, it seems too soon and too late to take this road."

"When we let Him, God sets the pace and it's always the right one. It took me a while to learn that. Wasted most of my life going down the wrong road. But you and me, we're on the right one now."

"Indeed." Mary couldn't argue with Sam's plainspoken wisdom. It was right on target.

"Getting back to Jacob, he'd decided to let the chips fall wherever." Sam's somber expression reflected a struggle. "I wanna explain it the way he did."

"Take your time," Mary encouraged. "Tell me in your own words."

"One afternoon Jacob was talking about regrets. His biggest one was not telling you about his brother. I suppose it rode his mind hard a few months before he started feeling poorly and went to see the Doc. Jacob planned on telling you and the kids at the same time. I reckon explaining once would be hard enough—considering how he felt about the whole thing. He'd picked Christmas because Nancy and Zack were coming home for the holidays."

"They did. Jacob didn't mention a word about his family or having a brother." Recalling the visit, she added, "It was a good Christmas. His last."

"Yep. And everybody knew it. He couldn't bring himself to add another burden to the ones you all were carrying. He figured you had enough on your mind, so he didn't say anything then. But he thought you ought to know—the kids ought to know—they had relatives they hadn't met. He always believed one day Gerald would come to his senses."

In the story, the boys had shared so much; they should have been lifelong friends—like her and Abby. Yes, they had squabbles and misunderstandings, but when life got tough, they always knew they could count on each other. "What could have been so awful that it drove a wedge between them?"

"I don't know." Shaking his head, Sam rubbed his palms on his knees. "Maybe he left the book so you'd go find out for yourself—if it was important for you to know. Or maybe he thought you'd have a better chance with his hardheaded brother, but I honestly don't know. Seems to me Jacob left you with a choice here: Let it go or keep trying."

"Choice," she murmured. She couldn't make his family love him, but had she known all those years ago, she would have tried and fretted over her failure. Rather than allow any form of dissension into their lives, Jacob had shut it off. Now, she understood his silence was an act of love. "You've helped me more than you know. Thank you. And thank you for being Jacob's trusted confidante."

In a flash of growing understanding, she realized she'd been looking at the problem too personally. The legacy of the manuscript wasn't about her or the kids—it was a testimonial of love from one brother to another.

CHAPTER ✾ SIXTEEN

T HAT'S EVERYTHING, IDA."
At her desk, Abby put a final checkmark on the lunch order.
"See you soon." Looking forward to the takeout meal from the
Springhouse, Abby hung up and retrieved her purse. Just as she
rounded her desk, the phone jangled another summons.

With her stomach rumbling, she shot a warning look at the
instrument. For such a time-saving device, it had inconvenient
moments. As if to prove her point, it rang again. Hoping the
call would be quick, she answered it.

"Joe Blackstock, here. I was wondering if I could take you
to lunch."

At first Abby wasn't sure she heard him correctly. His
Brooklyn accent was back in full force. Why, she wondered,
and whatever prompted him to ask her to lunch? "I, uh, can't
today. Hugo and I ordered takeout from the Springhouse. I
was just leaving to pick it up."

"Well, I'd sure like to see you for a few minutes, if you can
manage it. Can you swing by the marina, meet me at my boat?"

Her curiosity thrumming, she said, "Sure. I'll be there in ten minutes or less. Okay?"

"Terrific."

Abby hung up the phone. "Terrific?" she repeated. Joe never said *terrific*.

She stopped by Hugo's office and let him know of the slight delay. Soon she was driving past Stanton Farm on her way to town.

Low clouds scudded toward the horizon as she parked at the marina and walked across the asphalt to the wooden walkway. A fresh breeze skimmed the water, filling the sails of several boats tacking into the harbor. Salt air ruffled Abby's short brown hair. She turned her face to the wind and inhaled the scent of sea, wharf and distant evergreens. At the end of the dock, a pair of crows scolded a seagull with a crust of bread in his mouth.

"Ahoy, there," she called when she reached the *Island Hopper's Delight*.

"Welcome aboard." Joe's voice drifted up from the open hatch at the stern. "I'll be right up."

She climbed onto the boat and settled on a cushioned bench.

Moments later, he emerged from the hold, wiping his hands on a red rag. "You're quick. I figured I had enough time to get the oil draining before you arrived."

She blinked, removed her glasses, saw they were clean and put them on again. The Joe Blackstock standing in front of her appeared younger than the one she'd met here with Zack or saw at church yesterday.

"Is something wrong?" he asked.

"You look, I don't know, different." It struck her in an instant. "At peace. Happy."

Tossing the rag onto the toolbox, he shrugged a shoulder and sat beside her. "Could be because I am. I'm grateful too."

Abby kept looking at him, awaiting an explanation.

"See, I have a persistent and nosy friend," he continued in a teasing tone. "When she latches onto something, she doesn't let go until she's satisfied she has all the answers."

Abby played along. "Anyone I know?"

"Depends on how well you know yourself."

"What did I do?"

"You made me think about things I'd wanted to forget." His Brooklyn accent grew thicker. "Thanks to your pestering, I had to tell Margaret she was right and I was wrong. See, she insisted on keeping all the old photo albums when we moved here. Over the weekend, I went through them."

Wearing an enigmatic smile and shaking his head, he stared at the horizon for a long moment. "Ahh, the memories. They tumbled out of those old pictures like fish from a trawling net."

"Oh dear. I never meant to cause distress."

"It happened, just the same. See, Mark's guitar went missing first, then almost immediately we lost him. It was a one-two punch. He was gone and everything important to him and about him was gone too. Ripped right out of my heart." Joe brought an oil-smudged fist to his chest.

"I'm sorry," Abby said. "I didn't realize seeing the sketchbook would be traumatic."

"It was, but in a good way. If you hadn't brought it, I'd have continued my closed minded ways. Seeing it again made me realize I'd thrown the baby out with the bathwater. I'd been so busy hiding from the pain of losing him I wouldn't even think about him. So I lost all the good memories too."

"There seems to be a lot of retrospection going around Green Harbor," Abby mused. She had her predicament with Beth. Zack was in the process of measuring himself against his father's choices. And Mary searched the past for elusive explanations and an appropriate ending to Jacob's manuscript. "Amazing how the lens of time makes things look different, isn't it?"

"You bet. This morning, all I could remember was the good stuff. The fun. The sit-down-cause-you-can't-stand-up kind of laughter. Mark had a way of telling stories that made your whole body glad."

Joe pulled out a handkerchief and dabbed at the corners of his happy eyes. "You know the camping trip I told you about, the one out here for my graduation? I'd wake up every morning knowing my sides would split wide open ten times before lunch. Those were the days."

"Lunch!" Abby started. "As much as I'd love to stay and talk about Mark, I've got to pick up my takeout. Hugo's waiting."

"Right, right. Well, I'll be quick then. I told you I'd let you know if I remembered anything about the bats. And I did."

A new excitement began to simmer.

"I told you Rosario Strait, right?"

Abby nodded, hoping she and Zack hadn't wasted two precious days searching the wrong channel.

"Mark did more than talk about the bats; he showed me where they live."

Abby popped to her feet. "Where?"

"Can't place it." Joe winced. "Not yet. It was over fifty years ago. I remember the island was small. Measuring the long way, it's no more than half a mile—no less either. Hope that helps."

"It does, Joe. A lot." She didn't care if her order was burnt to a crisp or frozen as hard as a brick. Of course, it would be neither, but she was too elated to eat. She wanted to get back to her map.

"Well, that's about it. Just wanted to thank you in person for opening my eyes." Joe picked up the red rag from the top of the toolbox. "It'll come to me."

"What will?"

"The name of the island." He started toward the engine hold, then paused to look at her. "Memories I'd locked away are returning. I'll call you as soon as that one pops up."

AFTER LUNCH and leisurely conversation with her parents, Mary and Zack headed for home. During the short drive, she faced the uncomfortable realization that she needed to share Sam's revelations with Zack.

Upon reaching home and wishing she knew how to begin, Mary decided to ponder the problem outside. Tending God's greenery always filled her with peace and put her troubles in perspective. "What do you say we take advantage of this lovely day and do a bit of gardening?" she asked when Zack greeted her at the door.

"Sure thing, Mom." Zack rubbed his stomach. "I need to work off some of Grandma's lemon meringue pie. I probably shouldn't have eaten the third slice."

Grinning, Mary collected her gardening hat and tote and headed into the backyard. Zack took the larger yard tools and a garbage can out through the garage and met her at the corner rhododendrons.

After releasing Finnegan to run and play, Mary donned her gloves and began clipping the spent blooms. Armed with a second pair of pruning shears and a rake, Zack worked beside her. He started humming as they made their way along the hedge. Then they were both singing, leaving a manicured swath of greenery in their wake.

Mary treasured the precious moments with her son. Once she told him what she found out, the carefree melodies would end—at least for a while. Yet an inner certainty promised her this too would turn out for the best. Perhaps learning more about Jacob's family would help. Life didn't happen in neat little packages.

They finished the hedge, ending near the ramp to the back deck. "How about a break?" Zack asked.

"Sure. Come on, Finnegan." Now that the time had come, Mary's emotions resumed their churning. Resolute, she entered the house with Finnegan and filled two tall glasses with ice water. Before the trepidation inside could take over and silence her, she said, "There's something we need to discuss."

"Okay. What?" Zack carried Finnegan's replenished water bowl back to its usual spot, then took the frosty glass she offered.

"Come with me." Her pulse fluttering, Mary led the way to the craft room and gestured to a chair in the corner. "Make yourself comfortable."

Settling in, Zack stretched out his legs and crossed his ankles. He took a long drink and waited.

"I've racked my brain for a tactful approach." Mary folded her hands in her lap.

"Forget tact." Zack's eyes narrowed with concern. "You're starting to worry me. Is this something medical?"

"No, no. It's about your father's manuscript." She drew a calming breath. "It's more than a work of fiction. The boy, Jake, is your father. The younger one, Gerry, is his brother Gerald. Your uncle."

"You're kidding." Zack blinked, his expression growing stony. "No, you're not. How do you know?"

"I've suspected for a while. Today Sam confirmed the fact."

"What? Sam knew Dad had a brother, but Nancy and I didn't know we had an uncle. Is that what you're saying?"

The words stung, but Mary was determined not to wilt under the hurt in her son's eyes. It was up to her to lead him down the path to understanding. Keeping her head high and shoulders straight, she related her conversation with Sam, concluding, "Your father was a good man, Zack. He loved us and did his best to protect us."

"All these years, I've had an uncle," Zack mused, shaking his head. "Did you know?"

"No, not until I began connecting the links in your father's stories."

Mary took her son's hand and explained why she thought Jacob's family had passed on before they met. "The subject seemed so painful for him I stopped asking. When you kids came along, it was as if his parents had never existed. Jacob was happy. We were his family. His whole world."

"Leaving an unfinished manuscript is one thing." Zack's brow furrowed. "But leaving unfinished family business is totally not Dad. He wouldn't just walk away from family and pretend they'd died. There has to be another explanation."

"Or a very good reason," Mary added. "Don't glower at me, son. I love your loyalty to your father, but I'm trying to be realistic and practical."

"Sorry, Mom." Zack squeezed her hand and released it. "I know he wasn't perfect. No one is. Yet if the stories are true, then there was a bad falling out. Something unforgivable happened. And I'll never believe it was Dad's fault."

"We have to be careful about making assumptions. Life

is full of *ifs* and pitfalls. We need to deal with the situation as it is. That said, I agree, a falling out seems the most likely explanation."

Zack's heavy sigh reverberated in Mary's heart. "Sad as it is, if Dad was cast out of his family and the door slammed shut . . . well, it makes a certain kind of sense." He drew his feet back, leaned forward and rested his forearms on his thighs. "And gives me some answers."

"What do you mean?"

"Think about it, Mom. You aren't the only one who asked Dad about his family. Nancy did. So did I. We hit the same wall of silence. Dad was never harsh, just . . . skillfully evasive. He always found ways to divert us."

Smiling ruefully, Mary brushed an imaginary speck from the arm of her chair. "Well, you read the manuscript. What do you think caused the family rift?"

"My guess is the business. Jake hated it."

"Okay, you may be on to something. From the comments in the manuscript, the parents expected the oldest son to take over and step into the father's shoes. Obviously, he didn't. Perhaps his refusal caused the rift."

"Pretty lame, if you ask me." With a sudden puzzled look, Zack asked, "What was the family business anyway?"

Mary shrugged. "The manuscript didn't say, so I don't know."

"Another dead end. Now what do we do?"

"Ida said we need to think like Abby. I say we need to think like her *and* your father. After all, he was a mystery writer. When he packed away the manuscript, he included important links to Gerald." Mary picked up the paperweight from the craft table. "Catch." She tossed it to her son.

He caught it the way Jacob taught him to field a baseball—

with both hands. "Oh man, I remember this. It used to sit on his desk." Zack's tone softened. "You're right. The connection was there. I just didn't see it."

"There's more. Think of the one piece in his scrimshaw cabinet carved in elk horn."

Zack's jaw dropped. "The two boys playing on a tire swing. Just like in the book." He lowered the paperweight and looked up at the ceiling. "Good grief, Mom, I'm totally out of it. I've been away so much, I've forgotten the things that were important to my father."

"Posh!" Mary waved off his self-recrimination. "I've been here all along and didn't notice how odd the piece really is until I read the manuscript the second time."

Zack stood and paced the room several times. "Let's go over what we know."

Relieved he'd moved beyond an adversarial attitude to one of intense interest, Mary reiterated the clues she and Ida had gleaned from the stories.

She showed him the presentation box they'd found. Zack studied the horseshoe and the blue ribbon for a long time, his Adam's apple bobbing. When he next spoke, emotion rasped his voice. "I can't even imagine how Dad must have felt. Just the thought of never speaking to Nancy again makes me almost physically ill."

In that instant, Mary made up her mind. Sam had said the choice was hers. She could continue Jacob's efforts to restore the broken relationship, or let it go. Jacob never stopped hoping for reconciliation. Neither would she.

"What do you think about the incident with the wardrobe?" Zack asked.

Mary grinned as she imagined Jake and Gerry stuck in their

father's cramped wardrobe for an entire night. "I'm sure every kid who reads C. S. Lewis's *Chronicles of Narnia* goes looking for the land behind the fur coats."

"Nancy and I tried, but nothing happened. The wardrobe Dad built didn't have a lock," Zack mused. "I suppose he didn't want us to lock ourselves inside."

"Right!" Mary exclaimed as she made a mental connection. "Son, you're a genius. Your father left evidence for each of the major events in the book. I know exactly where to find the next piece."

CHAPTER ❦ SEVENTEEN

L<small>ATE IN THE AFTERNOON</small>, Abby headed for Hugo's office. Curious about the mysterious tone of his summons, she knocked once, then entered. Rebecca Cody stood by his desk, smiling wide enough to show her braces.

"We have the centerpiece for our bat exhibit," Hugo announced proudly. "Look what Rebecca has done!" He held up a large homemade poster titled "Bats—Myths and Facts". Black and white cartoons depicted common misconceptions, while drawings in sparkling colors portrayed the truth.

"Oh, this is perfect!" Captivated, Abby studied the teenager's work. Under a label declaring bats are blind, a black bat in dark glasses carried a white cane. Over it was the universal No symbol, a red circle with a slanted line through it. The explanation declared bats see as well as humans. Often, when they're flying, they catch insects with their wing and tail membranes. When they put the bugs in their mouths, their flight appears erratic.

The next myth under the universal No showed a bat tangled in a girl's hair. Next to it, a bat wearing a bib held a knife and fork over a plate of bugs. "Bats aren't interested in you," the caption explained. "If they come near, it's because of the insects drawn by your breath and body heat. The best of guests, bats want to dine on the bugs who want to dine on you."

Laughing, Abby turned her attention to the next montage. Along with the myth stating all bats carry rabies, were rows of tiny beds, each one occupied. The companion cartoon had bats in exercise gear working out with barbells.

Abby especially liked the factoids Rebecca had chosen. Folks needed to know that less than one percent of bats carried rabies. Statistically speaking, pets, playground equipment and sports were far more dangerous.

"Wow, Rebecca this is marvelous! I didn't realize cats are the most likely source of rabies."

"I didn't either," the teenager admitted. "But I went to the library like you suggested and Miss Naomi helped me find all kinds of information. Dogs used to be the biggest carriers. Now, most of them get vaccinated. Cats generally don't. I think if people knew, they'd get their cats vaccinated too."

"You're absolutely right," Hugo said. "You've done an excellent job with your research, Rebecca. I'm impressed."

"Thanks." A delicate flush rose in the girl's cheeks. "I learned a lot. I was kinda scared of bats before. Now . . ." She rolled her eyes and shrugged. "Do you know that besides eating zillions of bugs every night, many bats are considered keystone species? That means whole ecosystems depend on them. Without bats, we wouldn't have mangos, carob, cashews, bananas and a bunch of other stuff."

"I'm so proud of you." Abby put her arm around Rebecca's shoulders and squeezed.

Enthusiastically returning the hug, the girl said, "I'm really glad you came back to Sparrow Island. Some of the kids used to say science was nerdy. Now, because of you and Hugo and The Nature Museum, they think it's cool."

Hugo suddenly seemed to stand inches taller and Abby knew exactly how he felt. They couldn't have received a better compliment. "Thank you."

Rebecca glanced at her watch. "I've gotta go. I'm supposed to be in the museum, helping Grandma. The kids from Rev. Hale's Skills and Crafts Program are coming tomorrow. Bobby McDonald always has tough questions." With that, she bounced out of the office, leaving Abby and Hugo grinning at each other.

"Upon my word." Carefully, he laid the poster on his desk. "Do you think she knows she just gave us the highest compliment an educator can receive?"

Still savoring the accolade, Abby sank onto the nearest chair and gazed at the poster. "Young minds," she said slowly. "Sometimes we don't think they're listening, then they blow us away."

"Exactly."

While counting her blessings, Abby suddenly found herself wondering if Beth had found a similar fulfillment in her alternate career. Her enthusiasm suggested she had. What really stumped Abby was why Beth left the field of ornithology in the first place.

The phone rang, startling Abby. Hugo picked up the poster. "Would you answer that, please?"

While he moved Rebecca's work to a place of honor and safety on top of a filing cabinet, Abby picked up the receiver and identified herself.

"I tried your office first, then figured you'd be in there with Hugo," Joe chortled in her ear. "You two got time for a boat ride?"

Abby met Hugo's questioning gaze. "You remembered, didn't you?"

"Pretty sure I did, but I need to see if I'm right. Tell Hugo to lose the tie and put on his deck shoes. He needs to get out on the water now and then."

"Hold on a sec." Abby covered the mouthpiece. "Joe thinks he's remembered the island where Mark showed him the bats. He wants us to go check it out with him."

"What are we waiting for?"

"Okay, Joe. Hugo's on board. Are you going to tell me the name of the island?" Abby pressed.

"Nope. You'll know it when we get there."

"Joe, you are a minx."

"This *minx* is shoving off to see if he's right in exactly thirty minutes."

"Don't you dare leave without us. We'll be there."

"Better hurry," he teased. "The sea waits for no man or woman." Joe's chuckling ended abruptly when he hung up the phone.

Abby shuffled her feet in a mock tap dance as she handed the receiver to Hugo. "Don your deck shoes and windbreaker, my friend. Joe's taking us for a ride down memory lane. The boat leaves in—" she checked her watch, "—twenty-nine and a half minutes."

"What an incredible day. First Rebecca and now . . ." Eyes dancing, Hugo rose out of his chair. "A rare species colony right here in the San Juan Islands."

"I've got to make a call. We don't have much time to get to the marina and I've got to let Mary know I won't be home for dinner."

"You'd rather hunt birds than eat." Hugo loosened his tie.

"Bats are mammals," she retorted on the way out of his office.

"You know what I mean."

She heard him opening the cupboard where he kept a change of clothes for nature walks. "Five minutes and we're on the road."

Giddy with excitement, Abby called the house and left a message on the answering machine. Hopefully, Mary and Zack were out having a good time. Abby certainly intended to do so.

"WE'RE GOING TO SANDY'S to see Dad's armoire?" Zack adjusted his fedora and answered his own question. "Good idea, Mom. What are you going to tell her?"

"I'm vacillating between total silence and telling her everything." Mary pointed to the digital camera. Finnegan fetched it off the coffee table and brought it to her. "Good boy," she murmured, ruffling the fur on his back. "Sam said to do what I thought best and let the chips fall where they may."

"He has a point, but it's your call, Mom. I'm with you either way."

"Thanks for the support. I sure need it." Mary tucked the camera into the denim bag on the arm of the wheelchair, then looked up at her son. "There's been too much silence and secrecy about Jacob's family. I suppose there could be a dozen reasons for it—half being bad, the other half good. None of them can change the way Sandy loved your father. She was like a second daughter to him. She deserves to know why we want to see the armoire."

Zack opened the front door. "I'm not sure I ever told you, but I'm glad she ended up with it. It's easy to see you didn't have room for it here after the remodel." He held the front door open for Mary to pass. "Besides, you can always go visit if you get to missing it."

"True." She monitored her speed along the ramp leading to the driveway.

"I'll push you," Zack offered.

"Thanks, but no. I need the exercise. I'm keeping up my upper body strength." With Zack on her left and Finnegan on her right, they followed the driveway to the street and turned toward the McDonald home.

Mary swept a long glance into the green depths of her side yard. The elevated vegetable garden Bobby McDonald helped tend grew tall and lush. Farther down, pink and white impatiens nodded gaily as though happy to live at the rhododendrons' feet. Beyond the grass and flowers lay the glittering blue sea.

Thankful for the calm that had replaced her earlier uncertainty, Mary took a deep breath and savored the crisp scent of the evergreens bordering the road. A scant moment later, they arrived. Zack knocked on the door of the McDonald home, then stepped back.

With Sandy right behind him, ten-year-old Bobby opened the door. Laughter lingered in his big grin as he swiped a hand through his slightly mussed short brown hair. He had on his favorite clothes: a striped T-shirt, jeans worn at the knees and scuffed tennis shoes whose laces had a tendency to untie.

"Mary, how nice to see you. And Zack! Hi." Sandy hastily tried to restore order to her short, dark blonde curls. She too wore a loose T-shirt and worn jeans over her healthy, exercise-toned body. "Bobby and I were having a wrestling match."

"Hi, Mary. Hey, Zack!" Bobby hesitated before extending his right hand in greeting.

"Hey yourself." Dropping to one knee, Zack captured Bobby's wrist and tugged him forward. "I'm not too old for a bear hug." Wrapping his arms around Bobby's slender frame, Zack shook him and growled until the young boy's answering growl turned into giggles.

Mary relished the sight and Zack's unselfconscious burst of affection. A pang of emotion struck deep and she wondered if her son knew he'd make a great father. She prayed the answers he'd come home to find included the possibility.

"Come on in," Sandy invited, holding the door wide. An English teacher at Green Harbor Public School, she smiled knowingly at Mary. An acknowledgement of the bond between mothers and sons shone in her hazel eyes.

"Not so quick." Zack rose and collected Sandy in a brotherly hug. Her grin widened as she returned his affection.

"That's better," he said. "I've missed you all."

"Gosh, Zack." Bobby plucked at Zack's sleeve. "Your mom showed us all the postcards from the places you went. It must've been so exciting you hardly had time to miss us much. Did you see the Seahawks play the Cowboys when you went to Dallas? Did you go to the Smithsonian in Washington, DC? I wanna live there."

"In the Smithsonian Institute?" Zack teased.

"Oh yeah. Man, that'd be neat. Think of all the cool stuff I could see and learn when the people went home. I'd have the whole place to myself." Bobby glanced toward the kitchen. "Course, Mom would have to come. She doesn't like it when all I eat is peanut butter and jelly sandwiches. Dad would have to come too. We'd miss him too much."

Mary followed Sandy into the kitchen, the center of the McDonald family activities. Snapshots of Bobby covered the top half of the refrigerator. School photos marched across the wall behind the maple table. An assortment of African violets crowded together on the windowsill, the thick leaves and bright flowers overlapping.

After Zack related a few tales of his life on the road, Mary steered the conversation to Jacob and the manuscript. Sharing what she knew with Sandy felt right and gave Mary another measure of peace. When she finished Sandy sat for a moment, letting it all sink in. Then, Zack said, "There's a story in the book about the brothers going into an old-fashioned wardrobe."

"You mean like Lucy and Edward in *The Chronicles of Narnia*?" Bobby asked excitedly.

"Exactly," Mary said. "But unlike the one in C. S. Lewis's tale, theirs was just that—a wardrobe. No fur coats. No passageways to Narnia. Just woolen sweaters, heavy felt coats, mothballs and total darkness."

"Yeah, I figured that," Bobby said. "Bummer."

"There was a bigger bummer." Lowering her voice to a gravelly whisper in the hope of keeping Bobby engaged, Mary said, "They managed to lock themselves inside and wound up spending the night."

"Wow. It must've been scary. Bet their folks were looking all over for them the next morning." Uncertainty wrinkled Bobby's nose as he picked up a cookie from the platter on the table. "Spooky even." He dunked the treat into a half-full glass of milk.

"Don't even think about trying it," Sandy warned her son.

Mary stifled a laugh when Bobby, with cookie crumbs in the corners of his mouth, looked at his mother. "Why would I? Wardrobes aren't magic. Besides, I already checked. Ours doesn't have a lock."

"Speaking of yours," Zack said. "We were wondering if we could take a look at it. As I recall, the front feet were carved figures."

"Certainly." Sandy leaned close to Mary. "Do you think Jacob's armoire has a clue about his brother?"

"He left a memento for each of the major vignettes in the manuscript," Mary answered. "The armoire is the logical counterpart to the wardrobe story, so we'd like to see it and refresh our memories."

"You know you're welcome here any time." Sandy rose from the table. "Follow me. Neil and I put it in the guestroom that doubles as my office."

With Zack's help, Mary made the tight turn from the hallway leading into the room. Sitting in a place of honor, the big armoire gleamed in the late afternoon's golden light.

As though he was alone in the room, Zack walked up and tenderly traced the carvings on the door. "Until now, I didn't really appreciate the breadth of Dad's interests. He made his living with his stories, but his hobbies focused on beautiful things we can touch."

She met her son's contemplative gaze and glimpsed his struggle to achieve the balance his father had perfected. "He explained it to me as a way of keeping his creativity flowing. Some of his best story ideas came to him when he worked with his hands."

"It sure is pretty," Bobby said.

"Exquisite." The awe in Sandy's voice proved she still couldn't believe it was hers. The cost of her father's care in a Seattle nursing facility kept the McDonald family on a tight budget.

After the remodel on Mary's house to accommodate the wheelchair and Abby's decision to make her stay permanent, Mary had taken bids on her excess furniture. Sandy had garnered every penny she could lay her hands on, including her nest egg, to make a bid on the armoire.

On a dollar scale, she couldn't compete with many of their friends. But on the scale Mary used, Bobby out-bid his mother and everyone else. Love had fashioned the armoire and love purchased it. Bobby wanted the piece for his mother, not for himself, so he'd bid all he had—his time and his labor. He'd be weeding Mary's vegetable garden until he turned eighteen as payment.

Bobby plopped belly down on the floor. "Look, Mom. The feet are two guys. They're holding up the front with their heads."

Zack joined Bobby on the floor.

Mary and Finnegan retreated to give them more space. "As I recall, the one holding a book is facing the back of the one holding a hat."

"Right on," Zack confirmed. "Funny, I never noticed they had different things in their hands. But I always wondered why they weren't facing each other." He sat up cross-legged. "Nancy and I asked Dad about it."

"Did he tell you?" Sandy got on her knees and bent low for a better view of the carved footings.

"He said life isn't perfect no matter how hard we try to make it so," Zack answered. "You could look at these guys," he touched the one facing away, "and make up your own story. Maybe one was following the other."

"Or the one facing away is rejecting the other," Mary surmised. Considering what she now knew, it was more likely. "This is where the manuscript ends."

"Huh?" Sandy straightened. "You mean to say the boys in the story went their separate ways and never spoke to each other again?"

Mary winced. "The boy with the book kept trying to communicate with the one facing away, but to no avail."

"Why?" Bobby demanded. "How come he's so mean?"

Mary loved the straightforward way a ten-year-old cut through all the mire and dared state the obvious. "We don't know. Zack, Abby, Ida and I have read the manuscript. All four of us agree the book doesn't have an ending."

"But, but every book has an end," Bobby protested. The faint line of freckles on his nose scrunched with his confusion. "Maybe he just didn't have time to finish it."

"Or maybe he didn't know the ending." Zack stroked the figured footing before reaching into Mary's denim bag and withdrawing the digital camera.

"Whatcha gonna do?" Bobby asked.

"Take a few shots so Mom can see these guys as clearly as we can." Zack positioned the camera and began snapping away.

Bobby scooted back and laid an arm over Finnegan who turned his head slightly to avoid the camera flash. "Don't worry, boy. He's just taking pictures of two guys who had a fight. One of 'em doesn't want to make up. It'd be bad to stay angry for such a long, long time."

"Whoa. Look at this." Zack sidled out of the way so everyone could see.

"What?" Bobby asked.

"He moves." Slowly, Zack turned the figure of the young man in the hat one-hundred-eighty degrees until he faced the one with the book.

Sandy put her arm around Mary's shoulders. "Jacob was ever the optimist. I loved that about him. He used to tell me every story had a happy ending—if we have the courage and perseverance to find it."

Mary swallowed the sob in her throat and returned Sandy's gentle hug. Hope had kept the one figure mobile and hope had left the manuscript for her to find. Mary didn't know who had inflicted the wound that scored her husband's heart so deeply.

But she was going to find out—and write her own happy ending.

CHAPTER ❦ EIGHTEEN

As the *ISLAND HOPPER'S DELIGHT* approached James Island, Abby said, "I can't believe Zack and I were so close."

"Close is a relative term," Hugo said.

"With so many islands to choose from it's like finding one tree in the forest," Joe said.

Abby appreciated the men's understanding and their attempts to console her. Still, she wondered how she and Zack had overlooked this green jewel. They'd passed it twice during their investigation of the nearby islands. In a burst of insight, she realized how easy it was to overlook the small things right under her nose. She'd done precisely that with James Island and with Beth.

Until she and Beth had an opportunity to talk freely without the distraction of the bat hunt, Abby knew her niggling unease would persist. For now, the best course lay in finding the elusive little bats. The location of the colony was a meaningful gift she wanted to give.

Her spirits began to rise. She held on to her hat and turned her face into the wind.

Joe guided his big vessel through the water at a steady, smooth pace. His skill set Hugo at ease and reminded Abby of her father's practiced hand at the helm.

As close to their destination as the incoming tide allowed, Joe idled the powerful engine and they all looked at the island. Lazy waves slapped the rocks at the bottom of the timeworn cliffs. A red-tailed hawk dove out of the crags and soared upwards, drawing her gaze past the uninviting bluffs to the trees and thick vegetation crowding the uppermost edges of the precipices.

"What now?" Hugo asked. "Left or right?"

"There's a spot on the other side where we can moor the boat—if you want to explore the island on foot," Joe offered. "Mark usually went that way. He couldn't draw and steer the dinghy at the same time."

"Even if we knew where to go, we don't have enough light left to work our way through all the underbrush," Abby said. "I'd rather circle the island and see if we can find the bluffs matching this." She gave each man a plastic covered photocopy of the cliff drawing. She'd left the originals tucked safely away.

"Makes sense." Joe worked the throttle. "You two look at the bluffs. I'll get us as near as possible without running us aground."

"Thank you, Joe," Abby said. "I know these are treacherous waters, particularly when the tide is turning. If you want us to do anything, just holler."

"Will do. And if you find the bat cave, you do the same. I'd like to see the bats fly out this evening. Mark must've been impressed or he wouldn't have made a drawing with so many details." Joe turned his attention to navigation.

His reference to his brother gave Abby another reason to find the bat cave. Now that Joe had flung open the door to the past, each connection with Mark seemed to call forth more memories and flesh out others.

People's perceptions varied in such different ways. Joe knew the real Mark Blackstock. He was a loving brother, devoted son and nature enthusiast who always made time for his family. The world only knew Neville Sanborne as a singer, songwriter, performer and crowd-pleaser.

While Neville's songs wove memories in his listeners and became part of their lives, the heart behind the lyrics belonged to Mark's family. He was the person Joe cherished, the man whose legacy extended far beyond his music and embraced God's less appreciated creatures.

Watching the coastline, Abby marveled anew at the divine symphony of creation. Everywhere she looked, she witnessed the interdependence of birds and beasts, land and sea. Funny how some birds reminded her of people. The flashy and beautiful peacock lit up an area when he turned on the charm and spread his magnificent plumage. Neville Sanborne the performer became a peacock on stage.

Others, like the tiny Keen's myotis, labored far outside the limelight. Their role in controlling the insect population went largely unnoticed. Even when seen, they didn't inspire appreciation or respect because they lacked physical beauty or amusing behaviors. Too often, their uniqueness faded into the night with their songs.

Like Scott Kenai. A heaviness filled Abby's chest as she

thought about the young musician. He was like the little bat. He lived in the shadows and shunned the public because so many had turned away from him in the past. Only those who cherished his great talent, his gentle and courageous heart heard his true song. Like the bats, Scott enriched the lives of those who scarcely knew he existed.

Abby shifted positions as the boat changed course once more. Scanning the bluffs with her binoculars, she wondered how Beth had become the Western expert on bats.

"That's it," Joe said gloomily. "We've circled the island."

Clearly disappointed, Hugo frowned. "We couldn't have missed it. The cave must not be here."

"Or . . ." Abby studied the island for a long moment before checking the position of the sun. "Maybe we came at it from the wrong angle. We have two hours, Joe, maybe two and a half, before sunset. Can you take us around again? Back the way we came?"

Hugo and Joe both brightened.

"Sure," Joe said. "The tide is in now. I can get us in a bit closer."

"Excellent point, Abby."

"Thanks." On this circumnavigation, she determined to keep her thoughts as focused as her eyes. The insights she'd gleaned on her mental wanderings were important, but she couldn't afford to muff this opportunity.

Half an hour later, she saw a familiar looking shape on a jagged bluff—the same one etched into her memory from the sketchbook. "Cut the engine, Joe."

He responded immediately and set the big motor to idle. "You found it?"

"I do believe so." Keeping her binoculars trained on the spot, she reached out and pointed.

A moment later Hugo boomed, "I see it too. Excellent."

"What do you want to do now?" Joe asked. "Drop anchor and wait for sunset to see if they fly out?"

Abby lowered her binoculars. "We have time to go ashore, climb up and get a photo confirmation of the cave. If this site is deserted or just a look-alike, we'll know before dusk." She secured the binoculars and patted a different pocket of her birding vest. Feeling her camera, she gazed at their destination.

"A definitive solution," Hugo acknowledged. "What do you say, Joe? Let's find out what we're dealing with."

"I can't take you all the way to shore. Too rocky and too dangerous," Joe said. "You can't swim it either, but I've got an idea." He gestured toward the stern. "You can use the lifeboat if you're willing to row."

Hugo sized up the craft hanging from the davits. "I most certainly am."

Joe took the *Island Hopper's Delight* closer to the shore. Nevertheless, when Abby sat in the smaller boat as it bobbed in the waves, the island seemed much farther away. Hugo appeared undaunted. In fact, if she gauged his enthusiasm by his vigorous rowing, he relished their adventure.

After they made landfall, they secured the lifeboat to one of the boulders lining the shore and Abby led the way up the bluffs. Wind and water had scoured the cliffs, weathering the rock face. Smooth in some places, it broke into sharp points in others, making the climb treacherous.

"Watch for loose rock," Abby warned Hugo as she searched for a secure handhold. "Some of it's crumbling."

"I will. Mind your step too."

Soon, perspiration beaded her forehead. Grit speckled the lenses of her glasses and they slipped down her nose. Careful not to dislodge her straw hat, she used her upper arm to reposition the glasses.

Thirty feet above the waves, she found a narrow ledge. Off to the left, the rocks parted slightly, just as in the drawing. A puff of breeze cooled her face and carried the distinctive smell of bat guano.

"Hugo! They're here." Her excited whisper rode the air.

"Can you see inside? Can you see them?"

"No, not yet." Braced on the ledge, she took several pictures as she waited for Hugo. When his fingers reached her perch and he declined her offer of assistance, she moved aside to give him room. While he clambered up, she peered around the outcropping, and saw the opening to the cave was a ragged slit.

The bats had chosen their stony fortress well. It protected them from wind, weather, predators and most humans. The entrance presented a serious challenge to an inexperienced climber.

Secure on the ledge, Hugo moved beside her. Perspiration dampened his collar, but not his obvious love for the adventure. They conferred for a moment, then traded places so he could see the cave. "Only one of us should go inside, Abby. It's getting late and safety has to come first. This is your quest. You go."

He didn't sound as disappointed as she expected and she gave him a quizzical look.

"Of course I'd like to go in, but we're losing the light. If the bats are inside, as we think they are, they'll fly soon."

She beamed at him. Her boss was truly a man of quality and character. "You're the best, Hugo."

"Don't start, Abby," he said, returning her grin. "Let's get busy."

Together, they retreated to the widest portion of the sturdy ledge. Not wanting to get snagged by unseen obstacles inside the cave, Abby removed her hat and vest, keeping only her camera, which dangled from her right wrist. She tucked a small flashlight with a filtered shield over the bulb into the back pocket of her trousers.

"Poke your head in first. Let your eyes adjust before you step inside," Hugo warned. "For all we know, there could be a ten-foot drop on the other side of the entrance."

"Right." Abby maneuvered over the outcrop to the opening and slipped inside. With Hugo's warning ringing in her ears, she looked into the darkness and waited for her eyes to adjust. The inky air held a pungent smell and faint sounds of activity.

I wish Beth were with me. She'd know exactly how and what to do while keeping the bats' safety in mind. I want to do it right, but I feel so ill-equipped, so unknowledgeable about these fragile little creatures.

Abby ran her fingers over the bulb end of her flashlight. The filter remained in place. "Here goes." She wasn't sure if Hugo heard her. Even so, she had to turn on the light. She couldn't take a step without seeing where to put her feet.

The filter-muted beam illuminated a scant distance. Details disappeared in shades of gray. Everything in her wanted to charge ahead. Surely, her quarry was the source of the faint night song drifting through the cave. However, caution kept her in place. Despite her human advantages, she didn't possess wings or the ability to echolocate.

Without warning, the high-pitched squeaking sounds from deep in the blackness grew louder.

"Abby! Abby!" Hugo called worriedly. "Come out of there."

Reluctant to leave without seeing the colony, she hesitated.

"Please, Abby. There's another opening. It's smaller, but the bats are starting to fly out."

The urgency in his tone spurred her into action. A minute later, she was beside him, clinging to the rocks and sharing the small outcrop.

Almost as if the bats had chased her out, they began to emerge from the main entry. She raised her camera and took one shot after another, unconcerned about how well they were framed.

Below and just off the coastline, Joe sounded the boat horn. He, too, saw the bats fly. Grinning like a mustachioed Cheshire cat, Hugo gave a one-handed wave.

Her throat tight with emotion, Abby watched the bats disappear into the sunset shadows like wisps of smoke.

"We're losing the light," Hugo warned. "We need to get down this bluff."

"Go ahead." She shinnied against the rocks toward the opening. "I'll be with you in a minute or two."

"Abby . . ."

"Check your watch. If I'm not back in three—"

"You know I won't leave without you."

She did. Although she'd traveled extensively, Hugo had logged more miles and lived a far more adventurous life before settling down on Sparrow Island. Accustomed to leading expeditions, he made safety a primary concern.

"Okay Hugo. I promise. Two minutes, then we'll go." On his reluctant nod, she moved through the opening. This time, she immediately put the camera to work. Holding it out, she snapped one picture after another, stopping only when she heard a frightened high-pitched squeal.

Half an hour later, Abby, Joe and Hugo sat on the deck of the *Island Hopper's Delight*. One by one, they viewed the pictures she had taken on the cliff face and inside the bat cave. The flight of the bats exceeded her wildest hopes. As did her photos from inside the cave. The close-ups of the tiny mammals should be a big help for Beth.

"The WDFW will be thrilled we located a thriving bat colony. They'll have to make the official determination as to genus, but with all species suffering declines in numbers, this colony is a ray of sunshine." Abby patted Joe's shoulder. "Thanks to you and Mark's exquisite drawings, the site and the bats will receive protection."

Joe stroked his chin. "Yeah. To tell you the truth, Abby, I'd like an acknowledgement of my brother's artwork in helping locate the colony. No mention of Neville, just Mark Blackstock, nature lover." Joe grinned at Abby. "Bat appreciator."

Abby chuckled. "I like it."

"What say we go home?" Hugo vigorously rubbed the tip of his nose. "Abby needs a change of clothing."

She laughed. "And a good scrubbing from head to toe."

The trip to Green Harbor passed quickly as the trio took turns reliving their success. Eager to share her triumph, Abby returned home only to find Mary and Zack had retired for the night. Small wonder, she realized when she glanced at the clock. It was nearly midnight.

After showering, she took the plastic bag containing her unsalvageable garments down to the trash. On the way back, Blossom rubbed against her leg. Delighted, Abby picked up the cat and carried her upstairs. "Do you want to know what a fabulously exciting day I've had?"

Blossom's purr was all the encouragement Abby needed.

CHAPTER ❦ NINETEEN

MARY WELCOMED IDA TOLLIVER at the front door. "You're right on time. Breakfast is ready."

"I'm so glad you called and invited me." Ida stepped into the foyer. "My schedule's been a little crazy, but I wanted to touch base with you about the manuscript."

As she preceded Ida into the kitchen, Mary stifled a yawn. Last night, thoughts of Jacob, the armoire and the story within the stories had filled her dreams. A little boy with Jacob's adult face kept trying to tell her something she didn't understand. "We'll have plenty to talk about—after I have some coffee and breakfast."

Ida left her purse on the telephone table and asked, "What can I do to help? Oh! Hi Zack."

"Good morning. Just make yourself comfortable. Mom has everything ready."

Ida went to the sink and used the hand sanitizer. "If you're heading into town Zack, let me warn you. The hottest topic at the café is what you should do with the guitar."

Her son's grimace didn't surprise Mary. She knew very well, when he settled on a direction, nothing would change his mind. He had decided to keep the instrument, so he considered the subject closed.

He opened the oven to check the hot meal he'd helped prepare and muttered, "Why can't people just mind their own business?" He carried breakfast to the table.

Ida took the place he indicated. "I thought you'd want to know. All the interest and speculation hasn't gone away."

"What hasn't gone away?" Abby made a beeline for the coffeepot and filled her travel mug.

"The big controversy over the guitar." Zack shrugged. "You'd think people had better things to do. They should take a lesson from you or Mom and get a life. By the way, how'd it go yesterday with Hugo and Joe?"

Abby brightened and all traces of her short night vanished. "We found it, Zack. It was so exciting." She glanced at the kitchen clock. "I can't wait to set up a conference call with Beth, the WDFW and Hugo."

Looking wistful, Zack dropped a couple slices of bread into the toaster. "Were you there at sunset? Did you see the bats fly?"

"Yes. They're so tiny, about the size of a small hummingbird, but definitely not as speedy."

"Where were they?"

"You won't believe it. You and I were very close." She grinned up at him. "James Island."

"The little one? Just east of Decatur?"

"That's it."

"Man, if it'd been a snake, we would've been bitten."

Mary watched the exchange. "Did you two go right by the spot?"

"Guess we did," Zack said ruefully. "I'd sure like to see it—and see the bats leave the cave."

"You will," Abby promised. "I'll work out something." She stuck a banana into her jacket pocket. "Gotta run. I'll eat on the way to work."

"Wait for your toast." Zack finished buttering it. "And me. If you don't mind, I'd like to borrow your car today. Scott and I have a jam session later this morning."

"Wonderful!" Abby ran to the table and kissed Mary on the cheek.

Mary smiled.

Abby ran back and checked the lid on her coffee cup before dashing toward the garage. "Good seeing you, Ida. Bye, Mary."

"Bye," Zack echoed, snatching the toast off the counter.

The house sounded suddenly quiet. Then Ida burst out laughing. "I feel like I've just witnessed a whirlwind. Is it like that every morning?"

"No. Usually Abby and I are rather predictable." A startling realization struck Mary and she sat up straight. "My goodness, that's not quite true. Having Abby here definitely adds spice."

The two women enjoyed their breakfast and each other's company. When the dishes where done, Mary found Ida, head tilted in contemplation, studying her.

"Are you all right? You look—I don't know—tired maybe."

"I'm a little confused," Mary admitted. "I'm supposed to be the expert on Jacob Reynolds. I thought I knew him better than anyone."

"You did, and you still do," Ida insisted.

"I suppose you're right, but I'm questioning how attentive

I was to his needs. Good grief, I never pressed him about his family. Maybe I should have."

"And maybe he'd have resented it if you did. You loved him the best you knew how. Don't second guess yourself."

Mary met her young friend's violet gaze. "When did you get so smart?"

"The first couple of months after my parents died," Ida said evenly. "I nearly drove myself crazy with the 'maybe I should haves.'" A faint smile touched her lips as she lowered her shaking head. "I found help in the unexpected counsel of Frank Holloway. He made me understand we'd all like to rewrite parts of our past. But it is what it is. We can't change it. The best we can do is make amends where we can and trust in the Lord."

Mary made a mental note to do something special for Frank when he least expected it. Hearing his wisdom from Ida's lips reminded Mary how special he was. "Thank you, Ida."

"You're welcome. Now, tell me what you've found."

Mary did as Ida requested and brought her up to speed on everything she'd discovered about Jacob and Gerald Reynolds.

"Ah, it is an autobiography," Ida concluded.

"If not for your suggestion of a scavenger hunt, it might have taken much longer to put the pieces together. What made you think of it?"

"My mom and I loved scavenger hunts and Dad always indulged us. He believed every mystery could be solved."

Mary marveled at Ida's ability to recall the sweet memories with her parents.

"Unfortunately, with this mystery, we're stuck on the biggest part."

"Yeah, the ending of the book."

"It's as though we don't know enough to write it yet," Mary said thoughtfully. "Something is still missing."

"You're right." Ida stood. "Let's go back to the beginning."

"Okay. To the craft room." Mary turned her chair and Finnegan promptly came to attention. "Maybe we've overlooked something."

Two empty cardboard boxes lay atilt on the floor. The third sat on the staging table where Mary had left it. She gave Finnegan a hand signal to rest.

"Let's smooth the packing paper," Mary suggested. "There might be something tucked in a fold we missed."

"Or Jacob may have written a message on a piece."

"We can hope," Mary thought aloud. "He was a mystery writer keen on leaving clues."

They examined each piece while shaking out the wrinkles and folding the paper. As the pile of crumpled packing material dwindled, Mary said, "If we don't find anything, at least our neat stack will fit into the recycle bin."

"I'll bet Jacob was a hoot when it came to hiding Easter eggs," Ida said with a little laugh.

"Oh, he was imaginative," Mary agreed. "You know . . . sometimes he hid them in obvious places you'd never think to look. The kids rushed right by the best eggs."

"My mom once hid my basket in my toy box. I was six," Ida admitted. "I didn't find it until after Easter service when Mom told me to put all my toys away."

"What a good idea. Wish I'd thought of it."

"Well, we've gone through all the paper."

Mary looked around. "Let's check the boxes. Maybe something slipped under one of the bottom flaps."

"Sure. We need to break them down anyway." Ida reached for the craft knife and cut the tape on the bottoms.

The first two were just as they appeared—empty. From under the bottom flap of the last box, a business card fluttered to the floor. Ida picked it up and gave it to Mary.

The once-white card had yellowed around the edges. Mary's hand shook as she held it and read, "'Reynolds Clothiers, the finest name in men's fashions. Family owned since 1926. Yakima, Washington.'"

"Wow. Jacob's name is on it." Ida pointed at the center.

Mary stared at the card. "All those years . . ."

"In the book Jacob never mentioned what kind of store his father owned. Because of the inventory and the chores the boys did, I assumed it was a general store in a country town."

"Now we know it's a men's clothing store," Mary said. "It fits. Jacob had an excellent sense for coordinating his wardrobe."

"You mean the colors didn't clash or he didn't put stripes and checks together?" Ida lifted her hands in mock surrender. "My Dad was hopeless when it came to clothes. He was so color-blind, Mom had to check him every morning before he went to work."

"I had it much easier," Mary reflected. "Jacob knew more than colors. He knew what looked good and how to put things together. He usually took Zack and my father when he went shopping. I took it for granted then. Now I realize how Jacob acquired his fashion sense."

"He grew up with it." Ida agreed.

"Still, I'm having trouble seeing him as a haberdasher, even for a day. Not because he wasn't dapper, or service-minded—

he was. His imagination was too big for the confinement of four walls and a strict schedule. When he worked on a book, he was totally immersed. He worked all hours, walked at midnight and reconstructed scenes in the yard, the garage, the kitchen—wherever. Clerking at a store and checking inventory day after day would have killed his spirit."

Mary saw her husband as a young man afire with a passion to craft words into stories. His father's expectations would have doused that fire. Yet, the senior Reynolds had offered Jacob his life's work—a solid, tangible asset in an uncertain world.

As a mother, she understood a parent's desire to steer a child toward a stable career, one he could count on to support him and provide for a family. From the parent's perspective, it was the greatest gift a father could give a son.

But sometimes a parent had to keep an open heart and a closed mouth. She'd had to do that with Zack. Letting go so he could follow his own path was the only way to keep him in her life.

Mary tapped her open palms on the armrest of her chair. "I think we can safely say Jacob had been honest about his ambitions. Despite his family's wealth, or lack thereof, he paid his own way through college."

Still following the threads of her speculation, Mary mused, "I think Jacob broke his father's heart when he followed his own calling and walked away from the business." The conclusion felt right and explained so much. "When he did," Mary continued, "he may have done the one thing his parents and brother couldn't forgive."

"So they never spoke to him again?" Ida's eyes grew misty. "That would break my heart."

"I think it broke his too."

WITH ZACK DRIVING, Abby ate her toast and banana on the way to work and listened to his plans for the jam session. In practically no time, he let her off in the circular driveway in front of The Nature Museum.

As he cruised silently away, she walked to the bench under the big leaf Maple to spend a few private moments with God. She'd missed her morning devotions and felt off-kilter.

Sitting in the stillness, with a breeze soughing through the trees, she shared her concerns and asked for guidance. She needed to know if the missing letter had created problems. And why Beth had changed fields after graduation. Abby wondered if her fumble had played a role.

Regardless, Beth was due an apology and Abby wanted to make it. Forgiveness was a gift that blessed the giver and the receiver.

Abby experienced a sense of unhurried calm. When the time was right for discussing the matter with Beth, she'd know. Feeling energized, she went to Hugo's office. "Good morning."

He returned her greeting and asked, "Are you ready to share our news with the WDFW?"

"Just about. I was thinking of e-mailing the pictures to them before we set up a conference call."

"Excellent idea. They're bound to be as excited as we are. It isn't every day one locates a thriving colony of a rare species."

Abby couldn't help chuckling at his exuberance. "We hope it's a rare species, a Keen's myotis, to be exact."

"I know. I know." Hugo stood straighter and raised an eyebrow. "Neither of us has the expertise to make a positive identification. Nevertheless, the location of our bat cave is valuable information. I'm quite pleased with the idea we're giving them a colony they didn't know existed until now."

With a wave, she started out of his office. "I'll be back after I send the pictures." She laughed again. "I give them fifteen minutes before we're on the receiving end of a conference call."

It turned out to be twelve minutes. Abby had just returned to Hugo's office and taken a seat when the phone rang. Hugo answered and put the call through the speaker.

The joy of celebration on the other end of the line reminded Abby of the high-spirited gala in her dream.

"I'm on cloud nine," Beth gushed breathlessly. "You must have been right on top of them when they flew from the cave."

"We were," Abby said. "The opening is narrow and the approach precarious."

"Good, they're hard to get to," Beth said.

"Very hard," Hugo confirmed.

"From the last photos, it appears the pups are only a week or two old." Beth sounded more businesslike. "I'm glad you got the pictures, but equally glad you didn't take more. They must have hated the camera flash."

"I'm afraid they did," Abby admitted. "When the flight left, I presumed the cave was deserted. Of course, the minute I heard the cries, I stopped taking pictures. I'm sorry I distressed the little ones. When it comes to bat habitats and habits, I'm a rank amateur."

"You did fine. And found the colony so fast my head is spinning," Beth said. "We didn't expect you to locate them for months, perhaps even a year. This colony appears to be quite healthy. We couldn't be more thrilled or grateful."

"It was a most excellent adventure," Hugo said. "We had invaluable help—specifically Mark Blackstock's drawings. Without them, we would've remained ignorant of these tiny creatures. Perhaps when you're naming the sanctuary, you'll take Mark's contribution into account."

"Consider it done," announced the Deputy Director. "The WDFW needs the public's help to find and protect our wildlife. Their active participation should be rewarded."

"Thank you, sir," Abby and Hugo said in tandem. Then there was a flurry of activity, chairs scraping and papers rustling.

Beth asked, "Are you still there, Abby? Hugo?"

"Yes and we're astounded."

The bat expert gave a self-satisfied chuckle. "When I said we were grateful, I meant it."

"There is one more thing," Hugo said smoothly. "The Nature Museum is putting together a special exhibit about the benefits of bats. Your input would be most welcome. We want to educate our visitors properly."

"It'll be my pleasure. I wish all the requests coming into my office were like yours. Now, let's coordinate schedules for the official confirmation trip. I got my cast off yesterday, so I'm somewhat mobile. Even though the doctor insists I can't climb, my assistants are avid spelunkers and can handle the night vision equipment."

"Night vision?" Hugo echoed, his bushy eyebrows arching as he looked at Abby.

"It's much less disturbing for the colony. Especially now, while they're birthing. In fact, we have to ask you not to go up to the cave again."

"Oh dear," Abby blurted.

"Is there a problem?"

"My nephew is visiting and he was most helpful during the

search. I, uh, promised to take him to the bat cave before he went back to Chicago."

"I see. Maybe we can bend the rules. Let me check something." Pages ruffled. "Will all of you be available tomorrow?"

Hugo nodded affirmatively and Abby said, "Yes. That would be ideal."

"I'll see you then."

"Ah, Beth. Can I take you to lunch or dinner? Whichever works best?"

"I'd like that. Very much."

"Perfect. See you soon." Queasiness mixed with anticipation as Abby hung up the phone.

CHAPTER ❦ TWENTY

AFTER A TASTY DINNER, Abby excused herself and went into the garage. Refurbishing the camping gear gave her the quiet time she needed to think about her meeting with Beth.

Zack bounded out the side door of the house. "I'm here to help. It's only fair. We both used the camping gear."

She put her reflections on the back burner and engaged in the moment. "Okay, I'll move the cars into the driveway."

"No need. I'll do it."

Figuring where to start, Abby surveyed the equipment and began by checking the cooler.

After moving the vehicles, Zack returned and pointed to a pair of neatly stowed bundles. "The sleeping bags are good. I treated them and hung them in the sun for several hours. The tent too."

"Hey, you can go camping with me anytime. Not only do I get a campfire serenade, but you do most of the cleanup too." She opened a box of baking soda and put it inside the cooler. "I hope your plans for tomorrow are open."

"Hey, if I weren't free, I'd get that way. The opportunity to see the bat cave with experts is too good to pass up." He collected the eating utensils and set them aside. "When they fly, those little bats ought to scare away every mosquito around." He opened a nylon bag labeled "Quick Trip."

"I check that one regularly. It's basic medical supplies—human and avian—and some Meals-Ready-to-Eat for occasions when I have to leave in a hurry. Put it on the shelf."

"You plan ahead like Dad did." Zack closed up the bag and placed it beside a carton of bottled water. "Like I came home to do."

"Are you making any headway?"

"Some. I keep running into stumbling blocks." He hesitated. "I don't know. Maybe I'm supposed to. Looking for answers to questions I didn't know existed has shown me new ways to look at my dilemma."

He picked up a broom and started sweeping out the garage. "Naomi Yardley just called. She wanted to remind me how much the community would enjoy seeing Neville Sanborne's guitar on display." The sweeping picked up speed. "If I don't want to sell, I can loan it."

"She means well," Abby offered, not knowing what else to say. Naomi had good intentions. She was bent on preserving and sharing the history of the Sparrow Island community. "At least the sketchbook is a bonus. It solved problems Joe wasn't aware he had. Now, he's given himself permission to enjoy his brother's memory. He's richer in all the ways that count."

"And the two of them led you to the bats. Which was good, but it opened up a bit of a Pandora's box for you with Beth," Zack said dourly.

"It was always open. I just didn't realize it." Organizing the camp cooking equipment beside the Quick Trip bag, she mused, "The oversights of the past have a tendency to lurk in the shadows, then spring out when we least expect it. I have no valid reason—or excuse—for not tracking Beth down years ago and asking her forgiveness. I should've, Zack. But I didn't. Actually, I'm glad this happened the way it did. I had a lot of help finding the bat cave. Now, I also have a favorable setting in which to clear the slate."

"You know, Aunt Abby, I really like the way you look at things." Zack leaned on the broom. "I see your attitude of forgiveness in Scott Kenai. He's a great guy and fun to be around —after he lets his guard down. Since our jam session, he's been on my mind a lot."

"Any particular reason?"

"Balance is an elusive quality. Here I am struggling to find some in my life. Then I look at Scott. Talk about lopsided.

"He's got more talent and natural ability than I'll ever have. But he'll never go on tour. He doesn't have the physical stamina to cut it in this business. He never will."

"You're weighing his life on your scale," Abby said. "God's given him an audience. In church. Among friends and with his sister. Scott uses his gift to the best of his ability. That's his balance."

Zack scooped up the pile of debris. "I wonder how Dad dealt with the trade-off of his writing career and the rift with his brother and parents."

Abby hadn't had time to mull over all Mary had told her about Jacob's brother or the significance of the business card found in the bottom of the storage box. "I'm sure it was very difficult. Until Mary discovers the real reason for the rift—not conjecture or logical speculation, mind you—we won't know for sure."

"See? Another one of those double-edged swords. Knowing Mom, she'll track down Gerald Reynolds. Even if he gives her the time of day, why would he tell her anything? And if he does, how do we know he'll even be civil?"

"You're shopping for trouble where it isn't for sale. The short answer is—we don't. What's really worrying you?"

"This whole thing with the manuscript has been hard on Mom. She doesn't say so, but I know. I feel it too. Neither of us suspected Dad died with such a heartbreaking secret. It's wrong, Aunt Abby."

"I share your concerns for your mom. What's really driving your anger, Zack?"

"I feel cheated. Dad did so much for us. He didn't let us do anything for him—not even help him carry this burden."

"Hold on. The choice of silence was Jacob's. He did what he thought was best. Never doubt it."

Zack returned to the back of the garage and swept out the corners. "Dad was protecting Mom, and us, from his pain. All the things he did for us, for others, the way he led his life . . ." Zack's voice trailed off.

Hanging on every word, Abby remained quiet. The rhythmic swishing of the broom's bristles on the concrete moved with the precision of a metronome.

"Whatever happened started before Mom and Dad met," Zack continued as though talking to himself. "Despite Dad's attempts for reconciliation, Gerald never answered, never acknowledged their marriage or me and Nancy. Who knows how many times Dad wrote or called him? We sure don't. We don't know if Gerald married or if we have any cousins. Guess it doesn't really matter now."

Finally realizing Zack was venting a good case of frustration, Abby asked, "What are you getting at?"

He collected the sweepings and emptied the dustpan before hanging up the broom and facing her. "If Dad couldn't heal the rift, then in all likelihood, Mom will only get hurt trying to ferret out the causes."

"I understand your desire to protect her," Abby said. "But she'll do what she believes she must, Zack. It's who she is. What she believes."

"I know." He removed the fedora, slapped it against his thigh and wiped his brow with the sleeve of his T-shirt. "But what good will it do? Dad's been gone ten years."

A long, narrow white strip fluttered to the floor.

Abby started forward, curious to see what it was. "Something flew out of the inside of your hat."

"I didn't put anything in it." Zack bent and picked up the paper.

"Goodness, it's laminated," Abby whispered. She and Zack stared at the four washed-out pictures of two young men crammed into a photo booth. Elbows akimbo, they had their arms around each other's shoulders, trying to fit in side by side while laughing and mugging for the camera.

Standing beside Zack, Abby felt the angst melt from him. His eyes and mouth softened as his tension eased. Tenderly, almost reverently, he cradled the pictures in the palm of his hand.

"So this is my dad as a young man," he said so softly Abby barely heard. "And my uncle."

"They certainly do look like brothers," she agreed.

"At what? Around twenty? Twenty-one?"

Recalling the general age of the student body at Cornell, she nodded. "It's a good guess. They're no longer boys, but they still have the look of innocence. From their antics and camaraderie, it looks like they've grown up, but haven't parted ways."

"My uncle," Zack repeated, this time with a question in his voice.

Abby couldn't imagine what was going through her nephew's mind. He'd come home to sort things out and found much more than he'd bargained for—including an absent uncle. Putting a face on his estranged relative validated Gerald Reynolds' existence.

She wondered if he was still alive . . . if he remembered what once was—the friendship and closeness. Did he ever regret the distance and the lost years?

As if he could see into her heart, Zack warned, "We gotta pick a good time to show this to Mom."

"YOU TWO ARE JUST IN TIME to try out my new dessert," Mary said proudly. She'd made a crumb cake while Abby and Zack organized and cleaned the garage. "Janet gave me the recipe. If mine is half as good as hers, you're going to love it."

Abby went to the sink and washed her hands. "You've put on water for tea too. Fantastic." She bent over the single-layer cake cooling on a wire rack. "It smells wonderful."

Mary thought her son looked pensive as he arranged camping utensils in the dishwasher, then washed up. When she was about to ask if something troubled him, he spoke. "The car and van are back in the garage. I cleared a lower shelf for easy storage." He took the hand towel from Abby.

"That was very kind. Thank you." Mary watched him out of the corner of her eye. "Why don't you do us the honor of slicing and serving, Abby?"

Before pulling up to the table, Mary went to the back door and opened it. She removed Finnegan's service cape to let him know he was off duty. "Off the clock, boy. Stay in the yard."

As though understanding, he gave her a snuffle of agreement. She watched him trot across the deck, then turned to her son. "He's the smartest dog in the world. He knows what I'm saying and even better, he obeys. I have Lily to thank for his training and you and Nancy for his companionship."

Abby served the coffee cake and poured tea. Mary was pleased the dessert turned out as tasty as the one Janet had made for the reading group. As they ate, Mary listened to Abby's plans to return to James Island with Zack the next day.

"I want pictures of your adventure," Mary told her son.

"I'm afraid we can't take them inside the bat cave," Abby warned. "It's too dangerous for the bat pups."

"We'll take some of the colony when they fly." He glanced at Abby. "Speaking of pictures, Mom . . ." Zack handed Mary the photo strip.

She gasped, then held it tenderly. She couldn't stop looking at the photos. After he told her how he found the strip, she thought of the countless times Jacob had worn the hat and wondered when he tucked the pictures inside the band. Had they been there all along, or had he put them there when he packed the hat away?

It was just one more question without an answer. Whenever he'd done it, a single glance at the photos resolved any question about Gerry being his brother.

She picked up the strip again, marveling at the image of her husband on the brink of true manhood. "This is the final piece," she whispered. "The undeniable proof."

"I'll admit they look alike," Zack said.

"I've been thinking about this all afternoon." Mary looked at Abby, then at Zack. "Not the pictures, of course, but the whole situation. I did some research on the Internet and learned a great deal."

Zack folded his hands on the edge of the table. "Wouldn't it be better to leave it alone?"

"I can't."

"Mom—"

"I realize I may not get any further than Jacob did. But I want to try. Your father never stopped loving his brother. I think we should give his devotion the honor it deserves. So I'm going to. I know you're leaving next week and I'd like you to be here if—no—when, your Uncle Gerald comes."

"You know where he is?" Abby asked, leaning into the table.

"There are three Reynolds Clothiers in Washington State. They're all on the east side: Yakima, Spokane and Richland. The main store is still in Yakima. The president is Gerald Reynolds."

"Will you call him?" Zack asked.

"Maybe. I'm still trying to figure out the most effective approach, one he'd be receptive to." Mary fingered the photo strip as an idea started to take shape.

"It sounds like you're going after the lost sheep," Abby said. "I think trying to establish a relationship with your brother-in-law is a good thing—for all of us. The whole family gains if you draw Gerald into the fold. And if he refuses, well, closing the circle is important too. What are your plans so far? Can I help?"

Grateful for her sister's encouragement, Mary said, "I'm going to invite him to a family picnic at Stanton Farm." There were a hundred reasons Gerald might refuse—short notice, lack of interest, conflict of schedule, too long a drive . . .

Undaunted, she picked up the pictures and said, "I think the Lord just furnished the one thing that might persuade him to come."

"The photos? Why? Are you going to send them to him?" Zack asked.

"Just one. I'll overnight it with a letter and an invitation." Her confidence growing, she gave her son a reassuring smile. "If he doesn't respond, I'll know Jacob died in Gerald's heart long before my wedding day."

"And you'll drop it," Zack stated. "You won't let it eat at you."

"Yes, son. I'll let it go." She pushed away from the table. "Excuse me. I have a letter to write." A thought struck her and she pivoted the wheelchair back. "You know . . . Gerald's the reason Jacob didn't finish the book. He was holding out for a happy ending."

"I hope you're right, Mom," Zack mumbled.

CHAPTER ❦ TWENTY-ONE

Midafternoon the following day, Beth Bingham stepped into Abby's office. "Hey, this is nice!"

Behind her, Hugo grinned. Rising from her chair, Abby looked up at her slightly taller former student. "Thank you and welcome to Sparrow Island."

Time had been kind to Beth. Still as slender as her university days, the forty-five-year-old wore a huge smile and a wildlife researcher's typical uniform: jeans, a lightweight long sleeve shirt and a vest sporting a dozen pockets. Her sturdy oxfords were suitable for boat decks and long walks.

"You look great," Abby added. In fact, Beth looked better than great. The sparkle in her pale gray eyes and the smile lingering at the corners declared happiness was a regular habit. Reddish curls framed her heart-shaped face.

"So do you." She took Abby's hand in both of hers. "The photos on your books don't do you justice."

"You've seen my books?" Surprise raised Abby's voice several notes.

"Seen them? Heavens, there's a Dr. Stanton shelf in my office. I refer to it often. Your work is very helpful."

The sincere compliment touched Abby. Before she could respond, Beth introduced her colleagues. Harvey Kellogg, a tall outdoorsy man in a plaid shirt and khaki shorts ending just above his tanned knees, seemed reserved. Abby guessed him to be around fifty.

Brian Weber, his younger counterpart, couldn't have been a day over thirty. In jeans, running shoes and a bright yellow T-shirt, he dragged a Mariners ball cap off his longish blond hair and stuffed it into his back pocket.

Despite the difference in their attire, the men clearly shared Beth's exuberance and enthusiasm. With the introductions made, Hugo led the way to The Nature Museum's more spacious workroom.

When they'd gathered around the table, Abby handed out the binders she'd prepared. Each had a copy of Mark's drawing tucked into the cover's view pocket.

"Inside you'll find all the data we've collected," she explained. "I also included maps of the areas my nephew and I searched, along with our notes."

Beth leafed through the contents. "This is impressive. Seems you've done most of our work for us. Thank you."

Abby smiled warmly but remained silent.

Beth closed the binder and traced the picture on the cover. "Do you have the original drawings? And are you willing to part with them?"

"I'm afraid the answer is no on both counts. The originals

are part of Mark Blackstock's sketchbook. I've already returned it to his brother, Joe. However, I've included digital photos as well as photocopies for your records."

"Fair enough," Beth said. "We're grateful for Mr. Blackstock's help and would like to tell him so."

"The opportunity awaits." Abby picked up her hat and vest. "He's agreed to take us to James Island on his boat. My nephew, Zack Reynolds, is with him at the marina now."

"All right," said Brian jumping to his feet. "Let's get going."

Harvey gave Hugo an apologetic glance. "We're anxious to get started. The equipment Brian and I brought takes a while to set up and we'd like everything in position well before dusk."

As the group left the workroom and headed for the parking lot, Abby asked Beth, "Will you be staying on the island for a while?"

"We have rooms at The Dorset," she answered. "We dropped off our overnight gear before coming here."

Behind them, Brian added, "Nice place. And the folks gave us great directions."

Harvey laughed. "What he means is there weren't many places to make a wrong turn."

Obviously accustomed to their banter, Beth continued, "Our plan for today is to get what we need to make a formal confirmation. Tomorrow we'll go back to the lab and our real work will begin. I'm sure we'll be back several times before the end of the year."

The five of them climbed into the WDFW van. Harvey turned left onto Primrose Lane and said, "I noticed on your wall map that Decatur Island is much closer to James Island."

"It is," Abby agreed. With limited resources, most scientists preferred lodgings close to their sites. It allowed them to maximize field time. "Decatur is privately owned with no public lodging."

"If you're content with a sleeping bag, there's a campground right on James Island," Hugo offered.

"Works for me," said Brian. "Next time we come we should stay there."

"I don't know," Harvey countered. "We'll need to rent a boat."

Apparently unconcerned, Beth turned to Abby and asked, "Dinner tonight? Girls only?"

"Absolutely," Abby agreed. "Just you and me."

And You, Lord.

"WOW! WHAT A FULL DAY we've had, Abby. I hope we're not too late to order dinner. I'm famished," Beth said as Abby drove them to Winifred's, the best restaurant on Sparrow Island.

Despite the healthy snacks they'd eaten on the *Island Hopper's Delight*, Abby was ravenous. "Me too."

"Today just whizzed by," Beth marveled. "I don't know what we would've done without your nephew. He was so helpful carrying our gear up to the ledge, then when the rock fell on the recording equipment, I thought we'd have to pack it in and come back later. I'm still amazed Zack managed to fix it."

Abby parked at the restaurant. "He's often said life on the road with his band taught him how to improvise."

"Maybe I should send Harvey and Brian on the road and keep Zack." Beth laughed as they exited the car.

"They did a great job on the video," Abby countered. "I know Hugo, Joe and I thoroughly enjoyed sitting in the boat and watching everything on the laptop. Joe said it was better than a National Geographic special." She pushed open Winifred's teak and leaded glass door.

"It was," Beth agreed, "because we all had a personal stake in it. I'm just used to being at the front of the action."

As soon as they entered the foyer, the maitre d' picked up two embossed leather menus. "Right this way." Thick burgundy carpet absorbed their footsteps as he escorted them to a window table with an excellent view of the lights reflecting off the water.

Once they settled onto the well-padded chairs, Beth said, "I'm glad Joe invited the men to his home for a late supper. It was very nice of him. I hope he has an understanding wife."

"He does. Margaret's a treasure."

"Speaking of treasures,"—Beth glanced appreciatively at the plush decor—"This restaurant is one."

Abby tried to view the elegant room through her guest's eyes. An artful profusion of plants softened corners and high places. Cream-colored linen tablecloths and napkins adorned the surrounding tables. Fresh flowers graced the tables.

"Winifred's has been here for as long as I can remember. I've always thought of it as a special place." She put her menu down. Instantly, a waiter appeared to take their orders.

"I enjoyed your nephew immensely," Beth said as they waited for dinner. "So did Brian and Harvey. I'm glad I bent the rules and let him enter the cave."

Recalling Zack's amazement, Abby replied, "I am too. His expression when the bats took flight was something I'll remember forever. So will he. Thank you for allowing him to be part of a memorable day."

"You're most welcome. The awe of discovery is a thrilling experience."

"Do you still feel it whenever you find a new colony?"

"When I stop, I'll have to hang up my boots. I'm sure you

get just as excited when you locate a rare bird or find proof of a species you thought extinct." Beth's smile turned conspiratorial as she whispered, "Like the marbled murrelet right here on Sparrow Island."

Startled she knew about the discovery, Abby felt her jaw drop. Fortunately, the waiter brought their salads, which gave her a minute to regain her composure. "I'm surprised you heard about the marbled murrelet."

"I work for the WDFW. I keep up to date with the significant sightings in the state. Remember, I do have a degree in ornithology."

Oh, Lord, this is it, isn't it? Please, guide me. Help me address the old wrong. Give Beth a forgiving heart. "I'd like to talk about Cornell . . . and the master's program."

"I went to the University of Washington instead," Beth said lightly. "Call it water under the Thurston Avenue Bridge."

Rather than let herself be sidetracked by memories the busy bridge on the campus held, Abby said bluntly, "I call it neglect."

"What?" Obviously confused, Beth sat back.

"Neglect. My neglect," Abby admitted. "You asked me to write a recommendation letter and I did. A very good one." She leaned forward, willing Beth to understand. "I forgot to mail it before leaving for the Amazon."

Expressionless, Beth remained silent.

"I found it in my In box when I returned to my office. I looked for you so I could apologize, but it was too late. You were gone. Now that I find you at the WDFW in such a different field, I'm concerned that my oversight had a negative impact." The admission burned, but her regret, her inattentiveness burned even hotter. "I'm so sorry. Can you forgive me?"

"Okay." Beth shrugged a shoulder. "You're forgiven."

Perplexed, Abby eyed her friend. "Just like that?"

"Just like that."

The waiter brought dinner. Despite the delicious aromas drifting up to her nose, Abby's appetite fled.

Beth cut into the flaky salmon with her fork. "I'm glad you brought up Cornell, because there's something I need to tell you. You taught me one of the most important things in life is commitment to my passion."

"Excuse me?"

Beth speared another bite of salmon with her fork. "You have a passion big enough to encompass the entire realm of ornithology. I, on the other hand, did not. Shortly after graduation, while I was waiting on pins and needles for my acceptance into the program, I had a long talk with Jerome Winthrop."

The mention of Abby's mentor at Cornell brought to mind her recurring dream. The missing person was Beth. She was the one Abby kept looking for.

Thank goodness, Beth had turned to Jerome. He was a challenging teacher, a staunch friend and a constant pillar of encouragement. "He has a way of knowing how to direct students. What did he tell you?"

"I sat in his office, practically begging him to put in a good word. He reminded me there's only one Abby Stanton, and she was in the Amazon. Then he asked me if the world's one and only Beth Werling would be happy spending her life and her passion in your shadow. Or did I want to blaze my own trail."

"Gracious."

Beth smiled enigmatically. "We're different people with different paths. If I wanted to be a follower, he would have admitted me to the program. I chose the bats instead and never regretted my decision. Your letter—mailed or not—wouldn't have changed anything. The letter that opened the doors I wanted to walk through came from Jerome."

"I had no idea," Abby marveled and picked up her fork. "He never said a word. And I never asked because I felt guilty."

Beth tried to smile, but her lips quavered. "Now we come to my confession. I need your forgiveness too."

Abby blinked. "For what?"

"For not picking up the phone and calling you. For not dropping a line to tell you of my change in plans. You were my mentor. You spent countless hours tutoring me, guiding me. The very least I owed you was an explanation."

Beth swallowed hard. "I thought about contacting you over the years. Time passed, then I didn't know what to say." She shrugged helplessly. "I followed your career just in case I thought of something."

A rueful laugh escaped Abby. "What a pair we are. I could have called or written too." Suddenly, the absurdity of their mutual guilt spilled over into laughter. "How simple things could have been for both of us if we'd just picked up the phone."

"You're absolutely right, because in the meantime, instead of going away, my guilty feelings grew."

"Mine too." Abby reached across the table and Beth took her hand. "All is forgiven between us, right?"

"Absolutely," Beth agreed eagerly. "Clean slate."

"Let's promise here and now—we stay in touch. Holidays, special events and great finds in the world of bats and birds. Okay?"

Beth grinned. "I love it. I've missed you, my friend."

BY FRIDAY AFTERNOON, Mary had misgivings. Although she'd sent Finnegan to the mailbox three times a day and listened to every incoming call, she hadn't heard a word from Gerald.

She knew he'd received her letter. She'd phoned the delivery company and gotten their confirmation. He'd signed for it personally. What did he think of her invitation to reconnect after all these years?

How could he look at the picture and not answer?

Belatedly, she wondered how many times Jacob had experienced the same anticipation and been disappointed.

Still, she wasn't ready to accept Gerald's silence as a refusal. Love was never wasted. She'd acted in a spirit of love. Surely, some part of Gerald remembered the bonds of childhood and the deep friendship he'd shared with his brother.

Heaving a heavy sigh, Mary took heart from Sam's observation that even the hardest men cherished someone. No matter how long or how removed from their physical presence, those feelings didn't die completely.

Clinging to that thought, Mary sent Finnegan out to the mailbox one more time. He brought back Zack.

"What are you doing, Mom?"

"Waiting for you. I'm in the mood for a hot fudge sundae. Can I buy one for you?"

"You mean at Willoughby Pharmacy?"

"I think we need to smooth some ruffled feathers. Turned out he was right about the guitar."

"I know and I feel bad about it. I'm just not sure how to fix it and honor Joe's request."

"It's simple." Mary tucked her purse next to her hip. "You had it right the other day. Ed doesn't need to know how we know. We don't have to mention Joe. We'll simply confirm the guitar was Neville's and you're not interested in selling it—or getting any more phone calls about it."

"That ought to work."

"I'm sure it will. Ed's one of the good guys. He'll respect your wishes."

Zack motioned toward the garage. "Good. I want to square things with him before I leave."

Mary wheeled through the door to the garage. She didn't want to think about Zack leaving again. Particularly not until he had a chance to meet his uncle.

She hoped Gerald phoned soon.

CHAPTER ❧ TWENTY-TWO

Early sunday morning, before getting ready for church, Mary peeked out her bedroom window. Blustery winds ruffled the shrubbery and dark clouds lowered the sky. Both made her groan, "Oh no, not today!"

Finnegan's ears perked and he looked at her.

"Sorry, boy. I'd hoped we'd have better weather for the family picnic." She tickled the short fur under his snout. "Well, if we're getting a lemon of a day, let's make lemonade."

Wheeling to the closet, she selected a cheery skirt and matching blouse. One way or another, her big get-together would have blooming flowers and sunshine.

Gerald still hadn't answered her invitation. Instead of leaving her uncertainties at the door of Little Flock, Mary took them inside and placed them in God's hands. Immediately, she felt more relaxed, confident things would turn out as they should.

After Rev. Hale's inspiring service on helping others, she slipped out a few minutes early. She loved her church family, but when they all tried to help her down the ramp, she became a traffic jam of one.

To her surprise and delight, the dark clouds had drifted off, leaving only a few high wisps of white and a soft breeze. Gratitude filled her as she waited for the van's hydraulic lift. Abby and Zack waved as they hurried to her car for a quick trip to The Green Grocer for ice.

The McDonalds stopped to chat on the way across the parking lot. "We're so excited," Sandy exclaimed.

Her husband Neil nodded enthusiastically. "Are there any last-minute items you need?"

"I appreciate you asking, but I think we have it covered."

Sandy stroked Mary's arm. "We're delighted you invited us. You're family in all the ways that count."

"Yep," Bobby agreed, while hugging Finnegan. "And you're lucky, too, cause Mom's bringing her Chocolate Wonder cake." The boy's eyes danced as he licked his lips. "I love going to the farm. It's full of neat stuff. Will you let Finnegan take a walk with me there?"

"Sure." Mary rolled onto the lift. "He's earned some play time." As soon as her chair locked in place, Finnegan bounded inside the van.

Bobby ran around, jumped in and secured the dog's safety harness. Patting his head, the boy promised, "I'll see you over there. We're gonna have lots of fun."

In the middle of the line of vehicles heading to her parent's home, Mary prayed for the grace and wisdom to accept whatever Gerald's decision might be. She'd done her best with the handcrafted invitation.

Recalling the letter, she smiled. The missive was much

longer than she'd originally planned, yet surprisingly easy to write. The words flowed from her heart as though Gerald was an old and trusted friend.

In truth, they should've been friends, she thought fiercely—friends who'd known each other for years. They and their families should have celebrated birthdays, weddings and graduations. And when Jacob died, she and Gerald should have cried and grieved together.

"What happened to the bond between brothers?" she asked aloud. "Why couldn't it transcend the rift?"

Finnegan snuffled and she quieted. Second-guessing wouldn't help. No one had the power to change the past. But if Gerald gave her half a chance, together they could make a very different future for the Reynolds clan.

She turned into Stanton Farm just behind her parents and Ida. Abby and Zack were two cars back. Apparently, the trip to The Green Grocer had gone smoothly.

Mary pushed a couple of buttons and all the doors on the van opened.

Her father hustled up, reached in and released Finnegan. The dog stayed in place, waiting for her signal. "Can I help you unload?" George asked.

"Sure. The bags look bulky, but they're mostly paper products. Mom, Abby and I took care of the cooking yesterday." Mary fanned her chin at the reminder of a hot kitchen full of fun. "Too bad you and Sam were busy. Abby was in high spirits. Tales of her bat adventure kept us laughing."

Giving her shoulder a gentle squeeze, George said, "I'm proud of you, Mary. You're doing a fine thing with this reunion. No man could hope for a better welcome than the one you and your mother and sister prepared."

Her father's praise warmed her heart. "You're the best, Dad. You always know the right thing to say."

"Can't miss with the truth." He went to the side door and pulled out the bags of drink cups and napkins. "No time to rest on your laurels. Company's coming." Giving her a broad wink, he headed inside.

Suddenly nervous over the possibility Gerald might actually come to the picnic, Mary fumbled her keys and they fell to the floorboard. Finnegan squeezed into the close quarters and retrieved the jangling ring with his teeth.

Mary took them, then cradled his head in her hands. "What would I do without you?"

The dog licked his lips, his mouth curving into a familiar smile. "Dad's right," she whispered. "We've done all we can. Now, it's up to Gerald. Let's join the party."

Under Finnegan's watchful gaze, Mary exited the van. Her father returned for the rest of her cargo and said, "You're supposed to go around back and oversee there."

With Finnegan's help, Mary rolled across the grass toward the picnic tables set up beneath the old maple tree. Nearby, flames danced in the grill. Clad in one of George's utilitarian aprons, Sam raised a pair of tongs in greeting.

"I saw you dashing to your truck when services ended," she told him. "I figured you were going to start the coals. You must be hungry."

"Yep. Your mother's had me on the go since the crack of dawn. It's worth it, though." He gave the tongs a ceremonious click. "Ellen says we're having chicken, barbeque brisket and those fat stadium dogs I like."

He shot a knowing glance over her left shoulder and added, "Besides, I had to establish my position before the law arrived."

"The law . . ." Mary pivoted her chair and her heart leapt at the sight of Henry Cobb. Six feet tall, with a fringe of white hair around his balding pate, the deputy sheriff strode toward her. Even in "civvies"—a maroon jersey shirt and pressed jeans—he cut an imposing figure.

"Henry." Looking up into his warm brown eyes, she realized just how much she'd missed his familiar presence this past week.

"Hello, Mary," he said in a deep, velvety voice.

"It's so good to see you." Despite her churning emotions, she relished his look of care and concern. "I'm glad you're here."

His gaze locked with hers, he took her hand, raised it to his lips and pressed a kiss on the back of her fingers. "I missed you."

"Ahem."

"Sam." Henry's eyebrow arched though his gaze never left Mary's face. "Is it important? I'm kinda busy here."

"I just wanted to welcome you home from Whidbey Island." Sam airily waved the tongs. "And make sure you know today's my day to grill."

"Good," Henry said with an unmistakable ring of authority and warning. "The honor's all yours."

"Yoo-hoo, Henry," Ellen called from the back deck of the farmhouse. "Will you come here, please?"

Watching his frustration war with amusement, Mary struggled to contain her laughter. She loved his ability to keep the big picture in focus even when it interfered with his immediate plans.

Lips stretched into a grimacing smile over his clenched teeth, he teased, "How's this? Do I look okay?"

"You'll probably scare my mother to pieces."

"I'm that charming, eh?"

"Henry, dear?" Ellen called again. "Could you give Zack a hand?"

"Coming!" Henry kissed Mary's fingers again. "Don't go far," he ordered.

"Count on it," she answered.

After the deputy left on the first of what was sure to be many errands, Sam said, "So. What do you hear from Gerald?"

Her heart still pounding and fingers tingling, she said lightly, "Nothing yet. I'm hoping he'll just show up."

"Me too—for his sake. Regret is a harsh thing to live with."

"Yes, it is." She traced a circle on her chair's armrest. Although Sam's statement was a rare reference to the waste of his misspent youth, Mary knew regret came in many forms and often from unexpected sources. "This time, Sam, any regrets there might be won't belong to us."

"Right." He waved off a circling fly. "Glad you know that."

Appreciating his concern, she nodded and let the matter rest. "I'd better go help Ida."

By the time Mary made it across the yard to the drinks table, Henry and Zack were positioning a second, large cooler brimming with ice. She picked up a tube of brightly colored cups and watched the men return to the deck for extra lawn chairs.

"Did Gerald call?" Ida positioned large pitchers of lemonade and iced tea on the gaily-flowered tablecloth.

With a fresh insight into precisely why Jacob hadn't told anyone he'd invited his estranged brother to their wedding, Mary said, "No, not yet."

She handed the plastic cups to Ida and got busy pushing cans of juice and soda into the ice.

"He should have given you the courtesy of an RSVP," Ida said evenly. "You don't throw love away. It's precious."

Before Mary could respond, her father spoke over her head. "Not to worry, Ida. Love is never wasted. Why there's so much around here right now, the angels are jumping for joy. They know we're going to eat, laugh, tell stories and have a good time. Then we're going to eat some more and start again. If Gerald doesn't come, he'll be the only one missing out."

From the front of the house came the distinctive sound of a car door closing. Mary took a deep breath against the sudden thudding in her chest and waited.

MARY TRIED TO HIDE her disappointment when she saw that the car held Joe and Margaret along with Doug and Janet Heinz. After welcoming the family-friends and telling the women where to take their dishes, Abby retrieved a picnic blanket from her car.

Zack met her in the crowded parking area and explained, "Mom told me to invite the Blackstocks. Naturally, I invited Doug and Janet too."

"Good thinking. They're part of our extended family."

"Hey, I'm a sensitive guy. Nobody likes to be left out. I have a quick errand to run. May I borrow your car?"

"Sure. You still have the keys, right?"

"I do." Zack kissed her cheek and dashed toward the driver's door. "Thanks."

"Watch out for Hugo!" she called and immediately saw it wasn't necessary. The two men expertly maneuvered their vehicles in the limited space. In a matter of seconds, Zack was on the road and Hugo exited his car.

He beckoned her, then opened his trunk. "We can't have a

picnic without chips." Bags stuffed with half a dozen varieties stood in a neat row.

Joe appeared at Abby's elbow and looked wide-eyed at the array in the trunk. "You must've cleaned out The Green Grocer."

Hugo shrugged. "I brought salsa for the tortilla chips."

"Made in New York City?" Joe teased.

"Texas," Hugo countered, lifting his chin in mock effrontery.

"Excellent—as a good friend of mine says." Joe turned serious. "I hoped I'd catch you two together. I've been thinking a lot about the whole adventure with the bats. Mark's sketchbook opened doors, not the least of which was the one nailed shut inside my stubborn head."

"We all tend to get entrenched in our habits," said Hugo.

Thinking of Beth and herself, Abby simply gave a smile of encouragement. Habits were often an automatic response to the need for self-protection and seldom assessed for their actual worthiness. Some brought isolation and misunderstandings. She'd learned her lesson and didn't want to repeat it. "Sometimes it's best to try new approaches."

"I did and came to a new way of thinking." Joe's gaze traveled from her to Hugo and back. "I'm thinking Mark's sketchbook is like his guitar. Nobody hears the sweet sound of those strings if the guitar's hanging on a wall or hiding in a case. That's why I wanted Zack to have it."

Heaving a deep sigh, Joe looked down and studied his feet.

Sensing he wasn't finished, Abby glanced at Hugo. His bushy eyebrows rose questioningly and they both remained silent.

When Joe lifted his head, his gaze was steady. "I'm donating Mark's sketchbook to The Nature Museum. His sketches need to be seen. You can put them in your new bat exhibit or in one of the others with the birds."

"That's extremely generous, Joe." Abby touched his arm. "Are you sure?"

Nodding decisively, he said, "Since they're naming the bat cave after Mark, I figured people ought to know why. As Neville Sanborne, he had his glory moments on a hundred stages. But the Mark I knew, the brother I loved was so much more. Maybe sharing his nature sketches will shine a little light on that side of him."

"It will." Hugo clasped Joe's hand. "We'll take excellent care of his work and display it proudly."

"I know you will. You and Abby share his love for nature. This way, if I want to see his pictures I'll come over to the museum and maybe learn a thing or two while I'm there."

Eyes glistening, Hugo said, "Let me tell you about a teenager named Rebecca and what the bat adventure means to her. I have no doubt Mark's sketches will be a wonderful, positive influence on her young mind."

Abby backed away quietly, giving the two men privacy for the deeper bond they were forging. *Thank You, Lord, for love and friendships. Thank You for this day. The only thing missing is Gerald, and we're counting on You to send him to us.*

CHAPTER ❦ TWENTY-THREE

Looking for ways to be helpful, Abby surveyed the gathering in her parents' yard. In a patch of shade near the barn, Bobby, Ida and Finnegan played an energetic game of Frisbee under the watchful eyes of Neil and Sandy.

At a picnic table, George and Joe argued the finer points of crabbing and Abby chortled softly. She didn't think Joe knew her mom came from a family of crab-men and loved the delicacies. Naturally, her dad had made himself somewhat of an expert to please his bride.

Doug Heinz and Henry lounged on two lawn chairs indulging in an easy conversation too far away to be heard, but punctuated with good-natured laughter.

Janet in lavender and Margaret in royal blue with a flamboyant pair of granny glasses dangling from the chain around her neck helped Ellen fuss over the serving table. They organized the specialty dishes by food category, salads together, then vegetables on down to the desserts.

Hugo kept Sam company at the grill. Although she couldn't make out their conversation either, Abby suspected they were discussing the wildlife winnowing away the edges of the alfalfa fields Sam and her father planted every year.

Satisfied all was well, she went down to the drinks table for a soda. As far as their guests were concerned, Mary's picnic was a smashing success. *Mary! Where is she?*

Abby immediately hurried around to the front of the house and found her sister looking forlornly down the road. "Are you all right?"

"I guess so." Mary shrugged. "I can't find Zack. Do you know where he went?"

"He took my car to run an errand. I'm sorry I didn't think to ask what it was or where he was going. I assumed we'd forgotten something and he went home to get it. I'm sure he'll be back any minute."

Seeing her sister overly concerned about things that otherwise wouldn't have fazed her bothered Abby. However, she knew Mary's anxiety had been building since she overnighted the invitation to Gerald. Abby wasn't sure which disturbed her sister the most: the possibility of finally meeting Jacob's estranged brother or the prospect of never meeting him.

"I guess a small delay can't be helped," Mary said, clearly relieved to postpone the official start of the picnic. "We'll have to wait for Zack to return before sounding the dinner bell."

Wearing a questioning look and carrying a couple of glasses full of icy lemonade, Henry approached. "So this is where you disappeared to. I was waiting for you out back."

Abby shot him a meaningful look and said, "You're just in time. We're ready to rejoin the party."

"Good!" He offered the lemonade to both of them. "I'm here to organize an expedition."

Mary accepted the icy drink and murmured, "Thank you."

"An expedition?" Abby hoped he'd come with a diversion. "Don't tell me we're out of something important."

Mary straightened. "There's a problem?"

"Yes," said Henry. "Your mother has misplaced the mustard again."

"Oh." She turned her gaze back to the road.

Abby's hopes sank. Her sister wasn't easily fooled. They not only needed a diversion, it had to be something essential.

"I'm not kidding," Henry pressed. "She forgot where she put the mustard and the condiments. Everything from the bland stuff to the extra spicy was in a basket she misplaced. She asked me to get Mary and help her find it."

"Goodness," Mary said. "Let me drink some of this lemonade so I don't spill it on the way."

While she quaffed a healthy gulp, Henry took the cue and moved behind her wheelchair. "Abby, why don't you check with Sam? Ask him to slow down the grill if he can, while Mary and I give your mom a hand."

God bless you, Henry Cobb. And Mom, too. Relieved, Abby headed for the back and the big grill. She could trust Henry to keep Mary too occupied to dwell on their absent guest.

"Your sister looks as nervous as a cat in a room full of rocking chairs." Using his badge of office—the long tongs—Sam moved the brisket away from the hottest coals. He'd already cranked the grill surface as high as it would go.

"And you're buying time by slow-cooking our feast. You're a prince, Sam."

"If Gerald shows up, I am. If he doesn't, I'm just a pokey old chef keeping hungry people from eating the meal we promised."

Abby gave Sam's arm an affectionate squeeze. "The serving table is practically groaning under the weight of all the goodies. I seriously doubt anyone in this crowd will wither away from malnutrition before you pronounce the meat done."

"Probably not. But I'm working up quite an appetite smelling the barbeque sauce sizzle." He dipped a brush into a bowl of sauce and basted the brisket.

Abby leaned forward and breathed in the heady aroma of Sam's special sauce. In response, her stomach gave an insistent rumble and she discreetly stepped back. "You're about to have more company." She tilted her head toward her father, Doug and Joe strolling purposefully toward the grill.

Sam glanced their way. "Don't worry, I can handle them."

Laughing, she left the men to kibitz over Sam's grilling techniques. On the way to join Ida and Sandy, a flash of color caught Abby's attention and she detoured around to the side of the house. As she suspected, Zack had returned.

And . . . he'd brought Scott Kenai.

At the edge of the parking area, they extracted their guitar cases from the backseat of her car. A wave of delight swept over her. Her nephew had not only thought to invite Scott, he'd somehow coaxed the young man to accept.

Music was exactly what they needed. These two talented men were sure to hold Mary's attention and calm her nerves. As for Scott, perhaps if he mingled more he'd become less self-conscious of his appearance and more self-confident in the wonderful person he was.

"The entertainment has arrived," Zack bragged.

"Fantastic! Scott, I'm so glad you came. Can I give you a hand with anything?"

"We have it, Dr. Stanton. It's good to see you this afternoon. Thank you and your family for inviting me."

She would have given him a welcoming hug, but his reserve and the bulky guitar case stood in her way. Rather than cause him any discomfort, she gave him her warmest smile. The shy one he returned was ample reward.

Falling into step with them, she said, "I know the perfect place for you to set up."

"Under the maple and on the far side of the picnic tables," Zack stated, waggling his eyebrows. "We'll be in the shade next to the beverages."

"Oh, of course! I should've known you'd have the right spot picked out. I guess I'll never make it as a roadie."

"Nope. Better keep your day job, Aunt Abby."

Scott chuckled as they rounded the corner of the house. The happy sound faded when he saw all the people looking their way.

"No need for introductions," Abby said casually. "You know everyone here."

Ellen left Janet and Mary rolling napkins around silverware and made a beeline toward them. "Oh, Scott! I'm so glad you could join us." She spread her arms, clearly insisting on a hug.

Sheepishly he put down the guitar case and stepped into her embrace. At the warm welcome, he began to relax and as he did, Zack nudged Abby. "Keep him occupied for a minute. I'll be right back."

Mystified but willing to go along, she nodded. While her mother monopolized Scott, Abby recruited Henry and Doug to retrieve a couple of tall stools for the musicians. Word of a performance spread quickly. Eager picnickers carried chairs from various parts of the yard and arranged them near the improvised stage. Ida, Sandy and Bobby made themselves comfortable on a blanket spread on the grass in the shade.

Scott opened his guitar case. To everyone's surprise, Zack picked up his friend's instrument. "I'd like to try yours. Mind playing the other one?" Zack gestured to the tooled leather case holding the famous guitar.

"Uh, sure!" Wearing a look of pure pleasure, Scott carefully took out the Neville Sanborne guitar, then sat on the stool Doug had brought out for him. "This is really my lucky day."

Abby glanced over and met her sister's beaming gaze. It struck her how much generosity and consideration Mary and Jacob had instilled into their children. From her own experience with countless young people, Abby knew most of their values and beliefs were formed in their homes.

"Welcome to Farmfest," Zack announced, "an impromptu musical performance by a couple of local boys willing to sing for their supper. Right, Scott?"

Scott played a riff of intricate chords, then answered, "This'll be the first Farmfest. It's, uh, also my first public concert." He glanced over at Zack. "Hopefully, it won't be my last."

"Not a chance," Joe shouted, starting a round of applause.

Obviously pleased, Zack waited for the clapping to ebb. "Anytime I'm here and these folks want to cook for us, I'd be proud to sing and play with you."

"Me too. Ah, how about we dedicate our first number to Neville Sanborne. I kinda feel it was because of him—his guitar here—I got to know Zack."

At the opening bars of "Sparrow Island Night Song," Abby

closed her eyes and let the notes flow through her. Zack sang harmony during the chorus to Scott's melody. The rising and falling of their blended voices sent gooseflesh along her arms and made her own heart sing.

As she glanced around, she discovered she wasn't the only one affected by the beautiful sounds.

The hush in the audience was complete. Even the birds who'd been flitting noisily through the big maple now sat quietly on the branches. A pair of squirrels looked as awed as the rest of the audience.

After a long string of requests that kept the picnickers mesmerized, Sam rang the tongs against the side of the grill. "Dinner is ready!"

A chorus of yeas and nays greeted his call. Everyone wanted to eat, but no one wanted the music to stop. "The concert will resume after dessert," Zack announced. "We need to give this fine picnic the appreciation it deserves."

The good-natured crowd rearranged their chairs and got in line. Abby thought to help with the utensils and napkins and quickly discovered there was no need. Content, she hung back and waited for the musicians. Joe came up and joined her. Wondering why he wasn't in the food line, she looked up to ask, then realized he was watching Zack and Scott.

"Thanks for letting me play this," Scott said as he ducked out of the guitar's shoulder strap. Apparently not quite ready to part with the instrument, he caressed its sweeping curves. "It has great acoustics."

"It's yours," Zack said softly.

Scott gave the guitar one more loving touch, then placed it in the case and closed it.

Abby swallowed thickly. Beside her, Joe scarcely breathed.

"Did you hear me, Scott?" Zack secured the other guitar.

"I . . . I think my ears are playing tricks on me," Scott admitted, then gave a self-deprecating laugh. "It sounded like —aw shucks, it's so silly I can't even say it."

Zack picked up the tooled leather case and pressed it to Scott's chest. "You heard right. It's yours. The man with the best claim to it told me it's a musician's guitar. He said it needs to be played by someone who respects it and loves the sound."

Arms hanging stiffly at his sides, Scott shook his head. "That's you, Zack. You're a professional musician. C'mon, man, you're on tour."

"True, but the keyboard is my first love. On guitar, you are as fine a musician as I've ever come across. You make this one sing in a way I never will." Zack wiggled the case against Scott's chest. "Take it and play it. Carry on Neville Sanborne's legacy in the Islands."

Scott's mouth worked for a moment, but no sound came out.

Abby felt Joe squeeze her shoulder. Immediately she had a flash of understanding. Zack had set the whole thing up with his grandmother before he left to get Scott. When they returned, Ellen kept the younger man occupied while her grandson asked Joe for his blessing. Apparently, Joe gave it wholeheartedly.

Reaching up, Abby covered his hand with hers.

"C'mon guy. Your guitar's getting heavy," Zack warned.

Scott's arms rose as if of their own volition and closed around the case. "Th-thanks. I, uh, don't—Gee, thanks." Hugging the gift, he seemed to glow from within. "Thanks a hundred-million thanks. I feel like I'm dreaming."

"Great. Just so you feel like playing some more after we eat." Zack slung his arm around Scott's shoulders. "Now, there's someone you need to talk to right over here."

Reluctantly, as though it might vanish if he let go, Scott put the guitar down beside his stool. "Sure."

He'd talk to the whole town, if need be, Abby thought. And right now, he was dazed enough to do it successfully.

Joe stepped forward and said to Scott, "Let's you and I get something to eat and find a spot where we can talk. I'd like to tell you about the man who wrote his name in silver paint on the back of your guitar."

Knuckling the happiness spilling out of the corners of her eyes, Abby stayed with Zack while Joe and Scott meandered toward the dwindling food line. Despite the delicious aromas and the generous portions Sam dished out, she didn't think she could eat. She was simply too full of joy at what she'd just witnessed.

"You're the best," she told her nephew with a sniff. "You gave the most generous, thoughtful gift I've seen one person give another in I don't know how long. It'll make such a difference in Scott's life."

"It was easy." A note of wonder tinged Zack's voice, "Once I figured out why I bought the guitar." He tilted his head in Scott's direction. "All along, it was for him. And you know what the really odd thing is?"

Throat clogged with emotion, Abby raised her eyebrows.

"I feel like I'm the one who got the gift."

CHAPTER 🌹 TWENTY-FOUR

G ERALD ISN'T COMING."
Saying the words aloud, particularly to Henry, cemented Mary's realization.

"I knew you wanted him to. I didn't realize you *expected* him." Henry's gentle observation served as a reminder of his weeklong absence. During the whirlwind of the picnic, she'd managed to tell him of the manuscript and some of the mystery surrounding it, but not in any detail.

There'd been too many people around for her to explain her deeper feelings. Now, the fact her questions wouldn't be answered filled her with keen disappointment. She wanted to go forward without dragging the anchor of an unresolved past.

"You're right. I did expect him." She sighed at her foolishness. "I convinced myself he'd come. In fact, I'm still praying he will."

Time was running out. They'd just said good-bye for the day to the rest of their company, but she couldn't give up yet. "It's a long trip from Yakima," she mused. "He may have run into construction delays."

Voicing the obvious did little to assuage the resentment creeping up on her the way Blossom stalked a spider.

Abby and Zack, then Ellen and George drifted toward the house and backyard, giving Mary a little private time with Henry.

He sat on the edge of the front porch and faced her. "After all these years, it would take a great deal of courage to accept your invitation. Righteousness, pride and possibly forgiveness may be involved. Those three are hard pills for anyone to swallow."

He tilted his head and looked at the sky. "From the little you've told me, you've made some excellent assumptions about what happened. Unfortunately, even the best assumptions are only guesses."

"What are you trying to tell me?"

"If I've learned anything from police work, Mary, it's that things are seldom what they seem. For us, assumptions are dangerous. The minute we get complacent and start trusting them, we get trouble. It's just not good to make up your mind until you have all the facts."

"And if I don't get them?"

"Do what we do. Leave the case open. If Gerald doesn't come today, he might show up tomorrow. It could be he needs more time to consider your letter. Or he doesn't want to meet a crowd. Not everyone is comfortable in a group, especially when they're the only stranger."

"I truly have missed you, Henry. You're so levelheaded and cut right to the heart of things."

He shifted and grew somber. "Then let me cut a little deeper. You're my first concern—not Jacob or his brother. Every cop knows objectivity is the first casualty in any emotionally charged situation. I can interview five eyewitnesses right after a crime and none of them will agree on what happened."

It had never occurred to her to think of the situation in those terms. "But I know Jacob. And I've read the manuscript."

"It's only part of the picture. Those events took place a long time ago—as did the rift. It isn't reasonable to expect Gerald to view the past in the same light Jacob did."

"You're worried I'll be very disappointed."

"Yes, I am. You may hear things you won't like about Jacob."

"That's just it, Henry. On the one hand, I can't believe Jacob did something so awful he deserved his family's enmity. On the other, I have to consider it. The ostracism is so complete and so long-standing, they must have felt fully justified. Either way, I have to know. Leaving the manuscript was Jacob's way of asking me to finish what he couldn't."

Henry leaned forward, lifted the hair off the back of her neck and let the silver strands slip through his fingers. "I admire your courage. No matter how uncomfortable the truth is, it's the first step to resolution. I'm in your corner."

She looked up and studied him. Silent strength radiated from him. As far as she knew he'd answered every personal question she'd ever asked truthfully.

"What's going through your mind?" he asked.

"Do you have any secrets you haven't told me?"

"It's entirely possible, although I can't remember any. If I think of some, I'll let you know. Fair enough?"

Nodding, she answered, "Yes."

"What about you?"

"I'm not sure I know how to keep a secret about myself.

If it's someone else's, I most definitely can and have done so often. But as for my own, sooner or later I wind up sharing it." Thoughts of her most trusted confidante outside her immediate family brought a faint smile. "If I tell Janet . . ."

Henry chuckled. "You may as well post a notice in *The Birdcall*. However, Janet can surprise you. I've known her to keep secrets, even under pressure."

Remembering a few such instances in the past, Mary agreed. "Telling someone I trust shares the burden. Talking out problems or situations I'd rather not broadcast doesn't always solve them, but I usually see my troubles in a different light."

"Speaking of a new perspective on trouble . . ." Henry moved to the rear of Mary's chair. "I was nine when I found out humiliation isn't fatal. I just wished it was."

"What happened?" she asked, appreciating his thoughtfulness for taking the conversation into a new, lighter arena.

He pushed her chair down the path leading to the barn. When partway there, he angled them toward the backyard. "I was in the fourth grade. I'd been excused to go to the bathroom. Before returning to class, I did a few karate chops and kicks. I was better at it than I thought because I kicked out a window."

Mary imagined the scene. *Typical little boy. Like Zack was.*

"Explaining it to my father in front of the principal, a couple of teachers and the custodian who had to fix the window was humiliating enough. Then the school nurse insisted on examining my leg in front of everyone. She was sure I'd cut myself with the foolhardy stunt. At that minute, I thought I'd die. No. I actually hoped I would—right before I had to drop my pants."

"I'm so glad you survived." Feeling buoyed and hearing the

familiar sound of an approaching car, Mary turned to see who was pulling into the yard. "Janet probably forgot a dish," she guessed. "Or Bobby left a toy behind."

Henry pivoted her chair, affording them a better look. "I don't recognize the car," he said. "Do you?"

"No." Nor did she know the man behind the wheel. Her hopes soared along with a surge of nervousness. "I think it may be Gerald," she whispered.

"Let's go find out." Henry took them back the way they'd come.

The man getting out of the late model sedan and removing his sunglasses appeared uncomfortable and apprehensive. Dressed for traveling, he wore a light blue golf shirt with a designer logo on the pocket, casual trousers and brown leather loafers. He stood nearly as tall as Henry's six feet and gazed at the farmhouse with the same intensity as his rigid stance.

"Gerald Reynolds?" Mary asked in a tone as friendly as she could manage.

He turned toward her. Traces of the boy in the photo strip lingered in the shape of his eyes and mouth. The stylish cut of his brown hair revealed sprigs of gray at his temples. Hours in the sun—on the golf course, she presumed from his attire— had tanned his arms. Hazel eyes regarded her from a tense, but even-featured face with an air of authority.

"Are you Mary?"

"Yes, I am. This is my friend, Henry Cobb."

The two shook hands briskly, their businesslike manner showing they performed the formality often.

Gerald leaned against the car and folded his arms across his chest. "After all this time, I didn't want to come."

"I'm glad you did. It's high time we met." Mary sensed his

anxiety and suspected he was as uncertain about this meeting as she was, maybe even more so.

"Your letter wouldn't let me stay away." He looked down for a moment. "Let me correct myself. The truth is, it was the picture."

"I've heard one picture's worth a thousand words," Mary said lightly though her voice quavered. The touch of Henry's hand on her shoulder strengthened her.

"Now I'm here and it's . . . awkward." Gerald looked toward the front porch. "I assume this is your parents' home."

"They haven't bitten anyone in years," she teased with a trembling smile. "You must be hungry. Won't you come into the backyard with us? There's enough food from the barbeque to feed a horseshoe contestant."

Gerald paled under his tan. "Horseshoes," he repeated softly.

"Blue ribbon winners." Mary met his gaze and saw guarded curiosity.

"We were kids. He told you about the contest?"

"I learned about it only recently." Empathizing with Gerald's struggle, she tried to put him at ease with a small smile. "Come. I have a story to tell you." *Then maybe you'll tell me one.*

During the conversation, Finnegan had quietly moved to her side. Although "off duty," his protective instincts had him standing in readiness in front of the stranger.

"Maybe you should tell Finnegan that Gerald is a friend," Henry suggested. "At the moment, he's not sure."

Mary gave the signal and explained to Gerald, "Finnegan is my service dog, a gift from Nancy and Zack, your niece and nephew. He's my constant companion." As the dog trotted off to the backyard, Gerald abandoned his post by his car.

Henry pushed the wheelchair around to the concrete walkway.

"I have a golden retriever," Gerald said. "For years he jogged with me every morning. These days, I walk with him in the evening."

Mary asked the dog's name and learned it was Reg—an affectionate shortening of Reginald.

Sharing their common interest in dogs, they made their way around the house. Under the maple, Zack sat on his high stool strumming Scott's old guitar. His grandparents, Abby and Sam rested on the lawn chairs, watching him and enjoying each other's company. Closer to the house, a fine curl of smoke rose from the barbeque.

Gerald's steps slowed, then stopped as his gaze fixed on Zack.

"He looks a lot like his father," she said softly.

"The hat. I recognize it as one of ours."

"It was Jacob's. He always wore that style of fedora. When one wore out, he ordered a new one."

Gerald's Adam's apple moved in his throat as though he was trying to swallow something that wouldn't go down.

Zack slipped off the stool, set the guitar aside and approached, his expression unreadable.

"Gerald," Mary said watching her son, "this is your nephew. Zack, your Uncle Gerald."

"How do you do, sir?" Zack offered his hand and Gerald shook it slowly and carefully. From his expression, Mary knew this was very different from the perfunctory formality earlier with Henry.

"I'm glad to meet you, Zack. You . . . resemble your father." Undisguised amazement softened Gerald's features.

"Thanks. Fortunately, my sister favors our mother." Zack gestured to the picnic table with covered food dishes and several coolers on the benches. "How about something to eat? We had a feast and there's a lot left. If you're thirsty, Grandma makes a mean glass of lemonade."

Mary caught Abby's raised eyebrows and gave a slight nod. Zack seemed to have made it his mission to put his uncle at ease and make him feel welcome. Sam went to the grill and waved the tongs invitingly over the last batch of barbeque.

After piling a plate with food for Gerald, they joined the rest of the Stanton family beneath the big maple. Zack performed the introductions with whimsy and a humorous anecdote to describe their occupations.

His friendly manner had the desired effect. Mary saw some of Gerald's tension ease. In a lawn chair, surrounded by his brother's relatives, he smiled for the first time.

"In your letter"—Gerald looked at Mary—"and then again a little while ago, you said you had a story to tell me."

"I do." With a smile at Henry, she launched into the mystery of the manuscript in the storage box and the discovery of the subsequent links leading to the Reynolds in Yakima.

Eating slowly, Gerald hung on every word and asked few questions.

When the sun faded and the night chill rose, Zack retrieved sweaters and jackets from the house and they moved to the deck.

"Jacob wrote about us and put it in a box?" Gerald sounded incredulous. "And never told you about his family?"

"Correct," Mary confirmed. "He did more than that though. Throughout the years he made things. I now know they were meant for you. He wanted to show you he never forgot how much you meant to him. He never stopped loving you, Gerald."

She glimpsed the pain in his eyes when he spoke. "Go on. Tell me the rest."

"I understand he told you about our marriage."

The light streaming through the windows and onto the deck fell across Gerald's raised eyebrows. "He did."

"Man," Zack started, his voice filling with emotion, "didn't you want to meet his family?"

Gerald tipped his head and met Zack's gaze for a long moment. "I'm sorry to say, at the time, no."

"Will you tell us why?" Mary implored. "Help me understand what happened. I need to know."

"Jacob should have told you," Gerald said uneasily. "I guess I know why he didn't."

Sam shifted in his chair. "I know he planned to. The kids were coming home for Christmas and he was going to tell them then, as a family."

"Our Jacob was a loving, thoughtful man," Mary explained, aware Gerald might not regard him in the same light. "A few weeks before that Christmas, he was diagnosed with pancreatic cancer."

Gerald hung his head as though knowing the ultimate prognosis. "I don't blame him for keeping silent. There was no benefit in telling you about us then."

He took a heavy breath and exhaled slowly. "It's hard to know where to start. Jacob and I . . . we were so close growing up. Like two peas in a pod. The picture you sent reminded me of the good times.

"Like most kids, we wanted to go off and have fun but Father was stern. He didn't see value in goofing off. Only work counted in his book. While other boys played baseball or football, we worked in the store or had jobs picking apples, pulling weeds or delivering papers. He'd take our earnings, give us a few dollars and put the rest in the bank."

Mary's stomach churned. How Jacob must have chafed under that yoke of control. Yet he'd made no mention of his father's financial practices in the manuscript.

"Don't get me wrong," Gerald continued. "Our folks loved us. You have to understand, they were children of the Great Depression and in their early forties when Jacob and I were born. They viewed life much differently than we did. For them, tomorrow was always a risk. For us, because we grew up in the green lands of plenty, it held promise.

"Father wanted to expand the store, but didn't trust anyone outside the family to look out for his interests. When my brother went off to college, Father told him to get a business degree so he could come back and take over the expansion.

"I knew Jacob had bigger dreams, but I assumed—like Father—he would do as he'd been told. We always did. Even when we hated it.

"A couple of years after Jacob started at the University of Washington, I was accepted at the Air Force Academy and went off to Colorado Springs." A snuffled laugh escaped Gerald. "I'd planned to become an astronaut. For a while anyway. An eye injury sidelined me. A split second, and all my dreams of going into space were over. I was angry. Depressed. Wallowing in self-pity."

Gooseflesh that had nothing to do with the cooling night temperatures rippled across Mary's arms.

"At about the same time, Father opened a letter addressed to Jacob. He'd been accepted into some writing fellowship program at UW. Father blew a gasket, ranting and raving, but he had no leverage. Jacob paid his own college expenses."

Gerald took a long drink of lemonade. "Mother called me in Colorado. She told me Jacob and Dad had had a big fight and said ugly things." He gazed at Zack. "Things neither of them should have said. Once the words were out, there was no way to take them back. The old bull and the young buck locked horns and that was it for Father. He disowned Jacob.

"I was miles away and lost in my own valley of disappointment. I went along with Father." Gerald hung his head. "I envied Jacob. He was pursuing his dreams while mine had been dashed."

Sadness settling over her, Mary said, "I'm so sorry—for you and for us. Didn't your father ever consider Jacob's gift? Jacob was a writer. He'd have withered tending a store."

"Father didn't see much once he'd made up his mind. But I knew Jacob had to write."

"Tell us the rest of it," Mary coaxed. "Why did you keep your distance?"

"About four years after Jacob left, I was fulfilling my obligation to the Air Force. By then, I'd grown up some and missed my brother. I didn't know how to reconnect with him. For about a year after the big fight, he wrote and called. I didn't respond. Eventually I came to my senses and decided to go see him. The Air Force had other plans for me and I ended up overseas.

"Then Mother had a stroke. She knew her time was short and wanted to see her sons. I got emergency leave. Father contacted Jacob. I expected to see him at Mother's side when I got home. I'd hoped out of the tragedy of her stroke, Jacob and I might salvage a relationship. But he never showed. Worse for me, Mother died a few hours before I arrived."

"You mean . . ." It was hard for Mary to fathom. "Jacob refused to go see his dying mother?"

"So I was told. That single act was the *coup de grace* for me. We buried Mother and I buried my brother the same day. What was between him and Father was one thing, but Mother was a different matter."

Aghast, Mary put her fingers to her lips. "I can't imagine the Jacob I know not rushing to her side."

"Wait, Mary. There's more. I took over the business when I got out of the Air Force. The first thing I did was open a second store and move to Spokane. At the time there were too many painful memories for me in Yakima."

"I certainly see why," Mary murmured, her head spinning and her stomach roiling at what she heard. Suddenly she remembered Henry's advice. *Don't assume anything. Get all the facts first.*

"Father outlived Jacob. He died a few years back," Gerald said flatly. "A week before he passed, he wanted to unburden himself. He confessed he'd never contacted Jacob when Mother was dying. He knew what he did was wrong and it haunted him. At the time, Father thought he was punishing Jacob, but in reality he punished Mother and himself."

Abby gasped.

A small cry escaped Ellen.

George groaned and shook his head. "That's the trouble with lies. They take on a life of their own. How sad this one touched so many people."

Zack stood abruptly, anger hardening his features. "He punished Dad and you too. And all of us. What a waste."

Teary-eyed at the injustice, Mary took the handkerchief Henry offered. Although her son's assessment was right on the mark, her broken heart mourned for the entire Reynolds family and all that had been lost. "Oh Gerald. How awful for you."

"It was. After Father died, I hired an attorney to contact Jacob through his publisher."

"It was too late." Zack settled on the edge of his chair. "Dad was already gone."

"So I learned. How I wish I could roll back the calendar and explain to Jacob what I'm telling you now. In a way, I'm glad he was spared the extent of Father's duplicity."

In the ensuing silence, Mary realized the importance of the task Jacob had left her.

People often assumed time would blunt the sharp edges of a broken relationship and it could be repaired somewhere down the road. Few figured the unexpected twists and turns of life would end the road before they were ready.

Jacob hadn't made that mistake. He'd forgiven his family and extended that forgiveness through the scrimshaw, the paperweight, the horseshoe and the manuscript. And he'd left them in her care, trusting her to finish the journey for him.

Like a cracked vessel unable to contain the misery any longer, words continued to spill from Gerald. "The publisher also told the attorney someone had sent a copy of Mother's obituary. It was a long time ago and all they remembered was that it came with a brief note saying Jacob ought to know." He looked directly at Zack. "I have no idea who sent it. It wasn't from Father. Or me."

"Thank you, Gerald." Mary reached for him. "I know this has been difficult."

He slid off his chair and knelt by hers. Tentative at first, then sure and strong, he embraced her. She held onto him tightly. "We both loved him."

Gerald shuddered in her arms. When he regained control, he said, "Difficult to tell, yes. But it's a cleansing I needed." He released her and returned to his seat. "I hope what I've told you is more liberating than it is a burden."

"Rest assured, I needed to know the whole story. Now I understand why Jacob didn't talk about his family, why he found the subject so difficult and why he left the manuscript. He had a good life, Gerald. People he loved and who loved him."

"Still do," George added. "He knew the importance of loving forgiveness."

Ellen reached out and touched Gerald's arms. "What about you? Have you had a good life?"

"I'm glad Jacob had all of you. Ever since Father revealed his lie, I've lived with a horrible guilt. Not just because of him, but because of my role too. Most of all, I was afraid my boyhood idol may have become an embittered man because of us."

"'Do not let your hearts be troubled,'" Mary quoted from John 14:1. "My husband, your brother, put his trust in the Almighty and knew the power of love. Bitterness wasn't in his vocabulary."

Obviously relieved, Gerald sighed. "We both lost so much. He was my champion, my best friend. He had a way of taking the most onerous chore and making it fun. Not a day goes by when I don't think of him. He had a generous soul and so many ideas and talents . . ."

Gerald cleared his throat, took a long draught of lemonade and said, "I'm curious. Did Jacob ever learn how to balance his life?"

"Oh yeah, he did," Zack said with unabashed awe. "Every day in every way."

"Good," Gerald breathed. "Good."

Mary saw Abby duck into the house. When she returned, Mary said, "I have something for you."

"What more could you give me, Mary? Even though he's not here, it feels like I have my brother back. Like I've been forgiven." He laid his palm on his chest. "It means more than I can say to see what an excellent wife he chose. And to meet his son."

"Thank you." She took the box Abby had brought. "This is a copy of Jacob's manuscript. He wrote it for you." Mary placed the box in Gerald's trembling hands. "It's unfinished. He didn't know the ending. Now that you're here and part of *our* family, we can write the ending he'd hoped for."

Gerald looked up from the box cradled against his chest. "God bless you, Mary."

CHAPTER ✿ TWENTY-FIVE

O N MONDAY, ABBY'S WORKDAY went from good, to better, to amazingly great. On a scale of one to ten, it topped eleven and she was eager to go home and share the news. Although the extraordinary cause of her elation kept her busier than usual, her thoughts often strayed to Mary and Zack.

They'd invited Gerald over for a hearty breakfast to fortify him for the long trip to Yakima and he'd eagerly accepted. Zack had tried to get him to spend Sunday night, offering the guest room and volunteering to sleep on the floor.

Had Gerald accepted, they would have talked the night away instead of getting the restorative sleep they all needed after the emotionally intense day. But he'd held firm. He'd checked into The Dorset before venturing out to Stanton Farm and that's where he would stay.

Emulating his good sense, Abby had left home well before breakfast. The morning belonged to the three Reynolds. They had a lot of catching up to do. Last night's startling revelations hadn't allowed time for personal, getting-to-know-you questions.

Now, on the way home from work, Abby's curiosity burned brightly. Was Gerald married? Did he have children? What did they do? Where did they live?

No doubt Mary had learned those answers and many more. She had a gift for putting people at ease and getting them to talk about themselves.

Abby walked into the house from the garage and found Zack in the laundry room.

"Hey, Aunt Abby." He added a neat pile of white T-shirts to the basketful of clean clothes. "What a great visit this has been."

"Uh-oh. You're leaving."

"Tomorrow morning."

"I'll miss you." She stood on tiptoes and kissed his cheek. "I'm really glad you came."

"Me too. I can't imagine anyone thinking Sparrow Island is dull. We had a regular three-ring circus."

"It has been rather hectic. And tremendously rewarding, don't you think?"

He laughed. "I never dreamed my visit would include bats and brothers, music and a manuscript all wrapped in mysteries. I have a new uncle and gained a new friend. I even found some of the answers I was looking for."

"Care to share?"

"Sure, but you'll have to come outside. Mom and I have a project going."

Abby followed him into the kitchen and dropped her purse and briefcase by the telephone table. "I can't believe how fast the time has flown. It feels like you just arrived."

"Mom said the same thing." Zack glanced over his shoulder and grinned. "Lily doesn't agree, but she's not pushing me to hurry back to Chicago. She says to stay until I'm ready." He took three water bottles out of the fridge.

Abby knew better than to press. He'd explain his cryptic comments when he was ready. They went out the back door, across the deck and into the side yard. There, she stopped cold. "Good heavens, what are you doing?"

Mary sat at the far edge of a blanket spread on the ground. A big straw hat hid her face. Finnegan stood on the grass, watching his mistress curiously. In the center of the blanket, Blossom basked in the sun.

"Abby, glad you're home. We're planting. Come over here so I can see you. I can't turn around."

Flummoxed, Abby rounded the empty wheelchair.

Mary sat with her legs splayed around a large hole. Loose soil drifted off her dungarees and into the pit. "Zack did the digging and I'm doing the prepping."

She pointed at a bag of fertilizer. Finnegan dutifully fetched and brought it to her. "We're putting in a Reynolds tree. Sort of a memorial to the past—the roots we'll be burying—and a promise to the future—no more secrets and no hard feelings. Gerald suggested an apple tree. Zack and I feel it's appropriate. The real fruit is our new and restored relationships."

"When we're done," Zack said, "we'll send pictures to Gerald and Nancy."

Abby settled onto the blanket beside Mary. "A family tree is a beautiful idea and a fitting tribute." She gave her sister a one-armed hug. "I'm so happy for all of you."

"I know." Laughing, Mary returned the hug. "I don't mean to sound flip, I'm just so pleased and excited. On Gerald's next visit, he's bringing his wife, Pamela. They have two daughters and six grandchildren."

Suddenly, Mary bent so far over the hole, Abby feared she'd

fall in headfirst. Instead, she worked fertilizer into the soil, then just as abruptly, sat up.

"Wow, Mom, I had no idea you were so limber."

"Only the legs don't work. The rest of me is better and stronger than ever. I'm ready to set the tree. Abby, would you do the honors and take pictures?"

"Certainly. Where's the camera?"

Mary pointed Finnegan to the deck. "Fetch boy."

He raced up the ramp, and trotted back with the camera dangling from the strap firmly clenched between his teeth.

"Be sure you let Lily know about this," Abby told Zack. "Finnegan is so obedient and smart, he constantly amazes me."

"I will. She'll be pleased to hear it."

Already seated on the ground, Abby had a good angle for the planting and snapped several pictures. Then as she rose to her knees to better frame Zack and Finnegan, she called, "Lose the hat, Mary. It's hiding your face."

"Shall I take off mine too?" Zack reached for his fedora.

"No," Abby ordered.

"Absolutely not," Mary exclaimed. "It belongs in the picture with us."

When Abby was satisfied she had several good shots, she lowered the camera.

"Lord," Mary gazed up at the blue sky, "thank You for our growing family. Please help our relationships flourish with this tree and bear fruit of the Spirit."

After a few minutes of silence, Zack shifted his weight. "Mom, Aunt Abby, you've both asked if I've found answers. I wanted to wait for the right time and place. This is it. Do you two remember me telling you I sent an application to the pops orchestra a year ago?"

"Yes," they answered in tandem.

He reached into his back pocket and pulled out a folded envelope. "They answered. It came today in a packet Lily forwarded to me."

"Go on," Mary urged when he paused. "What does it say?"

"I have an audition next week. If it works out, I'll be able to continue doing what I love. I've come to realize the balance in my life has to come from inside me. If this doesn't work out, I'll keep looking for the door with my name on it."

While Mary and her son hugged, Abby fell back on the blanket and hugged Blossom. Nonplussed by the undignified display of affection, the cat immediately wriggled free and scampered off. Unabashed, Finnegan stepped up and nuzzled Abby's neck. Laughing, she reached up and hugged him.

"And the good news just keeps on coming," Abby said.

"You have more news?" Mary asked. "Share it or else!"

"Okay." Abby hastily sat up. "Joe and Scott came to The Nature Museum today to see the bat exhibit and meet Rebecca. Talk about perfect timing. One thing led to another and they decided to host a Bat Fest."

Zack joined them on the blanket, his eyes nearly as wide as his mother's. "Scott's going to sing about bats?"

"In public?" Mary breathed.

"Yes and no. Let me explain. The fest will start at the museum with our new display. Beth thinks it's a great idea. She's agreed to come and put on a full presentation. You're going to love her, Mary."

"I look forward to meeting her, but you're getting ahead of yourself. What about Scott?"

Abby took a deep breath and grinned at Zack. "Joe has a friend with a whale watching boat. After the program at The Nature Museum, everyone will board it. Instead of watching for whales, we'll be watching Beth. She'll have her displays set up on the boat and be available to answer questions. We'll arrive at James Island in plenty of time to see the bats emerge from the cave."

"By then, everyone will know how important it is not to disturb the colony," Mary reasoned. "It *is* a great idea."

"On the ride back, we'll have entertainment." Abby pressed a hand to her chest. She was so full of joy she felt she might float. "Wait until you hear Scott and Rebecca sing together. Their voices blend beautifully. She's asked him to sing duets with her for over a year, but he wasn't ready. Now, thanks to Zack, he's willing to give it a try."

"Man! Scott has his first gig. I'd give anything to be there for him. Cheer him on, you know. When is it?"

"We're looking at late August," Abby said softly, hoping her nephew wouldn't be too disappointed. If the pops orchestra took him on, she doubted they'd grant him vacation right away.

"Nancy and her family are coming then." Mary turned to Zack, her heart in her eyes.

He flipped open his audition papers and turned to the back page. With a finger, he followed the fine print, then sighed. "If they take me on, there's no way I can come."

His gaze turned to the freshly planted tree. "I think I'm beginning to understand the secret to the balance Dad found. Nobody gets everything. It's about choices. If I can't make it, take pictures for me, will you?"

Abby watched the little tree's leaves flutter. "You can count on it."

A NOTE FROM THE EDITORS

THIS ORIGINAL BOOK WAS created by the Books and Inspirational Media Division of Guideposts, the world's leading inspirational publisher. Founded in 1945 by Dr. Norman Vincent Peale and his wife Ruth Stafford Peale, Guideposts helps people from all walks of life achieve their maximum personal and spiritual potential. Guideposts is committed to communicating positive, faith-filled principles for people everywhere to use in successful daily living.

Our publications include award-winning magazines like *Guideposts, Angels on Earth, Sweet 16* and *Positive Thinking*, best-selling books, and outreach services that demonstrate what can happen when faith and positive thinking are applied to day-to-day life.

For more information, visit us online at www.guideposts.org, call (800) 431-2344 or write Guideposts, 39 Seminary Hill Road, Carmel, New York 10512.